A
Bed of
Scorpions

Also by Judith Flanders

A Circle of Sisters: Alice Kipling, Georgiana Burne-Jones, Agnes Poynter, and Louisa Baldwin

The Victorian House: Domestic Life from Childbirth to Deathbed

Consuming Passions: Leisure and Pleasure in Victorian Britain

The Invention of Murder: How the Victorians Reveled in Death and Detection and Created Modern Crime

The Victorian City: Everyday Life in Dickens' London

The Making of Home: The 500-Year Story of How Our Houses Became Our Homes

FICTION

A Murder of Magpies

A
Bed of
Scorpions

Judith
Flanders

Minotaur Books
A Thomas Dunne Book
New York

A THOMAS DUNNE BOOK FOR MINOTAUR BOOKS.
An imprint of St. Martin's Press.

www.thomasdunnebooks.com
www.minotaurbooks.com

The Library of Congress has cataloged the hardcover edition as follows:

Names: Flanders, Judith, author.
Title: A bed of scorpions / Judith Flanders.
Description: First edition. | New York : Minotaur Books, 2016.
Identifiers: LCCN 2015042577| ISBN 9781250056467 (hardcover) | ISBN 9781466860292 (e-book)
Subjects: LCSH: Women detectives—England—Fiction. | Book editors—England—Fiction. | Murder—Investigation—Fiction. | BISAC: FICTION / Mystery & Detective / Women Sleuths. | GSAFD: Mystery fiction.
Classification: LCC PR6106.L365 B43 2016 | DDC 823/.92—dc23
LC record available at http://lccn.loc.gov/2015042577
Library of Congress Cataloging-in-Publication Data

ISBN 978-1-250-11237-8 (trade paperback)

Our books may be purchased in bulk for promotional, educational, or business use. Please contact your local bookseller or the Macmillan Corporate and Premium Sales Department at 1-800-221-7945, extension 5442, or by e-mail at MacmillanSpecialMarkets@macmillan.com.

Originally published in Great Britain by Allison & Busby Limited

First Minotaur Books Paperback Edition: February 2017

10 9 8 7 6 5 4 3 2 1

For Frank Wynne

A
Bed of
Scorpions

1

The summer was rumbling on the way summer usually does in publishing, and I was ready to murder someone. Murder someone cheerfully. With a song in my heart. Because we had survived the London Book Fair, when thousands of publishing people from across the world poured into London, to be entertained and amused as well as met more formally for work, each one scheduled in at half-hour intervals throughout the day, even as, because it's our home city, we were also expected to get through our normal work. The Frankfurt Book Fair, in October, was always easier, because then we would become the thousands who poured in from across the world, to be entertained and amused as well as met more formally for work, each one scheduled in at half-hour intervals throughout the day. But then a bounce-back e-mail, "I'm out of my office at the Frankfurt Book Fair. . . . If it's urgent, please e-mail my assistant on . . ." and you're off, no office responsibilities for a week. But Frankfurt wasn't for another four months, which in publishing time is both an eternity, and tomorrow.

For the marketing and sales departments, October was tomorrow, and they were in full cry, hounding all of us in editorial for catalog copy, sales pitches, and advance information sheets, so they could produce the material we would need in four months. The art department also knew that October was tomorrow, and were also hounding us, this time for cover copy, design briefs, and the same damn advance information sheets we hadn't written for marketing, so they could produce the book jackets, which we'd also need in four months. Because book fairs are not about books as words. They are about selling, and if you work in publishing, the sooner you settle down and acknowledge that fact, the happier you will be. You may have bought the greatest novel since *War and Peace,* but if you can't sell rights—German translation rights, French translation rights, Japanese, and, if you're lucky, Norwegian, Turkish, and Polish translation rights, too—then the odds are your company is not going to see a return on its money. And if your company doesn't see a return on its money, you can't buy the author's next book. And if you don't have enough authors who write books that make money, you can't buy books from other authors, whose books probably won't make any money right away, but might one day, when they'll pay for . . . you get the drift.

But that's not the way to present it to an author who is struggling to produce *this* book. They know the rights need to be sold—they know, because they need the money. So hounding them for something you can turn into sales material for the people who are in turn hounding you, feels like prodding a sick

cow into being milked. The cow is having enough trouble pro-
viding milk for her calf, and here I am, Farmer Sam, coaxing,
"Just a little bit for me. It won't take you any time."

Which even as I say it, I know is a lie. Of course it will take
them time. Time they would otherwise spend on writing their
book. But if they don't take time off from writing their book to
produce sales material, I can't sell that book. And then they can't
afford to write it. Most authors earn less than the minimum wage
for their writing. The only time they make enough to live on
from writing is when they're so famous everyone wants to interview them, or profile them, or have them on TV. And then they
have enough money, but not enough time. If you feed the rav-
enous beast that is the publishing schedule, you penalise your
authors. If you don't feed the beast, you penalise your authors.
Don't try and work it out, because trust me, it doesn't make sense.

And so, come summer, when Frankfurt still feels far enough
away that we don't have to harass our poor authors, slaving away
in their salt mines (yes, I know I said they were cows a minute
ago, but bear with me, I'm an editor, not a writer)—come summer, all the editors collectively stick their fingers in their ears as
the sales and art departments rampage and sing, "La-la-la-la-la,
I can't *heeeear* you." That doesn't make sense either, but it makes
us feel better.

Those of us who are around. Publishing is not very well paid,
and it is therefore filled with women, mostly young women, who
also therefore have small children. And so an awful lot of people
vanish entirely during the school holidays. For some of that
time they are officially absent, on holiday. For a lot more, they
are "working at home."

In theory I have no complaints about "working at home." I do it too. There are no meetings at home. The coffee is better there, and no one steals the last of the milk. No one wanders in, saying, "I know you're really busy . . ." (at this point they give a winsome smile) ". . . but could you just take a quick look at this? It'll only take five minutes." It does take only five minutes. Then we have to discuss their new haircut, what idiocy the finance department has perpetrated by changing the format of the profit-and-loss forms, and did you *hear* (look over shoulder) about Meg and Dan. They were, you know, even though Dan's wife was *right there*. Then that only-five-minutes leaves, and another appears, and Meg and Dan get done over again.

Instead, working at home means you get some work done. But when everyone is working at home—and everyone also knows perfectly well that the home workers are taking their kids to the park, or are sitting in a café, or even just googling to find out how to get plasticine out of the carpet, and we can't do the same, because otherwise the office would appear so deserted it would be targeted by squatters—then it leads to a fair amount of passive-aggressive tutting and sighing from those left behind. And maybe a bit of eye-rolling. No more than that. We're British, so we're not going to say what we really think, now are we? Well, I'm a mongrel, only half a Brit, so I say it in my head. But outwardly I conform happily to the native passive aggression. Works for me.

I'd had my third conversation of the day about Meg and Dan. (And, really, apart from the tackiness of *where*, I wasn't very interested. I wasn't even entirely sure who Dan was. I knew he was in sales, but was he the one with the funny haircut, or was he the slightly geeky-looking one who piled up biscuits in front of his seat at meetings and then ate them in what seemed to be some carefully determined order?) Anyway, I'd had enough. I was meeting a friend for lunch, and I decided to set off early and walk, since finally, after a long, rainy month, it was one of those bright London days when you think, *Yes, it is worth living in this God-awful climate.*

I waved at Bernie at Reception and happily banged the heavy Georgian door of the building behind me as I stepped out into the sunshine. I raised my face, eyes closed, feeling the mild summer heat like a physical touch. As I walked along I saw everyone emerging from their offices do the same—step out, take a deep breath with eyes closed and face raised. It wasn't particularly warm, but the sun made everything feel like it was haloed.

I'd left myself enough time, so I cut through the backstreets. The more direct route would have taken me along Oxford Street, but as I didn't need a plastic bobby's helmet, a "My Parents Went to London and All I Got Was This Crappy T-shirt" T-shirt, or even a postcard with a pair of naked breasts painted red, white, and blue and captioned "I Love London," the extra ten minutes seemed more than reasonable. My office is three minutes' walk from the British Museum, and the same distance from Oxford Street, so the main streets are hot-and-cold-running tourists pretty well all the time, all streaming past the area's many offices without realizing that this isn't just a visitors' playground. London's zoning laws don't help, as the 1950s concrete buildings and the eighteenth-century brick houses alike all have 1970s fast-food-plastic frontages at ground level. But off the main streets, only a few hundred yards away, a much older London survives. Sometimes that older city is signposted, by blue enamel plaques that indicate where a famous person lived, but more often, noticing the odd old house, or a freak bit of ornament, feels like a private pleasure, a way of marking the city out as belonging to its residents, not the tourists.

I mooched happily along the back way, down streets my feet knew automatically, even though I'd never learned their names, toward the restaurant where I was meeting Aidan Merriam. He and I had known each other since I first moved to London, and had always been close—at one time, very close. But that was a long time ago. Now we had a friendship where we loved each other dearly, and saw each other rarely. Aidan had been married to Anna for—I stopped and thought about it. Since their children were now teenagers, they must have been married for more than fifteen years. Although they no longer had the baby thing to keep them tied to home Aidan, as the part owner of an art gallery, was almost permanently on the move around the world, zooming from art fair to auction to biennale to exhibition. I knew this because whenever I invited them to dinner Anna would list the two or three days a month when he might be in London. Anna was high-powered in her own field, a professor at UCL, with a speciality in Renaissance bronzes, which, happily, she never expected anyone to know anything about. And while she also traveled for work, not only lecturing but curating ex-hibitions, her job allowed her to have a home life. While she and I liked each other, we weren't friends the way Aidan and I were, and so once every two years or thereabouts he and I had a catch-up lunch on our own. Nothing sinister: Anna was entirely aware of our past, and all three of us knew it was past. None of us wanted differently.

This lunch had been in my diary for months, and Aidan had rung up only three times to change the date, which meant he was fairly unharried by his standards. It's true that he'd texted first thing yesterday to say he couldn't make it and would ring later, and then, an hour later, he'd texted again, to say he'd see me as planned. That was a little out of the ordinary, but I figured he'd tell me about whatever crisis it was when we met. We never had to say where. We always went to the same cheap 'n' cheerful Lebanese place, halfway between my office and his gallery on Cork Street, a small café that was all scarred woodwork and uncomfortable pine furniture. The staff were abrupt to the point of rudeness the first dozen times you ate there, until suddenly, magically, one day you had become family. Our pattern was to meet early enough to get the window table, then we'd order too many starters, fight over the last pepper, and catch up. The routine was part of the charm.

From across the road, I could see through the window that Aidan was there already. As I waited for the traffic to thin, I watched him. Seeing him behind a window made him look—I paused and thought about it—it made him look as if I didn't know him. People you know well somehow never change. I'd met Aidan when I was twenty and he was twenty-seven, so in my head that's the way he'd remained. But the through-the-window Aidan was, I suddenly recognized, much older. He still had all his hair—too much, in fact, since he never remembered to get it cut. But it had once been almost black, and it was now more than half gray. And the lines running from his nose to his mouth

7

weren't just strong, which they'd always been. Now they were deep grooves almost carved into his face.

The lines were particularly marked as he sat frowning down at his phone. The phone, at any rate, was familiar. It was how I usually saw him in my mind, although it was rare that he was waiting for me. I'm always early and, as I opened the café door, I checked my watch. I was today, too. Aidan never was. He was rarely late, but had that sort of businessman's timekeeping, one appointment dovetailing into the next, with Aidan neatly arriving at each one with no time to spare before, another meeting ticked off the list, he moved on to the next.

So when I'd kissed him hello and slid onto the banquette opposite, I didn't waste time with the how-are-you-fine-thanks-how-are-you formula. Just "What's up?"

He stared at me blankly for a moment, as if he wasn't quite sure who I was, or why I was talking to him. Then he put his elbows on the table and covered his face with his hands.

This was serious. Aidan was one of the most collected people I knew. Not reserved, exactly, but someone always on one level. Problems were, well, problems to him, things to be solved, and then, once solved, they were considered resolved and he shelved them. Since my method of dealing with problems is to run around screaming and carrying on like a headless chicken for a while before I knuckle down to deal with whatever it is, followed by chewing the same problem over afterward for months, sometimes years, agitating over how I might have done things differently, I'd always found his attitude very soothing. Except in that period when I was the problem. Then it was downright annoying.

I touched his arm gently now, joggling it to get him to let me see his face. "Aidan?"

He looked up, but he didn't see me. He was looking at something else, in some place I wasn't part of. Then he returned to me. "Frank is dead," he said.

"Jesus." Frank was Frank Compton, the other partner in their gallery, Merriam-Compton. He was Aidan's age, maybe a few years older, perhaps fifty. "What? When? Did you know he was ill?" I couldn't believe he or Anna hadn't told me earlier.

He smiled without a trace of humor. "You don't have to be ill to kill yourself."

"What? When?" I repeated, and then, more urgently, "Why? Why would he do that?"

Aidan shook his head, and then just kept on shaking it, as if he'd forgotten to stop. I slid around to his side of the table and sat close, holding his hand. Human warmth won't drive away death, but it doesn't hurt.

"Tell me," I said quietly. I didn't want to press him, but he wanted to talk. He must, or he would have canceled our lunch.

"I got back from Hong Kong yesterday morning early, on the red-eye, and went straight to the gallery," he said in a wondering tone, as if he was reading from a cue card and was surprised by what it was saying, as if it were news to him. "The alarm wasn't on when I got there, which meant that either Frank or Myra"—their associate, I wasn't sure what she did—"was already in. It was only seven, but that's not unusual, and I just went back to find them, to report on the trip. And then—" he broke off, covering his face with his hands again.

This was much worse than I'd expected. Even though he'd said

9

Frank had killed himself, it hadn't crossed my mind that Aidan had found him. I'd assumed that it would be somehow tucked neatly out of sight. Apparently not. I waited. As much or as little as he needed to tell me was fine.

Aidan took a deep breath. "I went into his office, and . . ." He paused, then continued in a rush. "He was there. At his desk. He'd shot himself."

I flinched. I'd only ever been in the office part of the gallery once, or maybe twice. Downstairs the exhibition rooms were the kind of modernist dream that a movie director would have rejected as being too clichéd: white floors, white walls, and nothing else except big, light-filled windows. Upstairs was different, a rabbit warren of small offices and cubicles, booby-trapped with random outcroppings of old desks that appeared to have been abandoned, and filing cabinets stuffed in anywhere. I imagined Frank, his reddish-blond hair shining out in that dark labyrinth.

Aidan's voice was hoarse. "There was blood. Across the wall, a huge spray of it." He was still staring at where I'd been sitting, as if he hadn't noticed I'd moved.

A black gun appeared in my picture, on the scuffed floorboards, the body in one of Frank's smooth, dark Italian suits thrown back by the violence Aidan was describing, the blood-red spray like an abstract painting on the wall behind him.

I tried to wipe it away by concentrating on practicalities. "Was he ill?" I asked. "Or depressed? Did you know?"

Something shifted in Aidan. "I hope the bastard was depressed." He wasn't looking at me, but he must have felt me flinch, because his tone became argumentative, as if I'd protested out loud. "He knew I would find him, me or Myra. Why would he do that to us? I've worked with him, we've been friends, for twenty years. Myra's sixty and got a weak heart." He became pugnacious. "What kind of bastard leaves someone to find that?"

I had no answer. Instead, "Did he leave a note? Do you know why?" Why—why kill yourself, and why kill yourself that way, and why there—seemed suddenly very important.

Aidan clenched his hands into fists. He clearly wanted to hit out. At Frank, though, not at me for asking. He barely knew I was there. "He left a note, if you can call it that. His computer was open and he'd typed 'I'm sorry.' That's it. 'I'm sorry.'"

I answered the pain, not the anger. "Oh Aidan, that's terrible." I put my arm around him and we sat there without speaking.

The lovely eastern European waitress who had worked at the café for as long as we'd been customers hovered by the table. She looked questioningly at the closed menus and then at the two of us, Aidan with his hands over his eyes again, me just staring blankly ahead. I leaped at the return of normality, grasping onto ordering lunch as something useful I could do.

I named a bunch of things at random. It didn't matter what, we weren't going to be able to eat anyway. I turned to Aidan. "Do you want a drink?"

"God, yes," he said, looking at me properly for the first time. I smiled back at him and ordered a bottle of wine, then moved back to my original seat.

Maybe focusing on detail, on the practicalities, would help. "What happened? Did you call the police? And how's Toby?" Toby was Frank's partner. They'd been a couple as long as I'd known Frank. Toby was a civil servant, but I knew nothing else about him. I didn't know them nearly as well as I knew Aidan and Anna. It was more the kind of friendship where we kissed warmly when we bumped into each other somewhere, saying how good it was to meet, and we must get together, and then none of us ever followed up. Not from anything except busy lives and, really, ultimately, lack of interest. Not dislike, but not like, or at least not affection either.

Aidan brought me back to the present. "Of course I called the police. What do you think, we worked around him for the rest of the day?"

I shrugged an acknowledgment. My question hadn't made much sense, and the anger in Aidan's reply was still for Frank, not me.

"We didn't open yesterday, and so far not today either. They've been there, taking pictures, going through the files. They're talking to his doctor, but if he was ill, he hadn't told Toby. Who says the two of them were very happy—as happy as any couple who have been together for nearly twenty years can be, at least, is the way he put it, whatever that means. So . . ." He shifted his weight, and I realized that only now had he got to whatever it was he wanted to talk to me about "So, they think it must be business problems."

"And were there any?" He wanted me to ask, or he wouldn't have told me that much.

"If there are," he said, and I noticed the change in the verb tense, although I wasn't sure if he did, "if there are, I'm not aware of them."

All I knew about the art world was the bits Aidan had dropped over the years, and what I read in the papers. Both suggested that money was far more important in their business than in mine. Even as I thought that, I knew that it was stupid. Money ruled my working life: how much could I offer an author, how many copies of each book were sold, at what price, how much could we squeeze out of subsidiary rights? But I never saw the money, never invoiced for it, never received the payments. I never had any real sense of the cash flow of the business as a whole.

The art world was different. A gallery like Aidan and Frank's—like Aidan's, now, perhaps—dealt with vast sums. Whenever I heard the two men talking about work, the commodity element was always right there on the surface. Art was about buying and selling, it was about trading an object for cash in a way books never were for their creators, or their version of art dealers, the publishers. Someone would say, "Fabulous show, I love what the artist is doing," and the answer was "Yes, we've sold six pieces," or "But no one's buying." I'm not saying that publishers don't think about selling books. We do. It's just that, at £7.99, one sale more or less doesn't matter; when you're selling a single object for six figures, it does.

None of that was relevant, though, so I returned to detail. "What happens now?"

Aidan looked blank at what I realized was a question vague to the point of inanity, and I clarified. "Can Toby make plans for the funeral? Does—did—Frank have family?"

Aidan sighed and rubbed his face again. He looked bereft. He was temporarily done with being angry with Frank, temporarily done with worrying about the financial havoc that might be lurking. Frank was once again his working partner of two decades, the man he probably spoke to more often than he spoke to his wife.

"His parents are dead. There's a brother and sister-in-law, and two nieces. He was close to them." He paused as the waitress brought our food. We looked at it, slightly nauseated, but automatically spooned random dollops of salads onto our plates. Neither of us picked up our cutlery, though. We waited until the wine arrived. That we picked up. Just as quickly, Aidan put his down. "I need to keep a clear head. And I don't think I've eaten since . . ." His eyes widened. "Since the plane."

That was more than a day and a half. I pushed his plate toward him. "Then eat something now. Even if you don't want to." I sounded like his mother, but that was a good thing at the moment, I decided.

He picked up his fork, but he just held it, as though he were pacifying me by making the gesture. He returned to where he'd left off. "One of his nieces, Lucy, works for us in the holidays. She's at university, but she fills in, and Frank was hoping she might join us full-time." He paused, his mouth thinning again. "How could he do that to her?"

I touched his hand, nudging it toward his plate. He smiled gently at me, and brushed his other hand across my cheek, a gesture of intimacy we hadn't had for years. Then he ate a couple of mouthfuls, although it was to show me he was OK, not because he was OK.

"The other thing is that I've had to cancel all my trips."

"You do? I know Frank does—did—the admin and gallery side, but is there so much that you have to be there?"

He looked at me as if I were an idiot. "It's not that. The police don't want me to leave the country for the moment."

I sat back, shocked. "They said that? That sounds like television."

"It was like television: finding him, being told not to leave London without checking in with them first. Oh, they were very polite. But I thought it was best to speak to a lawyer, and a forensic accountant."

I tilted my head. "What's that?"

"Not the kind who does your books, or your tax returns. The kind you use if you're being audited. Or, in this case, if the CID are telling you not to leave town."

CID. I sat up. "I don't understand. If the police think there are money issues . . ." I was circling around the words I didn't want to use, fraud, tax evasion, money laundering, or—or what? "Are you saying the police are looking at this as . . . as not suicide?" Now I was circling around the big word I didn't want to use. But otherwise, why CID, why not Revenue and Customs? I was hazy on the division of labor at the police, but this didn't sound right for embezzlement and suicide.

More importantly, it sounded worryingly close to home. "Um, I can't remember if I told you, when I last saw you . . ." I stalled, started again. "Do you know about my . . ." This was absurd. "Do you know I'm seeing a policeman?"

Aidan stared me dead in the eye. "Why do you think I'm here?"

Aidan had been looking at me as if I were an idiot for the simple reason that I was an idiot. I hadn't wondered why he was there at all. We were having lunch because we'd planned to have lunch. But that made no sense. If I'd found a colleague dead in my office—I flinched even at the thought—if I had, wouldn't I have canceled everything that could be canceled? And lunch with a friend I saw every couple of years plainly fell into the "could be canceled" category.

"What are you thinking? I'm not sure I'd know where to begin. I don't know who does what at Scotland Yard." I was burbling, I knew, but I couldn't stop. "Jake doesn't talk about his work. Sure, he moans about the office, or his colleagues, but nothing else. Not ever. I don't think he can—how can the details of violent death be conversation? And you know that's what he does, don't you? Murder, not fraud, or tax, or . . ." I steadied myself "Or embezzlement."

Aidan was grim. "Of course I know that's what he does. He's doing it. In my gallery. Now."

The breath left my body. I opened my mouth. And closed it again. Then I did it again. Until, "Jake is in the gallery," I repeated. Of course that was why Aidan was here. And of course that was why Aidan was here. "You canceled our lunch when you found Frank. And then, when the police arrived, and you realized Jake was . . ." I waved a hand. "That Jake was Jake, you reinstated."

He nodded.

I closed my eyes briefly, trying to gather my thoughts. Then, "I have no idea what to do or say. All I can think is that I need to stay as far out of this as possible. Far." If I'd been standing up, I think I would physically have been backing away. As it was, I felt myself pushing against the banquette, my hands rigid on the edge of the table. I tried to loosen my grip. Nothing. Because even as I said the words, I knew they weren't realistic. How could I possibly stay out of this? And whose side was I on? Jake's? Aidan's? He and Frank had been my friends my whole adult life.

I stopped short. Why was I thinking there were sides? Why did I assume Aidan's side was different from Jake's? If someone had killed Frank, then we were on the same side. Obviously. I said this to myself twice, to make sure I recognized how obvious it was. The bile sitting at the bottom of my throat replied that perhaps it wasn't so obvious at all.

And Jake. Jesus. That he wasn't going to be happy was an understatement of epic proportions. Even calling it an understatement of epic proportions was an understatement of epic proportions. We had met when he was investigating the death of a courier. First I was simply someone he interviewed for background, and then, involuntarily, I had become more deeply involved. And he had hated that. That I'd been in danger had made him furious, not with me, but with himself for letting it happen. That I knew Aidan and Frank, that Aidan was having lunch with me even as Jake was opening an investigation, wasn't going to get a five-star write-up in the *Crimebusters' Review*.

That was on the professional side. On the personal . . . On the personal, my stomach churned. We had been feeling our way gently. I had what Jake called a reflexive liberal-leftie attitude to the police, distrusting much of what I saw in the news. He, in turn, was, I think, slightly bemused by what I did for a living, or at least the passion I felt for it. He liked books, he read, but he didn't really think they were essential. They were a fun pastime, like football, not a reason for existence. I also had a sneaking suspicion that it was probably wildly against police regulations for him to have begun a relationship with me when I was a witness in a case he was investigating. But he had never said so, and I had never asked. There was rather a lot neither of us had talked about, in fact. I'd always known that while I talked a lot, it was only ever about things that didn't matter. Now I realized he was the same.

"Was Jake there yesterday?" I asked abruptly.

Aidan nodded, keeping his eyes on my face.

I'd seen him yesterday evening. We spent most of our free time together, but there wasn't that much of it. As a detective, Jake worked unsociable hours. Publishing also spills out long past the eight-hour office day. I do a fair amount of evening work-socializing—launch parties, readings, and events—as well as the more usual social-socializing. In between that, and work, whatever time was left, we were usually together.

I thought back to the previous night. Jake had arrived at my flat early and we'd cooked dinner together. Jake was a surprisingly good cook, and made things I was scared of, like pastry, so we worked in tandem, without getting in each other's way, with a couple of glasses of wine and idle chat. I closed my eyes, trying to remember what he'd said. He'd mentioned the politics that was holding back a promotion for one of his colleagues, and that he needed to prep for an upcoming court appearance, neither of which was about the day's work as such. After dinner he'd watched television, I'd read, and then we'd gone to bed, which was where we did some of our best communicating.

I gritted my teeth. He definitely hadn't mentioned a death in an art gallery. That wasn't the kind of thing I might have for-

gotten. I pulled back from my anger. There was no particular reason for him to. Maybe. "He didn't say anything about it. But did
you say you knew who he was? That you know me? You haven't
met him with me, have you?" I asked, even though I was sure he
hadn't. Jake's shifts meant he didn't often go out with me in
the evenings, and I hadn't seen Anna and Aidan in months,
maybe more.

"No. I mean, no, I hadn't met him before; and no, I didn't say
that I knew you."

"What do you want?" There seemed no point in tiptoeing
about.

"I don't know."

2

I took the bus back to the office. I didn't notice the way the sun struck the red-brick façades any longer, or the people enjoying its warmth. Instead, I huddled in my seat as if it were midwinter.

Miranda was lying in wait for me as soon as I appeared. She's my assistant, and her retro-Goth look puts some people off, but she's great. She's been with me for nearly six months, and I've been able to leave more and more to her. Now she picked up her mug and stood as I came down the hall, using a sheaf of cover briefs to gesture me into my office. The mug was ominous, indicating she expected a long session, and when she didn't lean on the door frame, but pulled a chair close to mine, I knew I was doomed.

I put my head down and slunk to my desk suitably chastened, but also very happy to focus on something I could do something about. She was right, and the work needed to be done; I might as well do it with good grace. Cover briefs are outlines to tell the jacket designer what the book is about (no, they don't read them, don't be silly), and how we want to position it in the market. Most of the books they pretended to describe hadn't been delivered—many hadn't been written—so they were written on little more than an outline and a prayer that the author would come up with the goods. Taking that into account, Miranda had done a good job, and we only needed an hour to tidy them up.

I was pleased to get it done. At least, I was until Miranda hitched her chair closer. Apparently there was more. She gave a brisk nod, and "Now" she said, as though she were getting a small child ready for her first day at school. I jumped inwardly. That was usually my tone—half editor, half sheepdog was how I privately saw my relationship with my authors. The notion that Miranda thought the same about me was endearing, and I grinned at her, despite being quite certain I wouldn't want to do whatever it was she had lined up for me.

"Now," she repeated firmly, "I've almost finalized your Frankfurt schedule." She pursed her lips when I shuddered. Give her a ticket to Frankfurt and watch her dust, her expression said. "In the meantime," she went on, not giving an inch, "you need to prepare for the Culture Committee panel."

This was much worse than I'd feared. In a moment of total derangement, I'd agreed to sit on a joint Arts Council committee, and what a waste of time that had turned out to be. David Snaith, Timmins & Ross's editor-in-chief, and my boss, had put me forward for it. With all the government spending cuts, it was undoubtedly sensible for various cultural bodies to pool their knowledge, and the committee was made up of people from concert venues, from museums, theater companies, and music festivals, as well as more book-related things like book festivals. Theoretically the range, from government-funded institutions like the Opera House to commercial outfits like ours, should have made an exchange of views interesting.

That was the theory. Back here in real life, however, a lot of time was spent whining. Yes, times are hard, yes, music, and books, and dance, and theater, don't have the stranglehold on entertainment that they used to. But moaning got old fast. Even when time was spent more constructively, discussions revolved around matters that, in general, applied to only a few people in any one meeting. Things that were essential to one art form—audio guides in museums, or live streaming for theater—had no relevance to the rest of us, and so we settled back to bitch and moan again.

And the panel. That was my lowest moment. I hadn't been bitching and moaning, I'd been daydreaming in the meeting when it was proposed, and so I hadn't heard when the committee chair volunteered me. I bet the son-of-a-bitch knew I wasn't listening, too. Now I was doomed to make a presentation on "Subsidy in a Commercial World." And since the area of publishing I work in barely deals with subsidies, it meant hours of setting up meetings with people in those areas that are subsidized. And all so that, when my turn came, I could say something that anyone who dealt with subsidies already knew, and anyone who didn't, didn't care.

I think I growled, because Miranda giggled, then hastily looked solemn, like a child with crumbs around her lips swearing she had no idea who had taken the biscuit out of the tin, hadn't even know there *were* biscuits in that tin. She hadn't giggled, no siree.

"I've set up meetings for you over the next few days, when it's quiet." I must have growled again, because she repeated "when it's quiet," now in full primary-schoolteacher mode, quelling the unruly through sheer force of personality. "You're seeing Emma Cotton from the University Presses Alliance, and Neil Simonson from the Riverside Literature Festival. They can both fit you in on Monday. There's also that charity that subsidises the cost of illustrations for art books."

I nodded gloomily, resigned. I'd had some dealings with the Daylesworth Trust because, although I mostly do fiction, every now and again I publish a fashion book. The costs of printing illustrations, and paying the picture fees, were so high that we couldn't do them on standard publishing terms. Either we had to get the fashion houses to contribute, or we needed some outside help. I hated relying on the fashion houses. They only knew what worked in magazines or advertising, and so what they wanted—what, if they were paying for it, they demanded—was often entirely unsuitable for books. So when a few years ago a friend who worked for an art publisher pointed me to the Daylesworth, it seemed a gift. The trust had been set up by some rich businessman who collected art, and it was entirely focused toward art books. But I'd decided that if you stretched the definition of "art," it could cover fashion, too. Maybe they had agreed, or maybe doing the odd frock book made them feel hip. I don't know. I'd never met anyone there. They had a grant application on their website, I'd filled it out the first time, and when it worked, I continued to do so. Maybe this meeting would be help for later books. *I feel almost positive about this,* I told myself. Then I added, *Liar.*

Miranda was still organizing me. "They've been playing funny buggers, but I've got them pinned down now." She paused, diverted. "It was very strange. I couldn't get a callback for weeks."

I didn't see why that was strange. I'd avoid meeting me to discuss arts subsidy, too, if I could.

I wasn't given much time to brood, however. Miranda had suddenly speeded up, clearly thinking that if she spoke very quickly, the content wouldn't register. "The woman there is Celia Stein, and she's apparently very busy at the moment, so I booked you in to see her this afternoon at four." And then she had gathered her papers and her mug and slid out the door before I could share my views on scheduling.

I'd been thinking recently that I should put her forward for the next junior editor vacancy that came up. She was new, but she had hoovered up everything I'd thrown at her, and she deserved a better job than the entry-level one she did for me. And the job's laughable salary meant that I couldn't keep her and just give her better work. But if she kept this up, I was going to get her promoted simply to get her out of my hair.

I called through the wall to the pod where she and her colleagues sat: "Where am I meeting her?"

"Her office," she called back. "The address is in your diary." I looked. It wasn't as bad as it could have been—just on the edge of Regent's Park, which meant I could walk home afterward. I tried to continue feeling martyred, but it wasn't working.

"Thanks," I called instead, my tone an apology for my thoughts.

She giggled again. I really would have to find her a better job.

At three thirty I gave up. I'd spent most of my afternoon worrying about Aidan, then pushing those thoughts aside and going back to the contract I was negotiating with a new author, before the picture of Frank in his office took over again. The image was so vivid I was barely aware any longer that I hadn't seen him myself.

Instead I checked out Celia Stein online. The Daylesworth Trust's website was remarkably uninformative. It said she had worked in "the arts," as though that were a job description, before she had moved to the charitable sector. And that was all. I googled her, too, but with no other information I couldn't disentangle her from the other Celia Steins the world was filled with, although for amusement I let myself imagine that she was the Celia Stein who was a competitive dirt-bike racer. Sadly, I decided the odds were against it, and so I set off knowing nothing, not a position I liked to be in.

I walked. The bus would have taken as long, and I hoped that the mindlessness of walking would stave off the pictures of Frank, that dark body in the dark room. It didn't, but it did make me realize that however much Jake wanted to keep me away from his job, we needed to talk. So when I reached the park, I stopped and texted quickly: *Are you working or am I seeing you tonight?* Then I looked around for the Daylesworth's offices. The address Miranda had given turned out to be a street of white-stuccoed, rather grand houses, on one side of the road only, as they faced a private square at the south end of Regent's Park. I'd always assumed the trust was a fairly small operation, but if it could afford more than a couple of rooms here, that was not the case. Or maybe the founder ran his business, whatever that was, from there, and they benefitted by the connection.

The office, when I found it, had no sign at all out front, neither for the Daylesworth Trust nor any other business. I went up the stairs past a group of three women smoking in the sun. Inside was even less informative. Where I expected a reception area, or a hall, there was nothing but a surprisingly small stone-flagged foyer, dominated by a vast double staircase, its large stone steps and elaborate gilt and wrought-iron railing making it look like it belonged in a seaside resort hotel in the 1890s. There was no sign, but also nowhere to go but up, so up I went. At the top of the first flight, tucked into the side of the landing, was an ugly 1960s veneered plywood desk. A plainly dressed, middle-aged woman looked up. "Yes?" she said, and it was only manners that stopped me from doing a carton-style double-take. She had the most beautiful voice, deep and gravelly, like Lauren Bacall, oozing sex and sin, but coming out of a completely ordinary face.

I contemplated asking her to marry me, just so I could wake up to that voice for the rest of my life, but I decided she might think it was too sudden. "Would you tell Celia Stein that Samantha Clair is here?" I said instead.

She picked up the phone and dialed. Then, "I'm afraid there's nowhere to sit, but she won't be long."

I smiled. An opportunity to listen some more. "Not to worry. This is a very strange building. What was it before?"

A snort escaped her. "It's nineteenth century, and it's listed, a building of historical importance. But for anyone who works here, it's a white elephant, is what it is. We're not allowed to touch any of the architectural features, so we're just shoved in wherever we fit, all over the place."

"Why are you here, then, if it's so impractical?"

She looked sour. "Good question. We were in a purpose-built office block not far away. When the building was scheduled for demolition, when Crossrail was given the go-ahead, we needed to move quickly. The upstairs here is lovely—the bosses have beautiful offices. That may have something to do with their choice." She stopped abruptly and picked up the phone. I couldn't tell if she had just realized she was spilling internal politics to a total stranger, or if she'd heard a step before I did. At any rate, when a woman appeared on the stairs above us, the receptionist was booking a cab and I was admiring the ceiling mouldings.

She came toward me holding out her hand. "Celia Stein," she confirmed. "How nice of you to offer to come to me. I appreciate it." She was the kind of woman I've always longed to be, looking at them wistfully in restaurants and theaters. She was neither terribly tall, nor terribly thin, but she looked both. Her hair, a reddish brown, fell in waves past her shoulders, and was held back from her face on one side with a comb. Her clothes were not dissimilar to mine—trousers and a blouse—but there the resemblance ended. Hers were two shades of elegant taupe, chosen to set off her russet coloring, while mine were black and white, chosen to reduce to the bare minimum the time spent thinking about them. And, I acknowledged to myself, that was why I would never look like women like Celia Stein: she took time and trouble and I didn't. Her hairstyle, so simple-looking, probably took half an hour of careful blow-drying every morning, and needed highlights once a month; my hair was cut when I remembered, and otherwise had to look out for itself. She also spent money, a neon sign flashing over her head: *Expensive to Maintain.* Her trousers were linen, her shirt silk, her watch thin and discreet, her shoes sleek Italian (maybe) leather. I bet the highlights cost a bomb, too, and her dry-cleaning bill.

I gave myself a mental shake. I had no idea why my hackles had gone up. She was watching me, and I think she knew it. "Please come up," was all she said, and, "Thank you, Denise," to the receptionist as she turned to lead the way.

Celia Stein's office was small and not particularly glamorous, whatever Denise thought. Or maybe she wasn't high enough up the pecking order. Her room was not dissimilar to mine, which was also in an old house converted to office use, and equally harshly carved out of a space that had once been beautiful. Hers was at the back of the building, and looked out onto a light-well and the rear of the house behind. Otherwise, it was run-of-the-mill: standard-issue office desk, filing cabinets, shelves. The only spot of color came from a print on the wall, an orange and gold mishmash of 1950s cartoon characters. Its colors suited her look, even if the style didn't go with her personality. Or what I had decided in the first twenty seconds was her personality. Sam Clair, the Sigmund Freud of snap judgments.

She sat at her desk and gestured to the single remaining chair. There was coffee in a cafetière on her desk, and two cups, which softened my mood considerably. We made small talk for the few minutes it took to pour us both a drink, and then she said, "Tell me how I can help."

I tried to look like those dewy-eyed ingénues everyone wants to help when they have a flat tire. Or, at least, that's the way it works in black-and-white movies. It's not my best look. "I'm not really sure," I admitted. "I was shanghaied into sitting on an Arts Council panel on subsidies, and since you're the only people I ever deal with on the subsidies front, I thought I'd come and pick your brains."

She gave a small, controlled smile. I suspected everything she did was controlled. "I can tell you about our own funding," she said, "and I can give you our guidelines for selecting projects to support. I've also put together the figures we release annually on our charitable allocations. Does that help? What more can I tell you?"

It was a good question, because I hadn't a clue. And what she had done could have been emailed over to me. She hadn't needed to allow me to break into her day for that, and she didn't strike me as the sort who went out of her way to have any of her days disrupted against her will.

"One area I'd like to explore is the future of reproductions in books. Given the spread of images online, and the costs of printing, the question, why illustrate books at all, is an obvious one. If the author can say, 'Vermeer's *Music Lesson*,' and the reader can look at it online, spending money printing it, or spending money paying a permission fee to the owner of the picture, is surely becoming pointless. Just what is the future of this kind of publishing?"

"It's a good question, but my job here deals almost entirely with works of art that are still in copyright, and protecting those rights," she said.

That didn't sound like a charitable activity.

She must have read my face, because she went on, as if I'd argued, "We give funds to publishers who want to use these works, who might otherwise not use them, or use them without clearing the legal hurdles. This promotes the spread of modern art, as well as protecting the rights for the artists and their descendants."

It still didn't sound like charity to me, but it was none of my business. I nodded as though she'd made valid points, and went through the questions I'd thought up on the way over, about funding and resource allocation. I was going to have to talk for twenty minutes, so the more concrete examples I could gather, the better. Celia, whatever her job was, had plenty of experience.

After half an hour, she made it plain without actually saying anything that we were finished, and I had to agree. I took her cool hand, held out as if she were dropping a charitable donation of her own into my indigent palm, and left. On the way down, I paused to say good-bye to Denise, just so I could hear her velvet purr again. It was just "Good-bye," but it made me smile as I left, and I was halfway across the park and only twenty minutes from home before I thought to check and see if Jake had replied to my text.

He had. *You know you're seeing me tonight. You had lunch with Merriam.*

Eek.

Jake arrived a couple of hours later. I heard the front door close, and the thunk as he dropped his bag. A few weeks before I'd been having a drink with my upstairs neighbor, Kay, when we heard him come in.

"He's got keys already?" she said, aiming for a neutral expression.

"Does it bother you?" We did share a front door, so it wasn't an unreasonable worry. I hadn't known him long.

"It's just, well . . ." she looked embarrassed. I waited. "It's fast. You've only been seeing him a couple of months."

I was amused. "I didn't realize we were discussing my relationship. I thought you were worrying about safety, and I was going to tell you that if things went horribly wrong and I ended up raped and murdered in my bed, at least the police had the keys."

She snickered, and then hastily covered, "I didn't mean to imply—"

I waved it away. "I know. It's fine. He has my keys because he works strange hours, and I don't want to have to get up at midnight to let him in."

I didn't call out when I heard the door. My bag was at the front and Jake would know I was in and come down the hall to find me. As I went up on tiptoe to kiss him hello, one corner of his mouth lifted in a small smile. A finger gently flicked my collar. "Battledress?" he said mildly, but his smile widened.

He was right, damn it. Unless I've had to wear what I think of as my posh suit to work, for a lunch, or an author event, my office clothes are casual enough that I don't bother to change when I get home. Since I hadn't known about my meeting with Celia, and lunch with Aidan never rates the posh suit, I hadn't been dressed up. But I'd had a bath and changed that evening when I got home, as some sort of unconscious preparation.

I bit back a sigh, which he also noticed. Dating a detective, I had discovered, could be a royal pain. All the stuff that most people remain serenely unaware of, he picked up on right away. Once or twice he'd tried to persuade me this was a good thing— "energy efficient" was the phrase he'd used.

I decided not to engage, or at least, not right away. "Drink?" I said, and turned automatically to get the glasses.

"Not for me. I'm probably going to have to go back to work later."

That made me pause, but I didn't turn around. After a second I moved over to the sink, where I'd been washing spinach for dinner, and continued where I'd left off. "Oh?"

Jake put his arms around me from behind. "'Oh?' yourself. We're going to have to talk about this, you know."

"Fun!" I said in an idiot-child voice. "Our best thing, talking." I hadn't planned on quarreling, but I found myself well on the way.

Jake pulled me away from the sink and gently pushed me into a chair before moving over to the glasses I'd abandoned. He opened a bottle of wine and poured me a glass without speaking. Then, "No, not our best thing, but we're smart, and we can get better at it."

I snorted. "A learning experience. It's the only thing my week has been lacking." Until the words came out of my mouth, I hadn't realized how angry I was. Or maybe I was frightened? I regrouped. "I'm sorry. Yes, I had lunch with Aidan, who told me you were at the gallery. I'm worried." I looked away, and then back. "Are you . . . that is, why are . . . I don't even know the words to use."

Jake took the glass from my hand and took a swig. In England it doesn't count as drinking if you don't have your own glass. Everyone knows that. He leaned against the counter. His usual work dress was khakis and a white shirt, so, glass in hand, sleeves rolled up over his forearms, he looked like a colleague I'd met for a drink after work. Or he did until his next sentence, which shattered that illusion, had I held it.

"Am I investigating a murder?" he paraphrased for me.

I nodded mutely.

"We don't think that way. At the moment, we have an unexplained death." He paused. "I thought about this on the way home. My job has issues of confidentiality, but all jobs have those. That's not why I don't talk to you about my work. Not because I can't, but because I don't want to. You're a clean space in my life, a place where I don't have to think about the things we wade through every day."

I nodded again, this time feeling some of my hostility, or fear, or whatever it was, dying away. Although not talking about what preoccupied him for two-thirds of his waking life was also a problem. For another time. I pushed it away.

Jake drank some more of what had now become his wine, so I got up to get myself a glass.

"There's nothing I can't disclose at the moment, but that's mostly because we know almost nothing. Given the situation, if you want to hear what we know so far, I'm happy to lay it out."

Wanted? I was absolutely sure I didn't want to know. But did I need to know? Yes. More than a little reluctantly, I nodded to him to go ahead.

He had obviously prepared it in his head, and it came out in tidy little bullet points. "We were called in yesterday morning, after the divisional detectives had been alerted to an unexplained death."

I would like to believe that I didn't smile at Jake dropping into policeman-ese—he really didn't speak like that normally—but either I must have, or he just knew me well enough to recognize that it was the use of language I would concentrate on. He tapped me gently on the nose, the way you do to tell a puppy to behave. So I behaved.

"There are several possibilities." Jake began to tick them off on his fingers. "That Frank Compton had an accident, which can almost certainly be discounted. That Frank Compton killed himself for personal reasons; or because he was of unsound mind; or for work-related reasons. Or that Frank Compton did not kill himself, and it was staged to look as if he did, for unknown reasons.

"At the moment, we are asking questions. His partner, Toby Stafford, knew of no health problems, but we are checking to see if Compton had physical or mental health issues he had kept to himself. Stafford also says that they had a good relationship, but others suggest it was volatile, and we are looking at that, as well as making preliminary inquiries to see if there was anyone else in the picture. The final area is business issues, and we are therefore looking at his finances, personal and business, to see if there are any irregularities that mean we should continue to investigate while we wait for the coroner's report."

"Irregularities," I said carefully.

He was looking at the floor, not me. "There was GSR on his right hand."

"GSR?"

He looked up and smiled apologetically. "Gunshot residue—the traces left behind when a firearm discharges."

I read crime novels, I knew about this. "Surely that's what you would expect? Why is that an irregularity? Was he left-handed?"

"No, he was right-handed all right, but the scatter is not entirely consistent with how he must have held the pistol, based on the angle of the wound, which was, in addition, much farther to the back of the skull than is common in self-inflicted wounds." He shrugged. "He could have held the pistol awkwardly, or it could have slipped, but it is an anomaly. More than that, though, is the weapon." He rubbed his hand through his hair, as though the problem itself could be rubbed out. "It's a 9mm Makarov semiautomatic."

I raised my hands to pause him. "I know nothing about guns. In the vaguest possible way I know the difference between a machine gun and a pistol, but that's it." I revised that. "Truth be told, whatever I know probably comes from World War I movies—I think I'm visualizing Erich von Stroheim carrying one—so it is unlikely to have any relationship to something used this century."

For a moment, the "unexplained death" vanished. He laughed, happy to be with someone who thought anything that went "bang" was an all-purpose "gun." "All you really have to know is that handguns have been illegal in this country since 1996, after Dunblane. So we have an illegal handgun, which even before 1996 was never registered in the UK. It's a Soviet make, and it has a fixed sight." He saw my incomprehension. "Makarovs with fixed sights were only sold in the Soviet bloc;

Makarovs manufactured for export had adjustable sights. The feature itself doesn't matter, it's just an indication as to where it came from."

"You say 'Soviet.' Do you mean that the gun is old? From Soviet Union days? Or is it just a way of speaking?"

"Old. Our people say the serial number dates it to the early 1960s, which means there are a lot of years to account for."

He returned to the present. "Frank Compton has never had any sort of firearm registered to him, he is not known to have ever had any interest in firearms, and as far as both his partner and his colleagues are aware, he never traveled in the Eastern bloc. So where he came by a semiautomatic is an open question."

"Isn't that what the serial number will tell you?"

"We've sent a request to our Russian counterparts. But the handgun was Soviet Army issue. There's not much point in finding out the name of the soldier it was registered to in 1962. It's not going to clarify how it got from there to here. We'll try." He didn't look like he expected much. "Then there's the note." He rubbed his face again. This part was troubling him. "The note is . . . It's not in his handwriting, and it's not addressed to anyone. He may have typed it, but even if he did, it may have been the beginning of a note to say he couldn't attend a meeting, for all we know. IT have confirmed the time the page was opened, and that and the time the automatic save was first generated are both consistent with the estimated time of death from the scene, but that adds very little. And opening a computer document to write two words is unusual.

"So." He was summarizing, although I wasn't sure if it was for me, or for him. "On one side, the GSR, the weapon's provenance, the unusual nature of the note. We'll get a report later today confirming time of death and letting us know if there are any other anomalies. Forensics are looking at the splatter pattern"—he saw the expression on my face and put his hand on mine, but continued—"and we'll know more about that in a couple of days. We're auditing the books and looking at Compton's financial situation. We'll speak to Stafford again. And to his friends."

I hesitated. "I understand why you would automatically concentrate on Toby. But what did you mean when you said Frank and Toby's relationship was volatile?"

He was in interview mode again in an eyeblink. "What did you think of it?"

"I didn't. Think of it, I mean. I don't think I ever saw them on their own." I considered. "No, I'm certain I've never ever seen them on their own. It's always been at a party, or at least a group of friends for dinner."

"And they've never fought?"

"Fought? Seriously?"

"So you've never seen it?"

"Never. Do you mean physically?"

He nodded, watching, but there was nothing for him to see. I'd had no idea.

"According to neighbors, they fought a lot. Lots of shouting and raised voices, according to the people on either side of them, some violence. And a spectacular row two days ago. Even neighbors across the road heard that one, including Compton walking out before dawn, shouting at Stafford that he'd have to clear his things out of the house in the next twenty-four hours. We've had a look. It was Compton's house, and Stafford's salary as a civil servant wouldn't begin to support him the way he lived there. He inherits the house and any cash."

"But . . . but . . ." I was speechless.

"But what?"

He waited. I tried again. "That's not evidence of anything."

To my surprise, he agreed. "It's not. Stafford says they did fight, and that the neighbors reported accurately. He also says that they'd been threatening to leave each other for the entire seventeen years they'd been together, and if we spoke to the neighbors again they'd tell us that, too." He shrugged. "There's nothing at the moment to say one way or the other."

I still couldn't get to grips with this. "People fight all the time. People break up all the time. They don't kill each other."

"Stafford was away for work, and we're checking the details. In London, at the moment, door-to-door hasn't found anyone who heard the gunshot, but that's not surprising. Merriam says Compton was dead when he came in at seven. It would be more surprising to find many people in the surrounding offices at that hour."

My eyebrows went up at "Merriam says," but I waited a beat before responding. "Don't you believe him?"

Jake may have attempted not to look exasperated, but without success, because he looked exasperated. "What Merriam told us fits within the onsite time limits for his death. Immigration have confirmed that his passport was scanned at Heathrow at 5:45; his Oyster card was used at Paddington tube station just after 6:30, so that does, too. I said 'he says' because that's what he says. I have no reason to disbelieve him right now."

Or believe him, I mentally added. I knew that what Jake was doing was Detective 101, but I still felt protective.

He was watching me, but now it was a considering look, as though he were trying to work something out. "He didn't tell me he knew you."

I'd been worried and upset about Aidan. Now my sense of grievance with Jake rushed back. "I could say the same to you." I wanted not to sound snotty, but failed. Spectacularly. I fought the urge to cross my arms and give him my librarian-handed-an-overdue-book stare in addition.

He knew, damn him, and I could see him working hard not to smile. So the hell with that. I crossed my arms. He took a careful sip of his wine. "I only found out you knew him last night. You were in his diary for lunch, but just as 'Sam,' and the PC going through it was, not unnaturally, trying to match it to a man's name in his contacts. It was only when it was all being collated later that the DS recognized it. From the previous investigation, not from—" he waved his glass at the kitchen and, I suppose, general togetherness. "She rang me at lunchtime. As far as I'm concerned, it's an unexplained death, and it may very well go no further. I didn't know how well you knew him—I still don't, for that matter. Your name's in his contacts, and it crops up very rarely in his appointment diary . . ." He wasn't asking me, except, of course, he was.

"I've known him a long time. Since I first moved to London." He didn't need a rundown on my two-decade-old love life, I decided.

Casually—far too casually—he drank again before asking, "How did he know you and I were . . . ?"

"It's not a secret that we're . . ." I mimicked his pause. "I saw Anna, I don't know, a month or so ago, at a friend's house for dinner. Aidan was away. Someone probably mentioned it then—we're fun gossip."

"We are? Why?" His voice was sharp. But this was nothing to do with Frank's death. I think his feelings were hurt.

I tried to make light of it. "Come on, 'Sam's shagging a cop.' Who could resist?"

His mouth smiled, but I don't think he thought it was funny. "Most people I know are shagging cops."

"You must be office gossip, too. 'Field's shagging a publisher, or a professor, or something.'" Nope. Not funny. I went back to the sink, and started to lift the washed spinach into the drainer.

Jake moved behind me again. "We have to make some decisions."

I didn't turn around, but asked the spinach, "Do we? What are they?"

"If I'm going back to the office, I won't be finished until the early hours, so I'll go back to my own flat. We have time for only one activity before I go. We can quarrel. Or we can have dinner. I suppose, if we're ruthlessly efficient, we can quarrel over dinner. Or we can go to bed."

"Hmm," I said, reaching behind me and drying my hands on the back of his trousers. "Tough call."

3

When I got to work the next morning, before I did anything else, I wrote to Toby. It was short, and more than slightly awkward, but then, when were condolence notes anything else? I didn't know him well, but I didn't want him to think people were avoiding being in touch because of the circumstances.

And so I e-mailed. My mother would kill me if she knew. *That's what pen and paper were invented for*—I mouthed the words for her—*if you can take the trouble to write, you can take the trouble to write properly.* I'm sure she was right, but I wanted him to hear right away.

Thinking about my mother made me realize I needed to tell her: she'd known Aidan nearly as long as I had. I checked my watch. Not quite eight, but she'd be at work. As always, she picked up on the first ring. Just one of her many annoying habits.

"Have you written to Toby?" she asked. No hello, no nothing. Honest to God, sometimes I want to smack the woman.

I put on my you-are-very-tiresome-but-see-how-patient-I'm-being voice. "Yes, Mother, you brought me up well. And I'm forty-three years old. If I haven't learned by now, it's no longer your responsibility. I was ringing, in fact, to make sure you'd heard."

"Of course I have," she said absently. "Aidan rang yesterday to ask who he should use as an accountant."

"He rang you? Why?"

There was a pause. "I'm his solicitor, Sam. I have been for twenty years."

Helena's a corporate lawyer, but when we were just starting out she'd helped several of my friends. Aidan must have been one of them.

I moved on. "Do you think there's anything I can do? Anything anyone can do?"

Helena paused, which was unusual. I paid attention. "Did you know Matt Holder when he worked for Aidan?"

"I remember him, but no more. Why?"

"He's a disgruntled ex-employee. They're always worth thinking about."

"Thinking about?"

"If Frank killed himself for personal reasons, there's nothing I need to do. If there were problems at the gallery, they will affect Aidan, whether he knew about them or not. So I'm looking to see what those problems might be."

"I remember Matt, and I remember, kind of, when he left. A year ago? More? Aidan said he barely sold anything, and since that was his job, they got rid of him. Was there something else?"

"Holder took them to an employment tribunal, claiming he'd been sacked after he started seeing an ex-boyfriend of Frank's."

"I definitely never heard that."

Helena's silence suggested that the list of things I had never heard was endless. Since I was fully aware of that, I plowed on. "Ex-boyfriend of Frank's? Before Toby, or during? Jake said that they quarreled a lot."

Helena was calm. "That's what Aidan said, too. That they quarreled. About everything, not about this man. And the ex was before Toby's time."

"That's really ex. Why would Frank care if someone dated a man he'd split from nearly two decades earlier? Why would he care if the man dated the entire trumpet section of the Grimethorpe Colliery Band?"

"They weren't mentioned in the suit." I could hear her smile, but she wasn't going to be distracted. "The man was named Werner Schmidt. Have you met him?"

"Me? No, why would I? From where?"

"He's the restorer the gallery uses when they need one."

I shrugged, a useful thing to do on the phone. "Why would I know a restorer? Aidan and I were together before he even set up Merriam-Compton. I vaguely know some of the gallery staff, but only vaguely."

"You mean, you should know them because you've been introduced a dozen times, but you never pay attention."

That was a low blow. Especially because it was true. But we were talking about Frank's death, not my social inadequacies. My phone would run out of charge before we got halfway through those. It wasn't often I could say this, so I took particular pleasure in it. "Mother, concentrate, please. Matt Holder. Frank. Employment tribunal. What happened?"

"Holder claimed he was sacked because Frank didn't like him dating this man. There was absolutely no evidence to prove that Frank had ever mentioned it to him, or to anyone else."

"So he lost?"

"No. Merriam-Compton, much against my advice, settled before the hearing. Holder agreed to withdraw his claim in return for a year's salary and a nondisclosure agreement."

I sat, thinking. Helena isn't one of those lawyers who loves a big brawl. She's pragmatic, more the do-you-need-the-trouble-and-expense-of-legal-action type. If she'd wanted the gallery to stand up to Holder, it was not only because she thought they could win. It was because she thought they *should* win. And yet, for whatever reason, Aidan and Frank hadn't thought the same.

"Goodness," I said feebly.

"Goodness, as Mae West said, had nothing to do with it, dearie." And she hung up. My mother was channeling Mae West? I squinted at the phone, as though that would help. Then I hung up, too. Frank's death and Aidan's involvement seemed much more important, but there was really nothing I had to contribute. And I was supposed to be earning a living. Time to get down to some work.

The morning was quiet, and quietly productive. I shoveled a bunch of admin bumf off my desk and onto Miranda's, and there were no meetings because everyone was either officially or unofficially working from home. There was an auction going on for a book I wanted, but nothing would happen on that for hours, because it was a New York agent, so even if she decided to start the action from home as soon as she woke up, it wouldn't be until noon our time at the earliest. Freakishly, therefore, I found myself with time to read submissions in the office. I pulled out the bottom desk-drawer, propped my feet up on the edge of it, pushed back and read for a couple of hours, only stopping to refill my coffee cup and check e-mails every now and again.

I also made a trip down the hall to the office kitchen. I have a coffeemaker of my own, because I drink so much that if I used the one in the kitchen I'd wear a path in the carpet. But there's an unofficial treat table in the kitchen that's always worth checking. Whenever anyone comes back from holiday, they bring some form of edible goody for the office. Remembering to circulate memos, checking holiday leave, consulting colleagues before you buy a book—compared to the iron rule of the treat table, everything else in the office is negotiable. But just once forget to bring treats back from your holiday, and people will "forget" other things. Not just about work. They'll forget to tell you about who is sleeping with whom, and watch while you make a disparaging remark to the wrong person. Or that Finance has issued a new diktat, and if your expenses aren't in by Friday, they won't be paid for three months. Or that builders are due to renew the wiring on the day you'd booked your most important author in for a meeting. Frankly, if you don't bring a treat back, you might as well not come back yourself: you're dead to that second layer of office life that is so much more important than the primary one.

I wanted to see what was on the table, and I also wanted a break. I wandered into the narrow galley kitchen, and found both Turkish delight, which I detest, and a group of colleagues from marketing. I poured some of the nasty communal coffee as my passport to the group.

"What's up?"

Nothing much, apparently. It was a bitch-fest about everyone working at home. Dull. I prepared to move away.

Then Alex, one of the designers, said, "I had a drink last night with Jim Reynolds. He said he's on that CultCo thing with you."

I barked out a laugh. "'CultCo.' That's perfect. We're a messianic-corporate combo. We play weddings, bar mitzvahs, and bookfairs." He laughed at that, and then laughed again when I admitted, "Which one is Jim Reynolds? I've been functionally comatose for most of the meetings."

"He said that what he most liked about you was how obviously you wished you were somewhere else."

Eep. I hadn't realized I was that transparent.

"Red hair, goatee?" he prompted. Yes, of course. I'd noticed him, too, because he contributed almost as little as I did.

"What does he do? Is he a designer?"

"He does installation work." Alex must have seen I had no idea what that meant. "He designs art exhibitions." Still nothing. "The layout, the design, the panels, and the showcases." I was with him now, and I could see why the Culture Committee panel—I was definitely calling it CultCo from now on—might be something he wanted to be involved with. "He also produces what he calls tourist tat for museum shops. Rothko tea towels, Holbein key chains. I think that's where his company makes most of their money."

"You can't have too many Henry VIII mouse mats," I agreed

as I tipped the rest of my coffee down the sink. I'd come back when people went somewhere where the sweets were nicer.

When I got back to my desk there was an e-mail from someone named Jeremy Compton. It was Frank's brother, thanking me on his behalf for my message, and adding that they had no information about the funeral yet, but that friends and family were gathering at Toby's that evening, and if I wanted to come I'd be welcome.

I couldn't think of anything I wanted less, but it seemed the decent thing to do, so after work I went home, changed, and headed out again. I'd never been to Frank's house, but from the address his brother had given me it wasn't far from where I lived. It turned out to be a mews house in what looked like a conservation area, all antique Victorian streetlights, and, in the mews at any rate, cobbles on the road. Hell if you were wearing heels, but I rarely did, so I thought it was charming. I might start a new school of philosophy: selfish aesthetics. Or maybe an Olympic sport.

Inside, the house was not big—it was in a mews, after all— but it opened up behind the front door like some sort of space-ship that does interesting things with a fifth dimension. The sitting room occupied the bulk of the ground floor, taking in a glassed-in extension at the back and giving plenty of space for two sitting areas, as well as a dining area next to a door that I assumed led to the kitchen. The style, however, wasn't remotely *Architectural Digest*, where the photographs always suggest that no one lives there—have you ever seen a room in a designer magazine that contained a toothbrush, or even a dog's bowl? Frank and Toby's house was clearly lived in. For the owner of a gallery where the display areas were white, with discreet touches of white, and white for contrast, his place was a riot of color, with a bunch of different colored rugs and bright modernist printed fabrics.

There were a dozen people or so milling about, some keeping Toby company in the main room, others I could see through the door into the kitchen, preparing food. I was quickly filled in. Toby's friends had set up a rota, and a changing group would take turns to bring food, try and make Toby eat a bit, and generally keep an eye on him. I agreed at once to join in. I wasn't a close friend, but I was an old one, and one look at Toby said he was only hanging on by a thread.

I went over to kiss him hello, and say those pointless things you say when someone dies. I've never worked out whether the banality and general uselessness of the phrases are worse than not saying anything at all. But what else is there? *How are you?* The answer to that was, obviously, Crap. *How are things?* Worse. *What's coming up in the future?* I'm planning a funeral.

So I did the I'm-so-sorry-and-please-let-me-know-if-there's-something-I-can-do thing. Toby's eyes were bloodshot, and he stared at a corner of the rug and didn't look up even when someone spoke directly to him. If the words were repeated a few times, he'd answer, but slowly, like he was waiting out an echo. There was a cup of tea beside him, but it had scum on the surface, and must have been there for hours. He looked far more like someone who had lost his life partner than someone who had been on the verge of splitting from a violent relationship. But then, how would I know? How would anyone?

I'm ashamed to say that after a few minutes I fled to the

kitchen. I know, no one else was having a good time either, and they were gritting it out. I didn't. In the kitchen I paused to take stock. The room must have been an addition the original house, with a glass roof, and two of the four walls entirely glass. Here you could see the modernist gallery-owner's hand: white walls, white cupboards, white table. They'd gone color-crazy out by putting in a beige floor, but otherwise the room could have been an extension to their gallery space. I thought of that dark body in the dark room again, and shivered. Which was no help. A couple of people were taking food out of plastic boxes and laying it out on plates. I saw some lettuce and salad vegetables and hunted for a chopping board. I could pretend I was being helpful, and avoid having to interact.

No such luck. A small, slight girl with hair so blonde it was almost white, came over and watched me for a moment, then produced a jar and started making vinaigrette beside me. I looked again out of the corner of my eye and revised upward. Not a girl, maybe twenty or so. She was wearing a T-shirt and jeans, and didn't look like she'd come from work. Apart from her startling hair, she was pretty rather than beautiful, but the hair would make anyone look twice. And then look again.

She smiled tentatively.

"I'm Sam," I said, putting down the knife and holding out my hand.

"Sam? Aidan's friend?"

I don't think of myself that way, but OK. I nodded. "And you're . . . ?" I prompted.

She blushed. "I'm Lucy. Frank's niece."

She was the one Aidan had mentioned, the one who had

worked in the gallery. "I'm sorry about Frank," I said. I'd said it a dozen times now, and it still never began to sound even halfway adequate.

She shrugged and looked down. Hadn't yet worked out what the conventional response was.

"You must have been close. Aidan said you worked with them, and they hoped you'd continue."

She looked up at that, as if she hadn't been sure. Maybe she hadn't. Frank wasn't very chatty. "I'd like to, but I've got another year at university. And now . . ." She chewed at her lip and ducked her head, shaking the salad dressing ferociously.

I tried moving on to something more neutral. "Which bit of art dealing do you like? Selling, or the acquisitions?"

She was definite. "The shows. Selling is what I'd do because you have to be able to do it to be able to show, but it's the idea of the show, putting the works together so that they say something, you know?"

I nodded. I felt like that about editing. But, "Wouldn't there be more scope for that in a museum?"

She looked mutinous. This was, apparently, a point that had already been made. "I'd need a PhD to be a curator, another three years at least, maybe more. And then I'd only be hired as a junior. It would be years before I could put on a show the way I wanted to." She looked at me defiantly, waiting for an argument. Which I had no intention of offering. "Absolutely. I see that. You might have a lesser range at a gallery—the artists the gallery represents, and mostly only what they're doing now—but the hierarchy isn't there. Or other curators eyeing up the space for their own areas of expertise."

She looked grateful that I understood, and expanded a little. "Frank and Aidan said I could do a summer show, when the gallery is quiet, with some of the pieces they own." She must have seen I wasn't following, because she explained, enjoying the chance to display her expertise. "Galleries usually don't own the work they show. The artist owns it, the gallery shows it, and gets a commission when they sell it. Sometimes they buy and sell on their own—maybe from an auction if they have a client who is looking for work by that artist, for example. But every gallery also ends up with works that they own. They buy works by artists they represent when they appear on the market, to keep the prices up, or to build up for the future when the prices will have risen. Or if they buy an artist's estate, the artist probably owned paintings by other artists, and they come, too. Or they just buy something thinking they can sell it, and then they can't."

She stopped, flustered by the blizzard of information she'd produced, but I looked encouraging. It was interesting, and anyway, it meant I didn't have to go out and mingle. I'm terrible at talking to strangers, so I nodded encouragingly, hoping she'd go on. Bless her, she did. "Merriam-Compton has some great pieces that never get seen, and Frank said I could do a little show of some of them. The summer shows never sell much—buyers are away, the art fairs take the business—so I think he was glad to have something that would cost nothing to mount, and might even generate some cash flow."

If I didn't keep her motoring along, I might have to go and sit with Toby again. "What were you planning?"

"Frank and Aidan thought it would be good if I did something with their Stevensons, so we could pick up some of the publicity the Tate is bound to get with their big retrospective."

I hadn't known there was going to be a Stevenson show at the Tate. That would be fun. I loved pop art, and I thought Stevenson's collages were great, although I'd seen most of them in books, not in real life. I made a mental note to keep an eye out for the exhibition. Then I noticed Lucy's phrasing. "'Their' Stevensons? Do they have lots?"

She looked at me curiously, then shrugged. "I suppose there's no reason you should know. Merriam-Compton are his dealers."

I looked around again and caught sight of Toby still staring at the carpet. So back to Lucy. I tried to think of something interesting to say, but my tank was empty. I made a stretch. "I love his work, especially the book ones."

She looked blank.

"There's no reason for me to know that Merriam-Compton represent Stevenson, and there's no reason for you to know I'm an editor. But that's why I like those collages he did with pages from books, or the covers. I know it's a bit tragic, but I actually read the pages he includes—you know, which Dostoyevsky novel is this taken from, and oh look, I have the same edition of *The Naked Lunch*."

She didn't quite back away from me, but I could tell she thought I was beyond weird. Oh well. I'd chopped enough vegetables to keep an entire commune fed for a season. I could move away without seeming rude. I wiped my hands on a tea towel and looked around for a bowl to put them in. I didn't see a bowl, but I did see that Aidan had arrived, and he was standing in the doorway attempting to catch my eye. I summed up, as though we'd had a meaningful conversation: "That sounds like a great plan," leaving whatever "that" might be carefully unspecified. "They'd be mad not to want you to go ahead." Then I mumbled the usual "see you later" and set off toward Aidan. He had retreated to the sunroom at the back, which looked as if it was barely used. There was a desk and a chair, a bench loaded with old newspapers and magazines, and not much else. Aidan was sitting at the desk, flipping through two vast piles of mail. I pushed the newspapers on the floor and sat on the bench.

"This is office post," he said, as though he needed to excuse himself to me.

I nodded and waited. He finally looked up. "I wanted to ask you if your policeman had said anything."

I swallowed a smart-arse response—"my" policeman?—and just shook my head. "He repeated pretty much what you told me at lunch: unexplained death, and they're investigating."

Aidan pushed a second pile of papers off the bench and sat down beside me, reaching for my hand. He didn't say anything else, and I didn't have anything to say, so we sat there quietly.

I wasn't thinking of anything much, when Lucy's plans ran through my head. I didn't think I'd jumped, but I must have.

Aidan looked at me.

I shook my head. "Nothing. A work thing I'd forgotten." Should I tell him? Jake? This was exactly what I'd foreseen at the start. Whose side was I on?

I was home by ten, and I spent half an hour online reading back issues of *The New York Times*. Then I phoned Helena. If she'd rung me at that hour, I'd have been furious, and more than half-way to being asleep. With my mother, I'd be lucky to find her home. She was, though, which was a relief.

"I was at Toby's, and I was talking to his niece, the one who works in the gallery. She says they represent Edward Stevenson."

My mother was as infuriatingly calm as she always is. "Yes, I think I knew that. And?"

"Didn't you see the papers last month?"

There was a silence. That was unusual. Then, even more unusual, she sounded like me. "Goodness."

I was too anxious even to think of mimicking her from earlier. "The question is, what do I do with this information?"

Helena knows me well. "Let's just revise first. I assume you've just checked the reports."

"I did. And they're creepily familiar."

Helena didn't have any truck with creepiness. Just the facts, m'lud.

So I gathered myself. "The first newspaper report I could see was in May. A family in Vermont decided to convert their unfinished basement into a family room. When the builders took out an old boiler, they found a skeleton behind a partition wall. There was a shotgun and a suicide note beside it. Dental records identified the remains as those of Edward Stevenson, who had lived there until 1993. But that's where the trouble seems to have begun."

"Go on."

I wouldn't be able to swear it, but I was sure Helena was making notes. So I pulled up the articles I'd bookmarked. "Stevenson vanished in 1993. He wrote a letter to his wife saying he was

leaving her and his family and going to join an ashram in India."
I double-checked the date. "An ashram, in 1993? That's what
it says. Anyway, at the time everyone believed it. He'd complained a lot about how commercialized the art world had become, he was interested in Eastern religions, and so on." It
sounded woolly to me, but it hadn't to his wife. At the inquest
her lawyer said she had never even considered that the letter
might have been untrue. "The letter had said he'd be in touch,
but when they didn't hear from him, after a few weeks they hired
detectives, who searched in India, and then everywhere else.
Even Cardiff, which was where he was from originally. But there
was no trace. Until this past May, when his skeleton showed up."

"What happened next?"

"There's a report from the inquest. The formal identification.
The coroner's report, which says that, as far as can be seen after
twenty-odd years, the wound in the skull was not inconsistent
with the shotgun beside him. Then the note found with the
body was reprinted." I read out: "I am sorry. I have recently been
informed that I have a terminal illness that will conclude my
life painfully within half a year. I have chosen this way to die,
in order to spare us all distress."

I paused. Helena was definitely writing. Then I continued.
"But it was typed, with no signature. After all this time, the type-
writer he used is long gone, although they compared the note
to other letters typed on that machine, and they matched. The
man who had been the family doctor—he was elderly, and is now
retired, but seemed from the reports to be absolutely compos—
testified. He said he'd checked his records, and that Stevenson
had had a checkup two months before he vanished, and he had

no illness of any sort. The police said they were checking to see if Stevenson had seen any other doctors, but the inquest was adjourned, and that's where the newspaper reports stop. After that there's just loads of stuff about his importance as a Pop artist in the 1960s and 1970s, and even more about ashrams, or suicide, or ashrams *and* suicide. But no information. There's nothing except speculation. I don't think the inquest was ever resumed: there's nothing in the big U.S. papers, and I think there would have been."

Helena made an affirmative grunt. She was still treating it, and me, like a legal deposition.

I was used to it, and waited. When I thought she'd finished, I summarized. (OK, I might not make notes, but I like things to be neat, too.) "So, an artist may, or may not, have shot himself twenty years ago, leaving a typed, unsigned note. A month after his body is discovered, his dealer may, or may not, have shot himself, leaving a typed, unsigned note. Mother, what do I do? Normally . . ." It worried me that I thought there was something I'd normally do when encountering violent death, but I didn't have the leftover brain power to think about it now. "Normally, I'd tell Jake. I doubt very much that he'll think it's coincidence, or at least, he'll think it's a coincidence worth investigating. But Aidan . . ." I trailed away miserably.

No trailing away for Helena. "You need to tell him," she said crisply. My mother drives me crazy because she is always so certain about everything. I often think how amazing it would be to be as certain about one thing—any one thing—as she is about everything. Today I was just relieved she was making up my mind for me.

"Do you think maybe he already knows? He might not have told me." I was wheedling.

Helena didn't play games. "It's extremely unlikely, and you know it, Sam. The discovery of Stevenson's body was news in the arts pages, and a month ago. Merriam-Compton represent Stevenson, but they also represent—what, three or four dozen other artists? Even if, for some reason, the police are going through the lists of the gallery's artists—and it would be extremely unlikely given the very slim evidence unless an inquest rules that it requires further investigation—even then, there would be nothing to make them pay attention to that one name. Apart from anything else, it's a fairly common and unmemorable one." Her tone sharpened. "They haven't got the Art Fraud team in, have they?"

"I don't think so. Jake didn't say. But he didn't say they didn't. It sounded as if they were thinking more along the lines of financial problems, not fraud."

"Then you need to tell him."

Welcome to the black-and-white world of Helena Clair. Just to maintain some sense of my own independence, I saluted the phone as I hung up.

I would tell him. But I'd wait until I saw him, which wasn't going to be tonight. A problem delayed is a problem, well, delayed so I can worry about it some more. Lip-gnawing anxiety is my major skill set. Everyone's got to be good at something.

4

In between worrying about what I was going to tell Jake, I spent an hour working on my presentation for the CultCo panel, before admitting finally that I couldn't concentrate. But Celia Stein had given me some good information, and I merged it with what I already had, figuring I could probably make it last for ten of my twenty-minute presentation. I'd agreed to meet the other panel members for breakfast the following morning, to map out how we wanted the seminar to run. At least now I'd be able to say I was halfway there.

The difference between publishing and the quasi-governmental, quasi-business world of arts charities came home to me when my alarm went off at half-past five. I'm an early riser, but that was plain silly. I'd agreed to breakfast, thinking it would be at eight, eight thirty-ish. I hoped I didn't visibly pale when they agreed on seven as though it were routine, but I bet I did. Because, frankly, who knew that there were two half-past fives in the day?

Things began to look up once I got myself out the door. There was only a pale, watery sun, but at that hour of the morning it seemed hopeful, and full of promise, rather than just ineffectual. And before the traffic really started moving, the scents of the early summer blossom in the front gardens lay like a blanket on the air. I walked along, ticking off my neighbors' wisteria and jasmine, sniffing the air ferociously as I passed each one. I was happy, even though I probably looked like a junkie ready for her next fix.

The Delaunay wasn't what I would have chosen for a meeting either—too big, too noisy—but at least it wasn't far from my office, and I could have a croissant to dunk in my coffee. I normally don't eat breakfast at all. In theory, I run first thing in the morning, although people who really run might take issue with that verb when applied to my early-morning outings. And when that's over, it's just a scramble to get to work. I don't have time for food, too. But if I had to be rousted out of bed in the middle of the night, I'd be hungry by seven, and besides, license to play with your food is never something to be passed up.

So I was moderately cheerful by the time I got to the restaurant. The panelists were a woman from a new City concert and theater space, an art-video producer, and a curator from a museum in Glasgow, who was not, therefore, going to be at this planning session. And, I was pleased to remember, Jim Reynolds, the installation designer Alex had mentioned to me the day before. He'd sounded, via Alex, no more enthusiastic than I was, which made me like him without ever having spoken to him.

Enthusiastic or not, he was already there when I arrived at ten to seven, a big red-headed man in carefully dressed-down designer scruffies. He waved away my comment on his promptness by saying he lived only five minutes away. I think if that were the case I would have had my first coffee quietly at home. But not Jim, it appeared. He was already halfway down a cafetière. I "borrowed" some of his and we ordered a fresh pot.

"Do you know any of the others?" I asked.

"I know Janey, the video producer. I worked with her once. The concert-venue woman, what's her name, Willa Phillips, not at all. I think she's only just moved into this job, and it seems like she's using the committee, and the panel, as a way of networking." I approved of the way he said "networking," as though he'd turned over a rock and found a whole bunch of slugs. I paused, wondering why I thought networking was such a bad thing. Maybe as long as you networked without wanting to do it, it was fine, while consciously setting out to make connections for the sake of career advancement was shabby? It was still unfair of me, but less unfair than before. I decided to drop it before I'd have to accept that I was a total bitch. Seven in the morning was no time for that sort of self-discovery.

Jim brought me back to the present. "Do we know what we want out of this panel?"

I was clear. "I want to not look like we've been wasting our time. Anything over and above that is a bonus." I have no idea what made me be so honest, but it seemed the right path to take.

It was. Jim relaxed back in his chair and laughed, uninhibited and strong. Several tables looked across at us to see who was having fun at this time of day. Either you were working, their expressions said, or you should stay at home. Having fun was not on the agenda until they got to "Any Other Business" that evening.

I was on mine now. Jim kept laughing gently. "Good to have ambitions."

I nodded seriously. "Mine are small, but perfectly formed." We were united, having somehow silently agreed we were allies. Which was good, because the other two now appeared, and I didn't think I would repeat my remark to either of them. They were taking this very seriously. Janey seemed pleasant, and more on my wavelength, but video art is not something that is ever going to make money. She needed to find regular subsidies, and the panel was a means to that end. As to Willa, I decided in ten seconds flat that Jim had read her correctly. This was career-advancement time. Fine with me. If she needed this, she could do the bulk of the work. Jim and I executed a deft pincer-movement, and it ended up that yes, to her surprise she found she would be taking on the bulk of the planning.

By eight, therefore, we were back on the street. Jim's office was in Soho, so we walked together.

We talked about Alex, as the only person we knew in common. "Where did you meet?" I asked.

"I did some work for him when I was first starting out. He hired me to redesign one of your colophons." Colophons are the little publisher's logos that go on the book spines. No one except publishers ever looks at them, but we treat them like small pets, lavishing time and attention and money on them, grooming them, giving them new looks, as though the rest of the world cares.

"One we have now?"

He nodded. "When you started your new paperback imprint."

"Cool. It's sort of geeky of me, but I love that stuff."

He looked down at me. "Geeky? That's my life you're calling geeky, there."

"Oops. Sorry." I smiled sunnily to show I wasn't sorry at all. "I worked for Tetrarch when I was first starting out, and one of my jobs was bringing a bunch of old books back into print, so I spent a lot of time looking at the colophons they'd had, deciding which needed to be revamped and which could be treated as 'heritage.' It was fun."

"It is, but unless you're doing it for huge corporations, where thirty-seven committees get involved, there's no way of earning a living at it, so we dropped it years ago."

"Who's 'we?' Do you work for a museum now?"

"No, I have two partners, and we do projects on contract. They mostly do corporate work, trade fairs or company headquarters. They make the money, I get us the publicity and kudos, because I'm the museum guy."

"So what are you working on at the moment, museum guy?"

"My big project is the Stevenson retrospective at the Tate. We're doing the installation, and also designing and producing the tie-in goods they sell in the shop."

There was no particular reason I shouldn't hear Stevenson's name twice in two days. Lucy had told me there was a big exhibition coming up, Jim was an exhibition designer. If Frank hadn't died, this would just have been the sort of coincidence where everybody said, *Gosh, what a small world.* But Frank had died.

"I heard about the exhibition just last night," I said. "From the niece of Stevenson's dealer."

"From Lucy?" he said quickly. He saw my surprise, and added, "She's been working on the show with the gallery, and we've become quite friendly." He flushed slightly, and I assumed that "friendly" encompassed more than having coffee together. Or even a gentle game of dominoes. I looked at him out of the corner of my eye as he slowly turned even redder, and decided that dominoes was definitely not on the list of what he and Lucy were doing together.

"She seems very nice," appeared to be a suitably bland response, so I made it.

"She is," he said, as though I'd argued. When I looked startled he backed off and shrugged. "Her uncle doesn't like me."

"Why not? You seem likeable to me." He was a bit older than Lucy, but not enough to be unusual, he had his own company, the Tate thought enough of his abilities to employ him. "Do you have a history of being unkind to small, furry animals, or is it that weekly strip poker game with the Bishop of Durham's gang that bothered him?"

Jim grinned. "The Bishop of Durham's strip poker night remains an unfulfilled ambition." He sighed theatrically. "One day . . ." Then he was serious. "I don't know why he doesn't—" He winced. "Why he *didn't* like me, and I feel terrible now. Everything was fine at first, so I must have said something, or done something, but I have no idea what. And then he decided he didn't like our work, either."

"Your installation?"

He frowned. "No, that was approved a long time ago, and anyway, even if he didn't like it, that's the Tate's side of things. This was only a few weeks ago. We'd come up with ideas for souvenirs for the shop that the Tate loved. And God knows, getting the Tate to love anything is a struggle in itself." He shook his head at the follies of art institutions. "We'd designed the usual things, mugs, posters, you know?" I did. "Then, because Stevenson used so many typographic elements, we thought it would be fun to do something with those. We chose a bunch of collages that had book jackets in them, and we reproduced the jackets to wrap around pads, so you had notebooks with the collage on them, on which you could see the book jacket, in which, you know, a Russian-doll thing of a reproduction in a reproduction."

"Sounds fun." Fun might be pushing it, but it sounded harmless enough.

"You'd think, wouldn't you? But Merriam-Compton kicked up this huge fuss, said we were sullying Stevenson's reputation, making him look like he was just a graphic designer. Which is absurd, but they have a lot of influence with the estate, and so we had to agree not to do them."

"So mugs equal artistic integrity, notepads equal commercial exploitation?"

He laughed, but he was angry, too. "Apparently so. Anyway, I ended up only communicating with the gallery through Lucy. And now Lucy's spending most of her time at Compton's house, but it feels wrong to go there now he's dead when I know he wouldn't have wanted me there when he was alive. So I'd feel bad visiting. And I feel bad not visiting."

"Why don't you meet her nearby? It'll get her out of the house for a few hours, and you can think of it as your Boy Scout daily act of kindness."

"That's a really good idea. Thank you." He looked around

vaguely, like I was leading him astray. Which I was, because he stopped suddenly. "Damn. I've walked past my office. I'll be in touch about the panel. And thanks for the suggestion. Very slick." And he went back to a door nestled beside a dim-sum restaurant and was gone.

In my entire life, no one has ever suggested I am slick. I preened. And tripped over the curb.

At lunchtime Jake texted to say he'd be home—by which he meant my home—around seven. We tended to spend most of our time at my place, for two reasons. One, his flat in Hammersmith was much farther from the Tube than mine was, and from there to my office needed two changes, instead of being on a direct line. Jake drove to work, so it didn't make much difference to him. And two, the first time I'd seen his flat, I'd looked around the nice cookie-cutter sitting room without a single personal possession on display and asked brightly, "When did you move in?" The conversation went downhill after he said, "Eight years ago."

As I said, Jake's very intuitive, good at reading people, but in many ways he's, well, he's just such a *guy*. I'm not starting a women-nest-men-live-in-caves rant, but he moved into this place after his divorce. His wife moved back to Lisbon with their son, and while Tonio came to visit once, sometimes twice a year, his was the only room that looked as if it hadn't been designed by the division at IKEA that creates room displays for their catalogues. No, it was worse than that. The IKEA people would have added fake photos of Auntie Mavis, or some ethnic rugs, or paintings on the walls. This place looked like it was ready to let out on short-term rental from an agency. There was some clutter, sure: books, magazines, those random odds and ends you never need until the day after you throw them away. But that was all. And so we mostly hung out at my flat. At least there was some color there, and I didn't fear I'd been struck with some dread neurological condition that made me only see beige every time I walked in the front door. All right, so maybe I was doing the men-live-in-caves rant. Beige caves. Impersonal beige caves. My point is, that when Jake said he'd see me at home, he meant my place.

I got back with an hour to spare, so I put the makings of a stew together and stuck it in the oven. I could have had a drink and read, but I felt restless. I went up to see my top-floor neighbor instead.

I live in a Victorian house that was converted into three flats a long time ago. I live on the ground floor, and above me are a couple of actors named Kay and Anthony Lewis, and their five-year-old son Bim. Bim's real name is Timothy, but Bim was what he called himself when he first learned to speak, and it suits him—he's gregarious and outgoing, and it's easy to imagine him bim-bam banging an imaginary drum as he marches along. Above the Lewises was Mr. Rudiger. I knew his first name now—Pavel—but I'd never contemplated using it. In the nearly twenty years I'd lived here, I'd seen him exactly twice. And then, a few months ago, my flat had been broken into, and he'd put me up for the night. And we became friends.

Mr. Rudiger doesn't go out. By that that I don't mean he mostly stays at home. I mean, he doesn't go out. At crisis point, those months ago, he'd left the house once, and after that he very occasionally came down to my flat for coffee or supper. Apart from that he never crosses his threshold. His daughter brings him groceries and any other essentials once a week, and as I see the post I know that the advent of Internet shopping has meant he isn't as reliant on her as he used to be. And now I know him better, I often exchange his books at the library, or supplement his daughter's shopping runs with the odd thing from the market.

Not that I'm boasting. I'm not a heaven-sent Lady Bountiful, scattering sweetness and light. If I were, it wouldn't have taken me nearly twenty years to meet him, or to discover he had been a hugely influential architect in the 1960s and early 1970s, but had retired, no one knew why, when he was still young. I still don't know why, and I wouldn't dream of asking. I think of us as friends, but he is thirty years older than I am, and his manner is very formal—as I said, I never even use his first name. As far as I'm concerned, "Mr." *is* his first name.

I tapped on his door, and when he answered, asked if he'd like to come down for a drink. That's the polite code we've devised for "I thought I'd see if you'd like some company, and if you have the inclination—I assume he has the time—I'd be happy to come in and visit for a while." That evening, as he mostly does when I go up, he stepped back and gestured me in, saying he was about to open a bottle.

His flat couldn't be more different from mine if we'd set out to do it intentionally. Despite his career as a modernist architect (raw concrete was his thing), the place looks like something from Hansel and Gretel—all Central European dark wood, that is, not that it's the home of a starving woodcutter and his family. The floors are polished dark wood, the furniture is dark wood and dark upholstery, and then red rugs and curtains warm everything up. It's like a very comfortable womb, if the womb had been decorated in the Austro-Hungarian Empire's heyday.

Mr. Rudiger poured us some wine, and we discussed household matters—did the hall need repainting, and would Anthony have time to hack back the ivy soon, and wasn't Bim getting big, basically just catching up on the week or so since we'd last seen each other. Then I filled him in on Aidan and Frank, which, I realized once I began to talk, was why I'd come up. Mr. Rudiger was a terrific listener, always interested, always ready to offer an opinion, but always, somehow, keeping himself apart. The world operated like television for him: it was a one-way street, and he didn't participate. Since he was not invested in the outcome, everything he said sounded sensibly impartial. Helena told me what to do. Mr. Rudiger somehow told me what I already knew I ought to be doing.

"I'm waiting for Jake to get home, and then I'll tell him," I finished.

Mr. Rudiger cocked his head. "He's home."

"He is?" I hadn't heard the door.

"About ten minutes ago, but I wanted the end of the story first."

That was slightly uncanny, and made me wonder how much noise I made when I got home. "I'd better go and get it over with then." I put my glass down.

"Do you want to ask him up here?" He smiled at me gently in the way he had, as if someone was telling him a good joke just out of my hearing. I knew, and he knew that I knew, that if I told Jake in front of Mr. Rudiger, Jake couldn't get cross with me for being involved. And, really, I didn't see how I could help being involved, I whined to myself. I hadn't become friends with Aidan twenty years ago in the expectation that his business partner would die in an unexplained fashion two decades later. And I hadn't chosen to sit on this sodding arts panel in the expectation that a fellow panelist would be jumping said business partner's niece. In fact, none of this was my fault, and I was becoming quite self-righteously outraged by Jake's potential crossness.

Mr. Rudiger's smile broadened. They weren't telling jokes out of earshot now, but right here in the room. I grinned back at him, since we both knew what I'd been thinking.

"Good idea," I said, and I texted down, *Dinner won't be ready till 8:30 earliest. Mr. R says would you like to come up for a drink?*

Mr. Rudiger looked amused again. "Do you text from room to room?"

I was appalled. "No!" I hesitated. "Hardly ever." My tone was grudging.

He laughed again, and moved to the door, hearing Jake on the stairs before I did. I waited in the sitting room while the two men greeted each other. I needed to work out exactly what I was going to say, and until that moment I'd successfully managed to avoid thinking about it at all.

When they sat down, I let Jake take his first mouthful of wine before starting. I told him about Lucy, and the gallery representing Stevenson, who had recently reappeared as another potential suicide. As Helena had guessed, if Jake had seen the news of the finding of Stevenson's body, he hadn't remembered it. And as I had guessed, he was not happy to hear about it from me.

He rubbed his head and stared at me angrily, as though I'd done it to spite him. "You couldn't have told me this morning, or last night, when I would have had time to get moving on this, send some e-mails to the States?" Then he looked away. Not cross now, just thinking out what to do. He stood. "I'll make some calls, send some e-mails. I'll need an hour before dinner." Even I could interpret the don't-call-us-we'll-call-you click to Mr. Rudiger's front door.

That was interesting. He was upset that I was involved, which I had expected, but he didn't think what I had told him was worth going back to the office for, which I hadn't. Or perhaps he just had a mad passion for my lamb stew.

I shared this possibility with Mr. Rudiger, who laughed out loud. I guess my stew isn't as good as I think it is.

5

In the morning, Jake had left for work before I got back from my run. That almost never happened, and he usually told me beforehand if he had to go in early. I didn't take it as a particularly good sign. He'd been quiet when I came down from Mr. Rudiger's, not irritated anymore, but absent-minded.

Most people now, when you say "absent-minded," are absent, but not terribly minded. Usually they (OK, me, too) are mentally absent because they're checking e-mails and texts, playing on Twitter or Facebook, giving the real people around them half their attention, or less, and scattering the remainder among a range of electronic distractions. I know that, truthfully, the only time I am entirely focused is when I'm editing. Then I shut down my e-mail and Twitter altogether, and concentrate absolutely on one thing. It's an inanimate thing when it's a manuscript. When I'm working on a new book face-to-face with an author, it's the same focus, but on a person, and my mind is split in two, with a constant assessment, like a voice-over, running in my head alongside, but separate from, whatever I am saying out loud: is s/he receptive now, if so, it's a good time to hit him/her with that major reservation I have about the first chapter; s/he is on the defensive now, so I'll fall back and go through the things I like and think really work. I am aware that I'm doing this—and I'm really good at it, if I do say so myself—but the focus is entirely on that other person, and I never think about me, much less about e-mail, or anything else at all. If you listen to the way fishing enthusiasts talk about fly-fishing, it sounds the same: you end up concentrating so hard, you're part of the river, and of the fish, and you somehow feel what they feel.

It sounds really wanky, I know. I assume most editors do, and think, the same, although I've never asked. But now I realized that this aspect of my job matched Jake's. Agreed, I don't generally mix with people who think violent death adds that vital soupçon of flavor to the day's routine, but when Jake interviews witnesses—and I know this from first-hand experience—he has the same honed-down concentration, and I'm sure if I asked him he'd say there was the same split-voice commentary. The only difference is that Jake also has levels of antagonism to overcome. Most witnesses don't want him to know what they are thinking. Even if they are not guilty of anything worse than not waiting for the little green man before crossing the road, there are always things that are no business of the police. Authors might be antagonistic, too—might? Hell, they definitely are—but they mostly recognize that we want the same things: for their book to be as good as it can be. The only divergence is on how to get it there.

So, when I said Jake was absent-minded, what I really meant was that he was concentrating, just not on me. That was fine, and for the most part I spent the evening as I would have done if he hadn't been there. Mostly. I didn't read while we ate, which I would have done if I'd been alone—that seemed a little too blatantly fuck you. But I flicked the radio on, and listened to that, and then after we'd washed up I put the TV on so Jake could pretend to be watching, while I pretended to read. On the surface, there wasn't much difference between this evening and many others. Except that he wasn't really there, and that when I went to bed, he just sat on, staring past the television.

And in the morning he left early. Without telling me.

It was the case, not me, I repeated. And for most of the day I believed it.

Helena rang at lunchtime to say Aidan and Anna were coming for dinner, and did I have anything scheduled that meant I couldn't come, too.

"I've got a book launch at six, but that's all." That was easy, but I paused. "Is Jake invited, too? I don't know if he's working tonight, but are you going to ask him?"

"How early can you leave your launch?"

I was surprised. Helena never got home before seven, and so she rarely ate before 8:30. This was breaking all her rules.

"If you can get here by seven, we can have an hour to talk, and I'll ask Jake for 8:30."

I still hesitated. "I think I'm uncomfortable with that. Would it be better if we didn't come?"

"I'm uncomfortable, too. But no one asked us about our comfort levels. We get on with the situation we've been handed as best we can." The lawyer's credo. Maybe I'd embroider it on a cushion for her birthday. If I learned to embroider first.

I thought for a moment. I was in the middle, and I couldn't change that. Helena was in the middle because she was Aidan's lawyer and my mother. She couldn't change that. Maybe I'd just embroider the damn cushion for myself.

"I'll get there as close to seven as I can."

My mother lives a twenty-minute walk from me. Near enough for a friendly back and forth, not so close I feel her terrifying efficiency bearing down on me all the time. I didn't bother to change, since it was just Aidan and Anna, and in effect a working dinner. Or a war summit. I brushed my hair and put some eyeliner on. That way I'd look as if I'd made an effort. I wouldn't really, but it would be enough to stop Helena from sighing when she saw me.

If I didn't love Helena, I would have learned to dislike her a long time ago. She seems to do everything perfectly, with no effort. I know that that's not true—I know it can't be true—but from my vantage point, that's what it looks like. She's been a senior partner at a big City law firm forever, she has an active social life, with dozens—hundreds? thousands?—of interesting friends, with whom she has dinner, goes to films, concerts and theater. She is well dressed without being a style victim. She exercises, she doesn't drink too much, she probably even flosses regularly and gets her five portions of fruit and vegetables a day. So you can see why she drives me crazy. Her private life is firmly private. She and my father divorced when I was a young teenager. I don't know why. I was too young to be told more than an edited version when it happened, and since then I've never asked and have no plans to. I've always figured if I stick my nose in her business, it gives her license to stick hers in mine.

I only spent twenty minutes at the launch. It wasn't one of my books, or I couldn't have done that, but I wanted to go and be a warm body to be counted. It was a book I admired, and it looked like it wasn't going to get much attention. Which is often what happens to books you admire but don't love. By the time I got to Helena's, Aidan was already there, and it looked like he had been for a while, papers in front of him, iPad open. Anna was coming from work, and would be there closer to eight. The plan was that the three of us would speak first, them as client–solicitor, me as unofficial conduit of police information. But it all felt slightly underhand, just as Jake being invited later felt underhand. And shabby.

Helena picked up her laptop, which she'd put down when I let myself in. "We're going through the Stevenson inquest reports," said Helena, answering my unspoken query. "As Stevenson's dealer, Aidan had a representative there."

"I read the *New York Times* reports, and I saw the English papers last month. What was there that wasn't reported?"

Aidan rubbed his eyes. He looked exhausted. "That's what makes no sense. There wasn't any more. The situation was weird, but not disturbing, you know?" He looked over at me, presumably as a connoisseur of the difference between weird and disturbing. Weirdly *and* disturbingly, I knew exactly the difference.

"Delia and Celia both told exactly the same story, there was nothing off," he continued, looking aggravated rather than worried.

"Delia and Celia?"

"Stevenson's widow and daughter."

"Seriously? A woman named Delia named her child Celia? And she wasn't convicted of child cruelty?" I shook my head, amazed by the sheer bizarreness of the world. I felt a laugh bubbling up, but then stopped, the smile left pasted on my lips, like a napkin I'd forgotten to untuck.

Aidan would have gone on, but Helena knew me better. "What is it? What have you just thought of?"

"Celia. She lives here in London, right?" I looked at Aidan. "A tall, cool redhead? Married to a man named Stein?" They were questions, but I already knew the answers.

"Divorced," said Aidan, missing the point, but Helena was on it like a terrier snapping at a cube of cheese. "How do you know about her?" She stiffened. "Or do you *know* her?"

"I know her. Sort of. I didn't know I knew her." I held up a hand to stop Helena telling me I was being incoherent. I knew I was, and so I started again. "I didn't know who she was when I met her, what her maiden name had been. And since I didn't know the gallery represented Stevenson, even if I had known who she was, it would have just been a sort of interesting 'Did you know?' thing." I replayed the conversation I'd had with Miranda in my head. Miranda had said she'd tried to get hold of someone at the Daylesworth Trust for weeks, but no one had been interested. Then, out of the blue, Celia Stein had phoned and agreed to see me. Phoned the day after Frank's death, and despite the fact that her role at the trust barely impinged on my subject. I thought about the meeting. She had a Stevenson hanging on the wall of her office, too. What else could those bright colors and cartoon figures have been? I just don't expect people to have pictures by world famous artists on their office walls. Even if I had recognized it, I would have assumed it was a reproduction.

I told Helena and Aidan what had happened, how she'd been in touch, ending, "But why? Why would she want to see me?" I tried to unpick it. "What is her function? Does the family run the Stevenson estate, or is it lawyers?"

Aidan was dour. "Good question. The legal situation is clear, the human one less so. Stevenson was officially 'missing,' not dead, for years, and the estate was administered by court-appointed trustees. But in reality Delia made the decisions. She was Stevenson's legatee, even if his will would only go into effect once he was declared dead, which since he'd written to say he was leaving, took the full seven years. We—that is, Frank—had represented Stevenson before his disappearance, and a few years after he vanished Frank bought everything he'd left behind. Stevensons weren't getting a great price, and Delia needed the money: Celia was about to start university, and Delia has two children from an earlier marriage. But in the last few years, Celia has taken over. She's on the spot, while Delia still lives in the middle of nowhere in Vermont. And Celia's field is art." His tone turned pugnacious. "Celia knows what she's doing. It's not like we're defrauding some little old lady. Celia's as sharp as they come."

Having met her, I agreed. "I don't understand. If Frank bought all the works, why does she have any say over what you own?"

"Usually when we buy an entire estate, yes, we would own the pieces outright. But it can be less . . ." He searched for the word. "Less absolute than that. With Stevenson, Frank had had a contract with him before his death. I don't remember now the precise terms of the deal—I may never have heard them—but it was along standard lines: unless they agreed otherwise for some reason, everything Stevenson produced was sold through Frank, who took a commission on the sale before the rest went to Stevenson. After Stevenson died, the situation could have remained the same, with the trustees, or Delia, or whoever was in charge, continuing to sell the works through Frank on commission. But Delia didn't want that. She needed the money, and so we cut a deal—Frank and I were in partnership by then— that we would pay the then-current price for everything, except a few things Delia decided to keep, and as the paintings were sold, any increase in the prices would go back to Delia, less our commission."

I concentrated. "So the deal was, essentially, the same, it's just that you paid some, or possibly most, of the money upfront."

He nodded. "And it wasn't a small sum, either. We had to stretch ourselves financially to do it. It was a good arrangement, it's made us decent money over the years, if not huge. Stevensons have never really found their market the way other pop artists have."

I looked over at Helena. She knew what I was thinking, and she filled me in. "Aidan's forensic accountant is still working through everything, but he says that he'd be very surprised to find anything untoward at this stage. Since yesterday, he's paid particular attention to the Stevensons Frank has sold over the years, and although he's just started, everything seems to be in order there, too." She flicked a glance at Aidan, who was slumped, staring down at his hands. "We'll tell Jake about Celia when he arrives." Aidan looked up again, but made no protest.

Jake and Anna arrived within minutes of each other, and we sat and had a drink, pretending to make bright chat, as though this were an ordinary evening where we'd gathered just because we liked each other. That didn't last. We moved to the dining table and passed the dishes, and then Helena brought us to order.

I'd watched Helena and Jake work together before. But that time Helena hadn't been representing one of the people Jake was investigating. Who was also sitting right there. The differences were stark. Jake didn't take the lead now. He might as well have hung a sign around his neck: OBSERVER. Helena laid out the information she had received from the gallery's lawyer in the States, the one who had attended the Stevenson inquest. Aidan filled in the background as necessary. And then Helena told him about Celia.

Anna and I said nothing, just pretended to eat. Jake nodded occasionally, to indicate that he was listening. But he kept his eyes on me as Helena and Aidan spoke, seeming to be more interested in gauging my response than in the facts Helena was relaying, or even deciding what they meant, or what she might not be telling him. He said almost nothing, and he didn't eat anything either, just sat, one arm crossed over his chest, the other hand at his lips. I contemplated throwing something at him, but I was afraid he'd just shift slightly out of the way and keep staring.

I'd like to say the conversation faltered after that, but that would imply that at some point there had been conversation. There hadn't. After giving his few bits of information, Aidan fell completely silent. Anna, who never talked much, at first joined Helena in pretending that things were normal, making a brief attempt to discuss a film they'd both seen. But then they gave up, too. Helena ate as she always did everything, neatly and temperately; Aidan, Anna, and I pushed our food around briefly, and then stopped even that. And we watched Jake out of the corner of our eyes, watching him watching me.

We all refused coffee. "No, thank you," seemed so much more polite than shrieking, "Are you kidding me? Just get me out of here!" at Helena when she asked. And for some reason we then sat silently on. Dinner was over, we could consider ourselves released back into the community, but instead we stayed at the table, playing with our cutlery, until Jake tossed his napkin onto the table and stood up. "We're going," he told me.

I've actually won prizes for bad temper, and being ordered around by strong silent types has never been one of my schoolgirl fantasies. But I told myself, the way harried mothers do, *Choose your battles.* So I stood up without answering, and went to find my bag.

We got in the car and I braced myself, but he still didn't say anything. I wasn't going to volunteer, so we made the short trip in silence. As far as I was concerned, I told myself, he could stay silent till the crack of doom. But that was too much to hope for.

I knew he wasn't angry with me. He was just angry I was involved. Or, at least, that's what I thought. We went inside, still in total silence, and I was halfway down the hall when I heard a thump. I jumped and turned. Jake had kicked the door—I could see the black scuff mark.

"You've slept with him."

I regrouped. "Aidan?"

Back to the strong silent type. He just stood, chin out, hands on hips. If all other forms of income failed, he could get a job modeling "male fury" in a life-drawing class.

The direction of the attack had taken me by surprise, and I couldn't even be angry. "Can we back up here? I'm happy to have a fight, but I'd like to know what we're fighting about. Last time I checked, you were pissed off because you didn't want me involved in your inquiry. I understand that, and I even agree—I wouldn't have chosen this. But." I closed my eyes and took a deep breath. "But you're angry because I slept with someone twenty years ago? Or, as I tend to think of it, I slept with someone *nineteen fucking years and ten fucking months before I ever fucking fucked you? Are you fucking nuts?*" Let me revise. Possibly I was angry.

My stance was now a mirror image of his, hands on hips, chin out. "Here's a sensible way to avoid this kind of problem in the future." My voice was saccharine with false helpfulness. "Next time the business partner of someone I slept with two decades earlier dies in a way that triggers a police investigation, I'll know that I need to go down to Scotland Yard very first thing and make a statement. Or maybe I can find it on the Met's website? It must be a routine scenario, so your office will have preprinted forms, right?"

Jake hadn't moved. He didn't look as if he'd heard a word I'd said. I was about to launch into a new chorus of the "are you nuts" song when he turned and kicked the door again. He stood staring at it, which made a change from staring at me. Then he walked out, closing the door very quietly, and very carefully, behind him.

I was filling the coffeepot when Jake came into the kitchen the next morning. He pulled me against him and said, "I'm sorry."

I nodded, but didn't turn around. I didn't know yet what he was sorry for. He'd come back sometime the previous night. I'd briefly woken when he got into bed, but he didn't say anything, and I didn't either.

He knew I was waiting, and he went on. "I'm sorry for shouting. I'm sorry for walking out. I'm sorry for being angry about Aidan and you before I even knew you. I'm not sorry for being hurt that you didn't tell me, but I am sorry for being angry." He pulled away and looked at me. "Does that cover it?"

I wasn't sure it did, but I couldn't figure out a way to say so without sounding petty. "It's pretty comprehensive."

"It was the figuring it out on my own. That you didn't tell me once Compton was found dead."

I looked at him for the first time. "I get that part. But it never occurred to me because it was so long ago. If it had mattered, I would have thought, I have to tell Jake. But the sex was so long ago, and so unimportant, I just never thought of it. The friend part, which is important, I told you right away."

He smiled slightly, which was a relief. "'The sex was so

unimportant?' You really know how to bolster a guy's ego, don't you?"

I went back to the coffee. "It was in another country, and besides, the wench is dead."

"Having a conversation with you literary types is always fun, but what the hell does that mean?"

"It means that that was then and this is now."

"This."

I nodded.

"I know talking isn't your favorite thing, which is why you end up quoting from books, but do we know what we're talking about here?"

I thought we probably did.

"OK. Let's let it go. If you have accepted my apology . . . ?" He waited until I nodded again, then he went and got down two cups.

I hunted through the fruit bowl for a banana that wasn't entirely black. I wondered if bananas were cunningly genetically modified by scientists in the pay of fruit companies so that they moved from green to black with nothing in between. Then I decided that this was probably not the ideal time to have a chat about that insight. Instead, "Do we need to talk about Celia Stein? I don't know why she popped up, what she wanted, or even if she really did want something."

Jake stood at the table, leaning on his hands where he'd put the cups down. I poured out the coffee and put his cup back in front of him and sat down. He didn't move. "I don't know either, but it doesn't matter. The weight of evidence suggests suicide. Unless the inquest returns a suspicious-death verdict, that's it for us."

I stilled. The bastard had let us jump through all those hoops last night when he'd known this?

He saw the thought and cut in before I had figured out what to say, his hands raised pacifically: "The file went upstairs yesterday; there was an e-mail with the decision when I woke up this morning."

Some of the tension left my body. "Lucky for you."

He carefully didn't smile. "So it would seem."

I'd expected another quiet day at work. Fridays were generally subdued in publishing no matter what time of year. Lots of people worked four-day weeks, and Friday was the favored at-home day. In the summer, even more people took long weekends, and then there were the ones who were formally or informally on holiday. I'd got lots of reading done the day before, and dealt with a backlog of contract quibbles I'd been sitting on for weeks. Truthfully, contracts I'd been sitting on for months. But no more than a couple of months. Three maybe. All right, they were contracts I'd been sitting on since before the dawn of time, but now I'd finally dealt with them, I felt I should get points for it, and even more points for all those months when I'd been genuinely pained at not having done them. Although neither the agents involved, nor even our own contracts department, seemed to agree.

At any rate, they were done now, and I was free to get on with the kind of work I liked. Submissions are great. There is always a sense of adventure when you pull the next manuscript off the pile. I still thought of it as a pile, even though most of our submissions were now sent by e-mail, and I read them on an e-reader. It's far more practical—the agents can send them over to us faster, the assistants don't spend their lives photocopying them, or unjamming the photocopier. But I still don't like these cyber-manuscripts. There are rational reasons for my dislike. I think it's important to know physically where I am in a book, how much farther to halfway, to the end, things that matter in terms of pacing and structure. And there are irrational reasons: the feel, the smell, the heft. An e-reader is less physically strenuous—carrying just three or four manuscripts home to read was hell on the back—but also somehow less of an adventure. And Bim has made his displeasure known, too. He was used to having lots of paper from me to color on, or cut into shapes and paste. E-readers were damaging his creative output.

That morning, however, it was a printed manuscript, from a Luddite agent who always sent her submissions by post. We rolled our eyes when we mentioned her name, but secretly I loved her. Miranda obviously felt differently when she came in and found me with my feet up, manuscript in my lap, cup in hand. She looked at me as if I'd asked her to go and pluck another quill from the goose and sharpen its nib. A few weeks ago I'd walked past when she was discussing manuscripts with another assistant. "How did they get submissions before?" they were exclaiming in wonder. I didn't break stride. "Papyrus," I said. Now she stared down at me as though she finally believed me.

I waited for her to remember what it was she'd come in for. She had plenty to be getting on with, and if she'd just needed advice or input, she usually e-mailed. She stayed leaning against the door jamb, but if that was supposed to make me think that she'd just come in for a casual gossip, she'd failed, because she'd closed the door.

"Have you heard?" she asked.

"Heard?" If it was minor office rumors, who was sleeping with whom, she wouldn't have closed the door.

"Olive. She's been having breakfast meetings all this week. And she hasn't told Evie who they're with, just to book her out till ten." Olive is Olive Robinson, the publishing director. In a larger company she'd have a fancier title, like chief executive. Evie is her secretary, which is another way you know how senior Olive is, because the rest of the senior staff have assistants. Whatever you call them, the administrative staff can, and do, forecast the major upheavals, because they book the meetings.

I took my feet out of the drawer they rest on when I read. Miranda's bulletin might as well have a caption: Important Enough to Sit Up For. "Wow," I said.

We stared at each other meaningfully. I drank the last of my coffee and kept hold of my cup. The kitchen would be where there was news, if it was anywhere.

A cluster of anxious-looking people stood by the kettle. I poured out some coffee, but didn't bother to look at the treat table. It was Friday, and no one came back to work from holiday on a Friday. I wasn't thinking about that consciously, it was just a Pavlov's-dog reflex response to office circadian rhythms.

I leaned against the counter and took stock: a couple of people from contracts, one from marketing, one from design. If there was anything to know, there was a chance someone would have heard.

Timmins & Ross is owned privately, by the descendants of the Mr. Timmins and Mr. Ross who had founded the company in the 1930s, diluted by a few others who had bought in in the late eighties when the company had needed a cash infusion. Happily, it was just before the period when venture capitalists had decided that investing in publishing would make them rich. Those companies had been swallowed up by conglomerates soon after, because there was no other way to make a speedy financial return. Publishing made an OK return if you didn't want riches beyond the dreams of avarice, but if an OK return was what venture capitalists were looking for, I'd missed the memo. Anyway, that was then. Now publishing barely makes any money, and an OK return would have us all conga-ing around Bedford Square wearing party hats made out of discarded publicity folders. Because in the last decade, book sales have declined overall, and even where numbers have held up, or even increased, the sales are made in supermarkets and online, places where publishers receive a declining share of the sale price. We are just like the farmers getting screwed over by the supermarkets: they buy from us at ever-lower prices, so even if they sell more and more, the money magically never increases. Same story for Amazon. Same story for e-books.

I know, not the world's biggest tragedy in the great scheme of things. But this wasn't the great scheme of things, this was our lives. And our livelihoods. But like everyone else working in a disaster zone, we had pushed the truth aside until it became background noise. We did what we could to make the new reality work. We offered our authors less money. That hurt every time we had to do it, but we did it. We spent less on marketing and promotion, which was self-defeating, but we did that, too. Staffing levels had been cut, thankfully so far through natural wastage rather than redundancies at T&R, but we were always expecting worse. And still profits dropped.

So if Olive was having long meetings with someone, or several someones, whose names couldn't be written in her diary, we automatically assumed the worst. A positive result would be a new investor. A negative one, that the current owners wanted to sell. Then it would be to one of the big corporate publishers, and most of us would lose our jobs. The big companies already had the back-office apparatus they needed, so finance, contracts, all those departments would go; even editorial and design weren't safe. T&R published a hundred books a year. If you were a giant corporation that already employed a few dozen editors and a few dozen designers, our whole list could be scattered among them. And since those editors and designers were just as scared of losing their jobs, they would quietly take on the extra work, no matter how burdensome.

I listened to the back and forth, but there was nothing concrete. It was all surmise, and a lot of fear.

Just before one, Sandra Stanworth, the head of publicity and one of my closer friends at work, put her head round my door and asked if I had lunch plans. I didn't, so we headed to a square behind the British Museum. It was part of the University of London, and would be packed with students, but the bigger squares nearby—Bedford Square on one side, Russell Square on the other—would have more tourists shuffling through from the British Museum and the stations. Malet Square was hidden, and there was less through-traffic. There was also a deli en route, where we could pick up lunch. A pastoral haven it wasn't, but it was the best central London could come up with on a weekday.

We stayed off the topic of Olive and her mystery meetings. We'd both been through it before—everyone in publishing over thirty has been through it before—and we knew that whatever would happen would happen. Instead we caught each other up. Sandra has a very small car, two large boys, and one vast dog, and they'd just driven back from a wedding in Ireland. As a mathematical equation, 2 (big) boys + 1 (huge) dog × 1 (tiny) car / (11-hour) drive = opening scene in comic novel. Then I filled her in on the Jake scenario—not Frank's death, which I couldn't bear to mention, just the dinner-with-Aidan-door-kicking story, which for her benefit I also turned into comedy. She was disappointed I hadn't thrown stuff. In another lifetime, I told her. I understand the attractions of throwing. But unless you organize your life better than I've managed to organize mine, if you throw stuff, eventually you have to pick it up again. Which is a terrible anticlimax, and would make me want to throw the stuff all over again. Which I'd have to pick up again. Which.

Despite our forced comedy, work was uppermost on our minds. Just before I'd left the office, I'd e-mailed Helena. She worked in corporate law, and if one of the conglomerates was circling, she might hear of it. Even a smaller bite would still need company lawyers. On a more personal level, when I got back after lunch I e-mailed my boss, David Snaith, and his assistant, sending them the manuscripts of two books I wanted to offer for, to get them listed on the minutes for next week's acquisitions meeting. I also sent copies to potential allies in sales, marketing, and publicity, as well as a couple of editors. The more enthusiasm I could work up in-house for a book, the more likely I would be able to buy it—if I couldn't persuade my colleagues that it was great, there was little chance that as a publisher we could persuade strangers. I'd done a sales number on Sandra at lunch, and sent her copies, too. If we were going to be bought out, I might as well acquire as much as I could while I could.

In the same spirit, I spent the afternoon sorting out my outstanding Frankfurt appointments. Miranda had done the easy ones, where it's just horse-trading—"I'll give you Sunday at 4:30 on your stand if you give me Monday 9 o'clock on ours"—but she couldn't do the ones where the horse-trading had failed, and the person I wanted to meet no longer had any free slots at a time when I had free slots, which meant a meeting couldn't be fitted into the working day. She couldn't know who I'd be happy to meet for coffee or a drink, but wouldn't be able to tolerate for a whole dinner (or, just as likely, who wouldn't be able to tolerate me for that long), or the people I could tolerate for dinner, but I'd whimper and refuse to get out of bed if I had to see them for a breakfast meeting, before I was properly caffeinated.

I got to the final entry on Miranda's list and read it twice before I called through the wall. "Did that guy from the small publisher in Oregon really send an appointment request with an urgent flag on it? Urgent, four months ahead of the book fair? From a publisher I've never heard of and who . . ." I looked a third time "who specializes in hiking guides?"

I heard her giggle. "Yes! I left him for you because I knew that would be one of your favorite things."

I was definitely going to have to find her a better job. "That was thoughtful, thank you. He's just been put at the very tail-end of my if-I-have-time-or-when-hell-freezes-over list."

There was a pause. "Who's at the top of that list?"

"He is. He is the only person on the list."

6

Jake had texted first thing to say he was working a late shift, and would go back to Hammersmith after. That was fine by me. I decided to be very un-Sam-like and not worry about it, although I worked around that by spending the time I'd saved by not worrying in worrying that not worrying was really a worrying sign. By the time I'd finished with that, Kay had invited me up for pizza and the new James Bond DVD. The pizza and the company were great, but the only person who understood the movie properly was Bim, although that may have been because he was the only one who was not drinking. But he explained to us the bits we'd missed by chatting through them, and he drew us pictures of the scenes he'd particularly enjoyed, in case I wanted to take them home and study them. It was kind of him, and he definitely had a better grasp of narrative structure than several of my authors.

When I went downstairs, I stuck them up on the fridge so that when he visited he would know I appreciated them. I used the ironic fridge-magnets that were shaped to look like paper clips, which I'd bought at a Roy Lichtenstein exhibition. Then I pulled one of the magnets off the fridge again. On the reverse, sure enough, there was "JR Installations." These were some of the "tourist tat" Jim designed. I thought they were charming and witty, and not tattish at all. I'd probably buy a Stevenson notebook if they'd made those, too. I stared at the magnet for a while, as if it might decide to speak if I left a pause in the conversation, a pause long enough for it to become embarrassed at not contributing. Apparently the magnet was not English, because it seemed unembarrassable.

I stopped being frivolous and thought about Jim, and Frank, and then, feeling like four kinds of fool, I e-mailed.

Hi, Jim

Just out of curiosity, I wondered which of Stevenson's collages you wanted to use for your notebooks. No real reason for asking, apart from having worked for Tetrarch, and I know Stevenson used their books a lot. If it's commercially confidential, please tell me to go away. I don't know how these things work, and don't want to step on any toes.

Cheers

Sam

P.S. I have entirely avoided thinking about the panel since the moment we left the restaurant. Hope your day was as good.

And for good measure I added a smiley. Queen of the faux-casual, that's me.

As I hit Send, I saw an e-mail from Aidan. It was actually from Myra, at the gallery, and was a group e-mail. The police had said the funeral could go ahead, she wrote, and it would be held on the following Wednesday, at a church in Highgate at eleven, and then at Kenwood House, on Hampstead Heath, immediately afterward.

I put it in my diary, and e-mailed Helena to see if she wanted to go together. I'd heard from her earlier in the day, when the police had notified Aidan of the date of the inquest, and that no further action would be taken until then. But she hadn't said anything else, and I guess there was nothing else to be said. I also e-mailed Myra back, to ask if she knew if we should send flowers. Or was it family only, or would Toby prefer a donation to charity, and if so, did she know which one? This kind of bureaucracy of death, normally so distressing to go through, now seemed comfortable after the previous week.

I hit Send/Receive a few more times, as though that might coax an otherwise shy e-mail to pop into my inbox. For good measure, I checked my phone. Nothing. I hadn't heard from Jake since his text that morning. In the couple of months we'd been seeing each other, we'd quickly found a routine. We either said if we had other plans for the weekend, or were working, otherwise we just assumed we'd spend the time together. After last night, followed by a day's silence, that wasn't an assumption I was making now.

And I went on not making any assumptions the following morning. There was no message from Jake when I woke up, so I got on with my day. I ran up to see if Mr. Rudiger wanted me to pick anything up for him at the market where I did my shopping on Saturdays. And I decided it might be a good time to go and see Toby, as the market was halfway between me and what I still mentally called Frank's house. If people were still keeping an eye on Toby, disguised as condolence calls, they'd probably be glad of a cake, or fruit, or cheese and biscuits. I could pick up whatever it was at the market and continue on to Frank's from there. I texted Anna to see if she knew what was needed, and she replied almost immediately with Lucy's number, saying she was in charge of kitchen supplies.

I stared at the text, as though it had some cryptic message for me. I was going to see Toby and pay a condolence call, I reminded myself. The police had suggested they would be surprised if Frank's death were anything other than suicide, and I was grateful for that. So why, muttered my subconscious, did you e-mail Jim last night? I have no idea, I told it wearily, and instead texted Lucy about cake. I was better at cake. I had talent there, and years of practice. Since I was being so sensible, I decided I'd better make at least a vague gesture toward maturity in other aspects of my life, and so I texted Jake: *Off to the market, then to Toby for condolence call. Back around noon.* I collected my bike from the hole under the stairs that we dignify by calling a cupboard, and set off.

It's barely twenty minutes' walk to the market, but the twenty feels like two hundred once I'm carrying a week's supply of fruit and veg, so I generally cycle. It's all quiet back roads, but the quiet roads sometimes feel more lethal than the busy ones. Because there are few cars, people step out without looking, crossing entirely by sound. And the cars hate the narrow roads where they have to pull over if they meet another car going in the opposite direction, so they rev their engines and spurt past cyclists in some sort of revenge deal. I know, it's the endless sob story that is the life of the self-righteous cyclist. All I'm saying is, I'm not a boy racer in Lycra, I'm a forty-three-year-old woman going to a farmer's market, for the Lord's sake. I'm as careful on the back roads as I am in the center of town.

Even more so between the market and Frank's house. I had my own shopping in a pannier on the back, but Lucy had replied that they needed desserts, and so I'd bought a big sheet of brownies, as well as flowers, to take to Toby's. Those were balanced, just, on my front basket, on top of my handbag, and I was cycling slowly, and looking out for anything where I'd have to brake sharply: not just traffic, but pedestrian crossings, bumps in the road. I heard a car behind me, but I didn't give it much thought. The road was too narrow for it to pass me, but the driver would be able to see that there was a gap in the parked cars less than twenty yards ahead, where I could pull in and let them pass.

I didn't get that far. Just as I was thinking that, there was a pinch point in the road, narrowing even farther for a zebra crossing. There was no one waiting, so I kept going. The car, however, roared past, pushing me toward the railings that marked the edge of the pedestrian crossing. There was nowhere for me to go. The car was on my right, there was a car illegally parked up against the crossing, and I was going to end up smashed against the iron railings. I had, strangely, time to think of this, even though it could only have taken seconds.

And then a rut in the speed bump that marked off the crossing snatched at my front tire. God bless our cheese-paring government and its vicious local budget cuts, is all I can say. The road hadn't been repaired in years, and that pothole definitely saved, if not my life, me from major injury, turning my front wheel away from the railing and pushing me to one side. I still flew off, right over the handlebars, but missed the barrier entirely. And just lay there.

The street, so empty ten seconds before, was now filled with people. I heard them talking over my head, but I'd had the wind knocked out of me, and I couldn't speak, much less move. Someone was phoning for an ambulance. I thought about protesting, but I knew they were right. I'd landed on my face, and then the rest of my body had continued on over my head. My face had scraped along the pavement, and I'd done something nasty to my shoulder, too.

Several voices were urging me to lie still, which was the impetus I needed to get me upright. I sat up and flapped at them with my good hand, like a cross penguin. "I'm fine," I said, even as I felt at my face gingerly. Possibly a broken nose? One cheek and my forehead was cut raw by the pavement. And there was blood everywhere. I lowered my head to my knees, feeling queasy and, only now, terrified.

Someone put a hand on my shoulder. I gasped loudly and pulled away. It was an older woman, with frizzy gray hair and worried eyes. The gasp had scared her, but the pulling away had scared me, too, producing a great wave of pain. I put my head down again until I was sure I wasn't going to be sick. Then the worst of it receded, and I heard her talking to me, ". . . do you want us to ring someone?"

I realized she had been trying to tell me she'd found my bag, and was, sensibly, suggesting I arrange for someone to meet me at the hospital. Two other good Samaritans were chasing down the groceries that had rolled out of my pannier.

I pointed one of them to the bike chain that had been thrown across the road. "Would you chain my bike up somewhere nearby? I'll come and collect it when I can."

He looked at me dubiously. But worrying about my bike, and how I'd get it home, was good displacement. I dabbed angrily at my tears, although I hadn't realized I was crying, and at more blood. "Please," I said, and gave him the key from my ring.

The need to make short-term decisions—phone, bike—was taken out of my hands as an ambulance appeared. Two wonderfully cheery men stepped out, and without seeming to do anything at all, managed to reduce the group of milling people to order in seconds. They listened briefly, then one rang the police to report a hit-and-run and failure to stop. My bike was locked up and the key returned to me. My pannier was put in the ambulance, and after a brief check, so was I. The woman who'd spoken to me tried to hand in the flowers I'd bought for Toby, but I asked her to keep them for herself. I hadn't been able to gather myself enough to say thank you for the help, and it was little enough for scraping me up off the pavement.

The two ambulance men consulted briefly. Then, "Do you know what road we're on, love?"

I laughed, which five seconds before I would have sworn was impossible.

"We're from Southend," said the larger of the two, who was covered from his neck downward with tattoos. "We've been brought in because of staff shortages. We got here via the sat-nav, but now it says that this street doesn't exist." He was resigned, but not surprised.

Swings and roundabouts. The government cuts had probably saved my life by preventing the council from repairing the road; the same cuts meant that the patients had to navigate their ambulances to the hospital. The younger, un-tattooed one, in the back with me, had been trying to get me to lie down. Now I brushed him aside so I could look out the front window over the driver's shoulder.

"Go to the end of the road and turn left. It'll take you to the main road, and it's easier to direct you from there." I paused. "You are taking me to the Royal Free, aren't you? I don't want to go to Essex."

They laughed. "No, we haven't got time to take you to the seaside."

That was a mercy. I hadn't thought to bring my bucket and spade with me to the farmer's market. Mr. Tattoo and I chatted across the backseat as I gave directions. Despite getting me picked up and into the ambulance in record time, he must have spoken to several of the bystanders. "No one got a car reg. Any chance you did?"

"It was too quick."

He nodded, unsurprised. "Maybe the police will get more."

Un-tattoo took my blood pressure and did a brief cleanup of my face, but there wasn't much point. My nose was gushing blood, and holding anything against it hurt too much. "It's fine," I said, trying not to sound impatient. He couldn't know it bled regularly, and I was entirely used to looking like a vampire after a particularly juicy meal.

In barely five minutes we had pulled up to the hospital, and they unloaded me—literally, because I wasn't allowed to walk. I've often wondered if hospitals use wheelchairs more for patient control than health. If you're in a chair, you go where they want you to, not where you want to.

The advantage of the vampire look is that you get seen very quickly. The Saturday-morning rush of small children with park- and football-related injuries was well underway, so A&E was seething with shrieks and scuffles and fights over Lego. And that was only among the parents. The blood on my face got me into a cubicle fast, although after they cleaned me off they realized it wasn't as bad as it looked. I'd need an X-ray for my shoulder, which was now agony, and my nose would have to be cauterized and—I felt it again—seemed to be lopsided. But I was not, rightly, anyone's priority. A nurse handed me a pack of swabs for my nose, and I was left to wait my turn.

As soon as she went, I sneaked a quick couple of Nurofen from my bag. I pushed the curtain ajar so that I would be visible, and they wouldn't forget to take me to X-ray at some point, and then I settled in, content to spend the morning reading on my phone, which is what I often do, wherever I am. Well, not on my phone, and the blood made turning pages messy, but as I say, that wasn't a novelty to me.

After an hour or so a text appeared: *Might be free around lunchtime. The Indian place in Whitechapel?* I could think of few things that sounded better than the Indian place in Whitechapel, and I reflected sadly on the diminishing odds of cumin-spiced lamb chops for lunch. I replied, *Fell off my bike. Nothing serious, but waiting to see doc.* I didn't even have time to flick back to the book app before a *WHERE* was on the screen. *Royal Free. But really, I'm fine.* And then nothing.

Half an hour later, I heard Jake's voice at the desk, which, if I shuffled down to the bottom of the examining table, I could see from my cubicle. There he was, looking official and—could it be?—showing his warrant card. He was pulling rank to get me seen more quickly? That was a terrible thing to do, and I was so grateful. He headed down the corridor toward me led by an orderly with a wheelchair, and then stood at the end of the bed, face impassive, arms crossed. No How are you feeling, just a nod and "You'll be taken down to X-ray now. I'll wait for you here."

We were barely around the corner before the orderly stopped and crouched down in front of me. "Are you OK?"

I tried not to look too abused. "Yes, everything's fine. Thank you."

He didn't believe me. He knew the police were waiting to interview me, even if I was too stupid to be worried. "Do you want me to slow this down?" he offered. "Often I can't find a technician."

"Really, there isn't a problem."

He still looked doubtful.

"I just need to . . ." I cast about, and then realized that being truthful was the answer. Which was a surprise. "It was a hit-and-run. They want me to give a statement, that's all."

Appeased, he stood up and moved behind me. "If you're sure."

"I'm sure. Everything's fine." Then I thought about Jake, arms folded, face grim. And his earlier silence. Pretty sure.

Back upstairs, I found Jake standing where I'd left him, but now talking to Mr. Tattoo and his friend. He nodded toward a registrar, whom he must have shanghaied in the meantime. "He'll do your nose now."

The registrar moved away my hand holding the swab, and great gouts of blood followed. We both jumped as Jake cursed under his breath. "It's fine," I said, ostensibly to the doctor. "It just needs cauterizing. This happens a lot."

He looked slightly revolted, and I agreed, but it was part of life's rich tapestry. Or something. Jake put his hand on my elbow. The registrar looked at me again. He hadn't thought I looked the type to do a runner. I knew Jake had done it for reassurance, but I still felt like a felon. The procedure was no big deal, and in three minutes it was over. The X-ray had come up in the meantime. My collarbone was bruised, and the ligaments had been wrenched, nothing more. My nose wasn't broken either, although it was leaning hard to starboard.

The doctor looked casual. "You can wait for orthopedics, or I can just straighten it. If orthopedics do it, you can have a local." He offered the anesthetic like a treat for a very good child, but I knew the way hospitals worked.

"You'll do it now, right?" He wasn't keen—I could see his eyes flicking over to the desk where, no doubt, more interesting patients awaited. So I spoke quickly, before he could move off. "Go for it."

He went for it. For a brief moment I thought he'd punched me, as everything sucked in and went black with the pain.

"All right?"

I nodded. I couldn't speak yet.

"Get her some water," said Jake, in the icy voice he might have used to an office junior. An office junior he didn't like. An office junior he didn't like and was going to sack in the morning.

The registrar thought he was going to point out that that wasn't his job. Then he looked at Jake again and realized that what he most wanted to do was get me some water. So he did.

Jake didn't move while we waited. I leaned back against him, and he swore again. Then, "Have you finished bleeding? Can we get you home?"

I nodded again. Jake wasn't any more talkative. In fact, he didn't say a word on the way out. Or in the car. By the time I was tucked up on the sofa and he'd brought me some tea, I was willing to confess to anything—murdering Frank, being Lord Lucan, or keeping the Loch Ness monster in a bucket beside the bathtub. Anything to end the silence.

So, finally, I did it myself. "I've never come off my bike before. I was overdue."

He didn't answer. I was about to try again, when, "Who do you know who drives a dark blue or green car, possibly a Volvo?"

I blinked. "You think the person knew me?"

He stared at me with the same stony expression he'd had ever since he arrived at the hospital.

"And you think I'd recognize a Volvo?"

That brought a small smile. I don't know what kind of car Jake drives. Or my mother. Or anyone. I am officially registered Car Blind, and am eligible for a handicapped parking permit for the ailment. Or I would be, if only I drove. And would have been able to recognize my own car.

Jake knew this, too, but I reminded him of the facts of life nonetheless. "Honey, I'm the girlfriend who knows about dead artists in Vermont. Did you think you were speaking to the one who spends her time at Brands Hatch?"

His voice warmed. "My mistake." He rubbed his hand fiercely through his hair. "The paramedics say the witnesses thought it was deliberate."

I thought about that. "It was deliberate, in the sense that someone saw me as a cyclist in his way—"

Jake broke in. "Her. Everyone who saw agrees on that."

I swallowed. "Her, then. She saw me as a cyclist in her way, and didn't want to wait. We all know there are drivers like that. But deliberate, by someone I know?" My voice had skittered up a few octaves. Minnie Mouse Does Helium. "Why?"

"It's a good question. Frank Compton killed himself, most likely. You met with his business partner and his business part-ner's solicitor to discuss the death, the three of you." He looked at me levelly. I might have managed to brazen it out under nor-mal circumstances, but my defenses were down. I shifted and looked away. He nodded. Point made. "That Aidan Merriam is a friend, and his solicitor is your mother . . ." He turned this around in his head for a moment, then continued: "You also had a meeting with Celia Stein, the daughter of an artist Frank

Compton and Aidan Merriam represented." He turned that over, too. "There's been no follow-up to that?" I shook my head, mutely, but he persisted: "You haven't been asking questions?"

"Questions about what? I don't know what to ask. Or who."

"When you visited Toby, did you discuss Frank's death with anyone?"

"Apart from condolence chat? Of course not." What kind of question was that? Sitting in a room with his partner? What kind of person did he think I was? Then I realized, he would have asked those questions. That's what the police do. "The only conversation I had there that was anything except the kind of thing you say when someone dies was with Frank's niece, the one who worked for them in her holidays. I told you about her. She was the one who told me that the gallery represented Stevenson." Jake made a rolling gesture with his hand—keep talking. "That's all. What did you think, that I'd march up to Toby and say, 'Where were you at seven on the morning of . . . ?' Speaking of which." I sat up. "Someone must have confirmed Toby's whereabouts?"

Jake's lips twitched. "He was with seventeen civil servants at a paintballing away day in Buckinghamshire."

"You're making that up." I laughed, which reminded me of how much my face hurt. That sobered me. "Paintballing at seven in the morning?"

"A few of them went the night before. He and three others went for a run at six. They got back just before seven, and were identified by the hotel porter. Compton's car park pass in central London was used at 6:25, and we've checked the CCTV footage. It was him. Merriam's call to report the death came in

at 7:05. Stafford's out of it. So." He shifted. Physically and mentally. "Who else have you spoken to?"

I threw out my hands. Which reminded me that my arm and
shoulder hurt, too. I didn't care. I'd fallen off my bike because an
asshole driver wanted to save three seconds. I glared at Jake. "I
told you, I haven't talked to anyone about anything because I
don't know anything about anything."

He considered smiling, but didn't. "That covers it."

"I can't invent things to tell you." I slid into a generic American accent. "'Oh, yes, Officer, you see I was Nancy Drew in a
previous existence, and so I got into my little roadster and . . .'"
I stopped. I'd e-mailed Jim Reynolds about Stevenson. So what,
said my sensible self. People didn't kill themselves over museum
souvenirs.

"What?" It was a demand.

I told him about the e-mail, vigorously adding my thoughts on
the lack of mortality figures connected to museum souvenirs.

"In the normal course of events I'd agree with you. And I
agree with you that this is most likely a hit-and-run. Common
sense, and statistics, would say that's what it is. But I don't like
coincidences, and I especially don't like coincidences when they
involve you. I'll keep an eye on the reports as they're filed, see if
anything stands out, although it's unlikely." He stood up. "I'm
going back to the office. I've got a deskful of paperwork."

"Why?"

He looked at me blankly. Then, "You're under the impression
we work one case at a time?"

I wasn't. I nodded and lay back, closing my eyes. My head really hurt. So did my shoulder. A nap was calling to me.

"Will you ring Helena?"

I opened my eyes again and crossed my single good arm. Preemptive crabbiness was the aim.

Jake was exaggeratedly calm. "You hit your head. You have a bloody nose and a badly bruised arm and shoulder. I don't think you should be alone."

Screw preemptive. "For heaven's sake. I fell off my bike. I'm fine. Now go away and detect something somewhere." I shooed at him, making the kind of gesture that really only gets made to dogs. In cartoons.

He shook his head at me. Not impressed. "Call if you need anything. If I'm not at my desk tell whoever answers it'll be easy to find me. I'm the one in the corner, banging my head against the wall."

"I'll be sure to remember that." I closed my eyes again.

When I opened them, I could tell from the light I'd been asleep for a good hour. Before Jake left to bang his head against the wall he must have gone upstairs, because Mr. Rudiger was sitting in an armchair, peacefully reading. He looked up when I moved, but he didn't close his book, indicating that he was happy to go back to it if I didn't want to talk. I started to yawn, then quickly stopped when I felt a pulling across my face. I reached up to explore. The grazes had scabbed over. I winced not so much at the feel as at the thought of what it must look like. I sat up.

As if that were a cue, Mr. Rudiger stood and went into the kitchen. *More bloody tea*, I silently groused. That would be my third cup that day, including the one they'd brought me at the hospital. More than I'd drunk in the previous year.

I should have known better. Mr. Rudiger was definitely going to win the Neighbor of the Year rosette, because he came back with coffee. And with sandwiches neatly cut into triangles, their crusts removed. I don't know if it was the thought of my elderly neighbor carefully removing the crusts because the injuries to my face might make chewing difficult, or if it was the reminder of childhood birthday parties, but whatever it was, it made me feel cherished.

I got creakily off the sofa and he was there without seeming to move. "Let me get whatever you need."

I shook my head. "Loo." His smile acknowledged that there were some things a girl just had to do for herself, but he trailed behind me to the door all the same.

I did have to go to the loo, but on the way back I scooped up my handbag and checked my phone. And there was an e-mail from Jim.

Hi Sam. Presentation done & ready to go. Lucky b/c Stevenson show really getting down to wire looking great tho. Images we chose, why shld I mind? We wanted the one w the naked lunch but any of the bk jkt ones wld hve worked. C u nxt wk. Jim.

No smiley for me, but he seemed happy to provide the information without thinking I'd had an ulterior motive. I forwarded it to Jake—I'd learned my lesson—with just a question mark above it. I was staying out of it. Whatever "it" was.

And then I sat down and, eating my sandwiches, I told Mr. Rudiger everything. Why not? The police thought there was no case to answer.

He was quiet when I finished. I assumed he was thinking it over, but the last thing I expected was his "It was a strange time, the sixties."

I tilted my head to indicate I didn't understand.

"From this time, looking back, the sixties were a big break, very different from the fifties. But at the time it didn't feel that way."

Mr. Rudiger wasn't prone to talking for talking's sake. He was going somewhere.

"The people we now think of as typical—Bob Dylan, or Warhol, or"—he dipped his head toward me "Edward Stevenson, they were the exceptions. And they were the exceptions partly because of their talent, but mostly because of their . . ." he stopped, searching for the word he wanted. "Because of their vanity.

"When I look at Stevenson's pictures, I like them, they're good, but what always strikes me is how they shout, 'Look at me!'"

I sat suspended, sandwich halfway to my mouth. I couldn't have said why this seemed important, but it did.

He continued, speaking almost to himself. "I remember when the news came that he'd gone to India to join an ashram. That sounded right to me, that the man who'd made those pictures would want to do something that let him think, and talk, about himself." He sounded almost bitter, in a way I'd never heard from him before, this man who always appeared so gently amused by the world. "But when his body was found, that I didn't believe. I know suicide is unpredictable. But I still didn't believe that the man who had made those paintings would make that choice. His work screamed out that he loved himself too much to imagine a world without him."

I had no idea what made him feel this strongly. He didn't say, and I wouldn't presume to ask. We sat quietly together as the room got dark.

7

I slept on and off through most of the weekend. While Jake theoretically spent it with me, and technically we talked, in reality we both avoided saying anything of importance. He said he'd asked for the local divisional police's report of the accident, and the statements all said the same thing: a woman driving a blue or green car, maybe a Volvo, who had tried to pass me where the road was too narrow. The only unusual aspect was that she'd driven off. Women, according to Jake, mostly didn't do that. We left it there.

It was therefore Monday before we faced off again. When the alarm went off and I hauled myself out of bed he looked at me as if I'd lost my mind. "Where are you going?"

I gave him a who-has-lost-whose-mind evil eye. But it was early and without caffeine I wasn't prepared to talk more than I had to. "Work," seemed like more than enough explanation.

Apparently not. "No, you're not."

"Um-hmm," I said mildly, heading for the shower.

He stood in front of me, arms crossed. "No. You're not."

I walked around him without bothering to reply. He was naked, and it's impossible to look truly ferocious when you're naked. That's just a scientific fact. The mirror in the bathroom though did give me pause. I'd seen the grazes on my face several times the day before, when looking in the mirror was unavoidable. But I had managed not to think about the rest. The stiffness had shrieked out at me when I woke up. Being the mistress of denial, I ignored that, too. But my shoulder was a mass of bruises, and was swollen, too. In fact, I was a mess. But staying at home would just give me time to brood, and I was more anxious to deny the coincidences Jake was seeing than I was to deny the serious mess that was my body.

By the time I was showered and had dried my hair, Jake was dressed and in the kitchen. Clothed he might be trickier. Coffee was imminent, so I decided attack was the best form of defense. "Why aren't I going to work?"

"You're ill."

"I've got a sore shoulder and a scraped face. I don't work in the construction industry. We don't need to be physically fit." I thought about my colleagues. And me. "If we did, only four books a year would get published. Worldwide."

He brought out the big guns. "You're not going in to work because someone tried to kill you."

He thought that? I dropped down into a chair and stared at him. Then, "No. No one tried to kill me. You know it and I know it. Stop. Just stop."

He didn't reply.

"You've seen the reports, and all anyone saw was an impatient driver. Don't make this more than it is because my getting hurt upsets you."

He didn't deny that.

"And definitely no one's going to try to kill me on the way to the bus. The only people who want to kill me are my colleagues, and they've wanted to kill me for years."

Jake must have realized he was on a hiding to nothing. "I'll drop you on my way in."

I nodded. I didn't believe anyone had tried to kill me. I couldn't let myself think that. But I'd appreciate a lift to work even if the reasons for it were far-fetched. Whatever I'd said to Jake, my arm still hurt like stink, and the thought of a rush-hour commute was not enticing.

At the office I stopped to chat to Bernie at reception. If I told her what had happened, she could start the story moving. That way I wouldn't have to explain it over and over. I didn't want to because talking hurt, the scabs pulling every time I opened my mouth. And I didn't want to because I didn't want to think about it.

By the time Miranda put her head around my door, around ten, she had already been primed, but I must have looked worse than she'd expected, because instead of a quick hello, as usual, she just stood there staring.

I held up a hand. "It's all right. It looks much worse than it is."

"I hope so," she said bluntly. "Because it looks terrible."

I winced. I'd been hoping for "not great," or, at worst, "fairly bad." "I've moved a bunch of appointments. Talking is hard, so I've canceled whatever I could. I'll give you the dates when they're rescheduled. But I've got to keep the two meetings for the Culture Committee panel. It's only five days away and I've got at least another ten minutes to fill."

I spent a quarter of an hour fooling around in the kitchen, listening to various theories about Olive's mysterious breakfast sessions, and then, unable to postpone anymore, I set off. I was meeting Neil Simonson at his office on the South Bank, before Emma came to me later that afternoon

Neil was the director of London's biggest literary festival. It was only recently that book events had begun to take off in London in an organized way. You'd think that if literary festivals could succeed in the wilds of Wales, the way the Hay Festival did, then they'd do even better in densely populated urban areas. Lots of people had gone broke thinking that. It turned out that people went to festivals in the country, driving for miles, because there wasn't that much live entertainment near them. London had more live entertainment than you could shake a stick at, if stick-shaking was your hobby. So literary festivals had risen and died over the years. Only now, at arts venues that already had established audiences and great programming, were they beginning to find their way.

Neil's summer neighborhood festival was in full swing as I got off the bus on the bridge and headed down the stairs to reach the center's offices. London was having one of its prolonged fits of good weather, showing what it could do if it really tried, all designed to taunt us the other forty-nine weeks of the year. I walked past several school groups planting herbs in wheelbarrows that, signs said, were going to decorate the pavements and terraces of the surrounding streets for the rest of the summer. Residents could "adopt" a barrow, keeping it watered and weeded, and in exchange they were welcome to use the herbs. And, said the same notices, this would be accompanied by talks from gardening and cookery writers, demonstrations from television chefs and more gardeners, and a competition to find the next big cookery blogger.

So by the time I reached Neil's office, a combination of sun and good-neighborliness had put me in a better mood. That only increased as Neil bounced out to meet me. We were friendly without being friends, in the way people are in small but sociable professions. I'd known him for years, liked him very much, and knew nothing about him or his life, and cared less. And I was quite sure he felt the same about me. In an industry where friendship and work are so tightly entwined, it's very enjoyable not to have to ask after somebody's partner, or child, or dog, or breakdown.

I'd be willing to bet that Neil had never had the latter, though. He was like Tigger, all energy and exuberance, as though, if anyone thought to suggest it, he would happily wrangle those gardening schoolchildren singlehandedly into planting the entire riverfront. Now he pushed his glasses up his nose with a characteristic gesture, using the back of his hand, stared at me for a moment, and carefully kissed the single unscabbed bit of my face. Then he acted as though I looked the way I always did. I considered asking him to marry me on the spot, but then I remembered I was already going to marry Denise-with-the-wonderful-voice. Denise who worked with Celia. That punctured my mood of general benevolence.

Neil said, "Do we need to be in my office? Or would you like to get coffee and sit by the river?"

On a day like today, that was a rhetorical question. We collected the coffee and sat like an old married couple, staring out at the tourist boats as they went past. I was conscious of taking up his time, though, so I quickly laid out the aims of the panel, and my need to produce a twenty-minute talk that didn't make me sound half-witted. "I'm shamelessly picking the brains of people who *do* need subsidies, and, in exchange, I'm offering to be the conduit to get across the points they want to make," I ended.

He grinned. "If you put forward the points I want to make, I'll even write that section for you."

"Deal."

He snorted a mouthful of coffee at the speed with which I'd replied. "Don't you even want to know what my points are, and if you agree with them?"

"Neil!" I'd explained this. "I haven't got any ideas for your points to agree with. I'm on this panel because I wasn't paying attention at the committee meeting; I wasn't paying attention at the meeting because I'd drawn the short straw at the office to attend in the first place. I'm sure there's lots to be said about subsidy and publishing, but I'm not the person who knows. You are, so tell me what needs saying."

He didn't hesitate twice. "I'll e-mail it over to you by tomorrow. And I owe you one for presenting our case."

He knew perfectly well that I owed him equally, for taking the work off my hands, so I didn't bother to reply. Instead we sat enjoying the sun. Ten minutes later, coffee and gossip finished, he walked me back to reception, where I'd left my bag. As we got to the door, we merged with a large group that was filing into the venue's main auditorium. Someone pulled at my elbow and I turned. Jim Reynolds.

"Hey," he greeted me, with the enthusiasm of Stanley discovering Livingstone. "I didn't realize you were coming. That's great. I've got to do the presentation, but will you wait for me at the end, and then we can talk about the panel?"

Before I could ask what presentation he was called away by a woman with a clipboard who looked as if she'd either cry or hit someone with it, or possibly both. I figured if I stuck around, I'd find out. I thanked Neil for his time, warning him that if he didn't produce the material he'd promised I'd hunt him down and press-gang his firstborn into the navy. He seemed relatively unperturbed.

I slipped into the back of the auditorium and looked around. Fifty or sixty people, and from their scruffy clothes and their general aura of having got lost on their way to the job center, I made a guess that they were arts journalists. On stage, four people stood in a little huddle. One I recognized, the director of the Tate. He was standing with a young, round, anxious-looking man, as well as an older woman with silver-white hair, and very elegant silver-white trousers and a jumper to match. She stood beside—I swallowed hard—she stood beside Celia Stein, as immaculate as before, in the only pair of linen trousers I'd ever seen that had not a single crease in them. She probably willed creases out of existence.

I decided that if I could produce mental commentary on her clothes, I couldn't be frightened. Frightened of what? the little voice taunted. Since I had no idea, I willed myself to be calm, and looked around. Jim was standing beside the stage with three others, and I guessed that I had stumbled across the press conference for the Tate's Stevenson show. Jim was gesturing toward a laptop, which must have controlled the AV, because at that moment the director nodded at him, and on the screen behind him appeared *Poppity Princess*, Stevenson's most famous work.

It is so ubiquitous, and used so frequently as a shorthand to say "pop art," or even "the sixties," that I hadn't really looked at it in years. I did now, and was reminded involuntarily of Mr. Rudiger's comments. With Warhol, the pictures were superficial because the artist wanted to reflect the superficiality of the world around him. Looking at *Poppity Princess*, I didn't feel that. It was as clever, funny, and subversive as it had always been, but it was also—I groped, not really sure. It was interested only in itself, I decided. It was an odd way to think about an inanimate object, but it almost smirked, as if saying, *Look at how lovely I am.* Once I'd seen it that way, I couldn't un-see it.

And as I moved my eyes down from the screen as the director of the Tate began to speak, I looked again at Celia Stein. She stood very quietly at the side, doing nothing to draw attention to herself, but she said the same thing as the painting. *Look at how lovely I am. Look at how much I matter.*

The director handed the microphone over to the silver-haired woman. I'd missed the introduction, but from her words she was Delia Stevenson, the artist's widow. Her speech was bland, generic—she was so pleased to etc., etc.—so I tuned her out, and watched Celia some more. She looked very much like her mother. Both were very lovely. Both were very elegantly, but quietly dressed. But the resemblance was only skin-deep. Despite their chilly beauty, they couldn't have been less alike.

Delia was very plainly unhappy to be onstage, unhappy to be the center of attention. She was there because her husband, and his work, in that order I thought, mattered to her, but if she could have avoided playing a public role, she would have. Celia, by contrast, had officially no public role—the presentation was over and she had not said a word—yet she had chosen to stand on the stage. Did she like being looked at, as Mr. Rudiger thought her father's work did?

The journalists dispersed, and Jim ambled toward me. Celia and her mother had been walking to the exit, talking quietly to each other, but she followed Jim's path, and as she looked up and saw me, she paused in midstride. Then she continued. It was nothing, fleeting, but the odd part was, she looked frightened, too.

I had no time to think about it. Jim and I did the hellos, and then the extra yes-doesn't-my-face-look-terrible-I-fell-off-my-bike. Then he said he was heading back to his office, so once more we walked back together.

"The pictures looked great," I said, figuring most of his mind would be on the upcoming exhibition. "Are you happy with the installation?"

He shrugged. "I suppose so. As happy as I ever am at this stage. I'm mostly seeing what doesn't work. And the souvenirs for the shop haven't been delivered yet. The change in images was a nightmare in terms of scheduling." As though that had reminded him, he looked over at me. "Why did you want to know?" He was curious, not worried.

I shrugged, too, or half-shrugged when my sore shoulder stopped my attempt at insouciance. "I was looking at the paper clip you did for the Lichtenstein show—it's on my fridge"—if he hadn't been a thirty-something hipster with a goatee, I would have described the expression on his face as a simper—"and so I was wondering how the decisions about what to use got made. When I think of Lichtenstein, I don't think of the paper clip, I think of those comic-strip paintings."

"And we used them, too. Most of the souvenirs have the most famous images, but it's also good to have a few less well-known ones, for people like you." He looked at me mock severely over his spectacles. "For mugs or cards, we tend to go for fame, but sometimes there's a piece where the subject matter suggests a use, just like the paper clip suggested a souvenir that would be used to clip things up. For Stevenson I wanted to use a piece with a book jacket in it to wrap around something book-shaped." He shrugged. "Not rocket science."

"No, and you'd think fairly uncontentious, especially as they hadn't argued with the paper clips."

He snorted. "It was never the Tate. The Tate was fine with the idea. Or as fine as they ever are, after they pick and fuss and meddle. . . . Never mind, standard freelance complaining. But it wasn't them. It was the estate that said no."

"That's odd. You'd think that they'd want the lesser-known pieces to have a moment in the sun."

Jim made a face. *Don't ask me*, it said. So I didn't, and changed the subject. "Did you go and see Lucy in the end?"

He could have been eighteen, he was so transparent. "I did what you suggested, went up and took her out for breakfast on Saturday morning. I think she was glad to get out of the house for a while. She's usually laid-back, but she was really stressed."

She probably was. Sitting with Toby and her family and friends waiting for a funeral couldn't be much fun. I made a mental note, I really had to go over and see Toby again.

The phone rang before I'd been back in the office for ten minutes. I was eating a salad at my desk as I went through my e-mail, and I contemplated letting it go to voice mail. I looked at the caller ID. Helena. *Even more reason*, I thought. Then I was ashamed, so I picked up.

I had spoken to her the day before, telling her briefly about my accident, although I only said I'd been knocked off my bike, leaving out that it needed a trip to the hospital, and definitely not adding that Jake had decided an unknown crazy had decided to exterminate me. I know, I'm exaggerating, but he'd frightened me, so I'd decided to blame it on him. Anyway, I assumed Helena was ringing to check up on me. I can be so dim.

She didn't trouble with a greeting. She rarely did. Her view was, she was busy, the person she was speaking to was busy, why waste time? "I'm going to Thomas and Stella Wynford's for dinner tonight. I've asked them if I can bring you."

I pulled the receiver away from my ear and stared at it accusingly. That was no help, so, "Why?" I said in an anguished voice. I knew from long experience that saying no would make no difference. Hell, dying between now and dinnertime probably wouldn't make a difference.

"Since he left Merriam-Compton, Matt Holder has been working as a private curator for a hedge fund owner. He's a client of Tom's, and he'll be at the dinner they're giving tonight. I thought it would be a good idea to see him."

I'd completely forgotten her questions about Holder. It had sounded so tenuously connected to Frank's death. Helena thought that anyone who had bested her at law was suspect, and I thought she was fixating. I still thought so.

"If the police aren't continuing with their inquiries, why would we do that?" I bit my tongue. I'd said "we." Now she knew that I knew that I was going to this bloody dinner.

"The inquest hasn't been held yet, so it's not final. And all we're doing is going to dinner at friends.'

Last chance saloon. "I can't go. My face looks like hell—it's covered with scabs and raw." I'd played down the accident yesterday so she wouldn't worry, but if it got me out of dinner with a bunch of lawyers, I'd be happy to tell her they'd had to amputate my nose and the stump wasn't healed.

"It can be a conversation opener."

Fabulous. I hung up, my mind a jumble, zipping back and forth between trying to remember if my posh frock was clean and thinking up new and inventive ways to torture Helena. I also needed to let Jake know I wouldn't be home for dinner. I picked up the phone. Then I put it down again. Did he know about Matt? Theoretically, there was no problem, case closed for him. But did I need to highlight a problem at the gallery, just in case? Finally I texted, *Going to dinner w Helena. See you after? Or tomoro?* When in doubt, prevaricate.

The Wynfords' house was what you'd expect for a senior QC and his McKinsey consultant wife. Large, elegant, and neutral-toned, and with a sprinkling of good contemporary art, everything the best that money could buy, but as personal as a five-star hotel, just with extra family photographs. I don't know why I felt so hostile. They'd been friends of Helena's for years, and her friends were usually people I liked, even if we didn't have much in common. I valued her judgment.

But tonight it was as though everything was a personal insult: a bunch of rich, smooth people enjoying their rich, smooth lives. I wanted to bite someone.

Spencer Reichel appeared to be an excellent candidate to be the bite-ee. The hedge fund employer of Matt Holder was the opposite of the caricature of the City fat cat, being thin, stooped, and vague-looking. If I'd been told he taught geography in a secondary school and played the organ in church on Sundays that would have been entirely believable. Believable until I'd listened to him for two minutes, because he had the City fat cat essentials, and then some. He thought he was the smartest man in the room, and he had no time, nor desire, to listen to anyone else, particularly not women.

And, oh joy, I was seated next to him at dinner. He looked me up and down, as if to check I wouldn't damage his expensive pinstriped suit by putting my nasty non-brand-label dress in close proximity. I gritted my teeth and gave my well-brought-up-girl smile. It's not as if I hadn't had practice making polite conversation with men who thought they were wonderful. There isn't a woman on the planet who hasn't. "Have you known the Wynfords long?" Anodyne was definitely the way to go.

He barely bothered to look at me. "They have an early Hockney drawing I want."

I was channeling middle-class manners so hard I nearly

snapped "I want never gets." I thought of telling him to take his elbow off the table while I was at it. Instead I substituted a mild, "I didn't know they collected."

He looked around their really beautiful dining room as if it had been a Travelodge. "I wouldn't call them collectors."

He began to expand. And expand. Truth to tell, I stopped listening after the fourth "I." It was all about how clever he was, how he'd outsmarted somebody about something, or lots of some-bodies about lots of somethings. It didn't matter. I knew how to do this. I smiled and nodded and said, "No, really?" intermit-tently, in an admiring little-pixie voice.

Then something went wrong. I don't know what, because I wasn't paying attention. Either a "No, really?" was in the wrong place, or he'd realized I was off on the planet Zog communing with a more interesting life form, because all of a sudden he barked, "You fell off your cycle, I hear?" It was presented as if it were a joke, but he was sneering, making me sound like a three-year-old who'd come off her trike. And if the patronizing contempt in his voice weren't enough, he actually held my chin with his hand, to get a better look.

I jerked back sharply. Helena was directly across the table from me, and her eyes signaled, *Do* not *throw anything at him.* There was no point, anyway, we were only on the first course, and the white wine wouldn't make a permanent stain. I thought briefly about waiting for the red, and then I lost my head, and kicked him sharply on the shin.

I don't know what came over me. I'm never physically violent, but he'd pushed all my buttons. It looked like I'd pushed his too, because his face turned a deep purple.

His voice was terrifyingly calm, however. "How *dare* you. Do you know who I am?"

If he'd stopped after that first sentence it might have worked, because I didn't quite know how I'd dared to kick a total stranger at a dinner party. But *Do you know who I am?* Come on.

I put my head to one side, the picture of someone giving a question deep consideration. "I'm not sure. Maybe if you were taller? Or shall I ask if anyone here recognizes you? Somebody must know who you are." I bared my teeth. I don't think even the most optimistic would have called it a smile.

He stared at me, speechless. Apparently no one had ever told him in so many words (all right, so many words and a good swift kick to back it up) that his behavior was unacceptable. I let my smile die and we both, with the precision of a long-established synchronized dance team, turned our backs on each other and began to speak to the people on the other side.

I didn't look at Helena. I knew that her social mask would be firmly in place, but my daughterly X-ray superpowers enabled me to see her eyes rolling to the heavens, wondering why with all her years of hard work, her training still hadn't taken hold.

Tough. *No one should be trained to put up with behavior like that,* was the message I stared back across the table. I didn't unfurl a suffragette banner and sing the famous suffragettes' song, but that was mostly because I hadn't thought to bring a banner, and I didn't know if the suffragettes had had a song. I'd come better prepared next time.

The man I'd turned to made me half-hope that there would be a next time. As I took a steadying sip of my wine he smiled and said, "I'll keep my hands on my cutlery, where you can see them at all times."

"I'm not armed, I promise." I couldn't believe I'd behaved that badly, much less that everyone knew. "Did you really see me kick him?"

He looked at me pityingly. "*Everyone* saw you kick him. And," he smiled again, "as an officer of the court I am legally obliged to disclose that there isn't a woman here who didn't cheer you on. And more than half the men. So who are you, and why did Reichel want to intimidate you?"

That was interesting. I'd only thought Reichel was a prick. It hadn't occurred to me he'd done it deliberately. My new friend watched me work it out, and nodded when he saw I'd got there.

I smiled, sincerely this time, and put out my hand. "Sam Clair," I said. "And you can put your fork down whenever you like. I'm not ready to go cold turkey yet, but I'm cutting back: one kick a night is my new limit."

"Alan Derbyshire," he replied, and we shook hands. He smiled with tired gray eyes that looked like nothing surprised him. At first glance there was nothing to make this man stand out in a crowd, but one look at those eyes and you'd quickly revise. In his way, he was as formidable as Reichel. But his power was contained, and he didn't need to make a show of it. Maybe that made him more formidable.

I answered his last real comment. "I'm not sure why he wanted to intimidate me. I'm sort of an add-on here. Helena"—I nodded across the table—"is my mother, and I'm her date. She and the Wynfords are old friends."

"Helena and I are old friends, too. I can't imagine why she's kept you hidden." He let his gaze drift down to where my feet would be under the table. "I'm a solicitor, too, and we've occasionally worked together." He glanced down toward the end of the table, where a dark man sat quietly. I'd noticed him earlier, as he and I were the youngest people at the dinner by at least twenty years, if you didn't count Reichel's wife, who was in her twenties. And no one did count Reichel's wife, including Reichel. And she'd always be in her twenties, because he'd trade her in for a new model each time she hit thirty. Some people have children, some people marry them.

"The last time we were on opposite sides. That was my client."

I refocused my attention on my neighbor, and on the young man he'd pointed out by not looking at him. "Who is he?"

"I was advising him on a termination of employment, a non-disclosure agreement. Not very interesting."

"Matt Holder," I said. I knew Helena was a magician who waved her wand, and abracadabra, rabbits fell over themselves to jump out of her hat, but that she'd got me sitting between Holder's lawyer and his current employer—even if I'd been foolish enough to declare open war on the latter—was pretty nifty rabbit-wrangling.

Derbyshire raised his eyebrows at my instant identification and I answered the unspoken question. "Aidan Merriam is a friend."

He nodded. "It was nastier than it should have been, and the agreement was . . ." he smiled in Helena's direction "forceful. More than necessary. Especially as Holder moved straight over to Reichel. I assumed then, and now, that the job was already lined up."

I was puzzled. Why would Holder's solicitor be talking like this about his client? Even if Holder had only hired him once. Then I saw the flat, dead look he flicked over my shoulder, at Reichel. There was hostility there. "If he had a job lined up, why do you suppose he bothered? I don't want to disparage the legal profession, of course . . ."

"Of course." He smiled quietly, looking down demurely, like a cat. I suspected that for him that was the equivalent of a huge hyena laugh.

". . . but Helena said he'd never had a case to begin with, and to bring you in to advise on the settlement? The legal costs had to have been a killer for someone who had been working as a junior in a gallery."

"Makes you wonder who was paying for it, doesn't it?"

I put down my cutlery and glanced slightly to my right before answering Derbyshire. "Yes. Yes, it does."

I was quiet for the rest of the meal. Which was probably a relief to at least one of my dinner partners.

When I got home, Jake was sprawled across the sofa watching football. He rolled his head along the sofa back to say hello, but he didn't lift it, although his glance paused consideringly when he saw I was dressed up. He patted the cushions beside him, but I shook my head. "Let me hang my clothes up first. I don't want to have to iron."

Back in jeans and a T-shirt, I recapped on my meeting with

Jim that morning, and then on the evening. I told him about Holder, too. It didn't seem to matter anymore, now the police were officially out of it.

Jake was smart enough not to comment on the fact that I'd had this information for a week, although I watched his face smooth out when I got to that part. He waited until I'd finished, and then said, "The interesting thing is that every loose end in this case returns to money. But the books are clean."

Another interesting thing was that he had never told me that. I knew it from Helena. But if he was smart enough not to comment on Holder, I should really be smart enough to keep my mouth shut, too. Part of me recognized that, since as far as he was concerned the investigation was closed, there was nothing to tell. The other, larger, and more unreasonable part said I didn't care what officialdom said. I narrowed my eyes at the thought, and his lips quirked. Now I was annoyed at him for not telling me, annoyed at him for knowing what I was thinking, and really annoyed at him for thinking it was funny.

That way madness lay. "If the books are clean, why does the story keep coming back to money, then?"

He shrugged. "It might mean something, it might not."

"That's the accumulated wisdom of Scotland Yard: it means something unless it doesn't?" I stared bleakly at him. "Lucky you people have crime novelists to burnish your image. Imagine if people wrote down what you really did."

He grinned full out. "That's like the giant rat of Sumatra. The story for which the world is not yet prepared."

There was no answer to that. I pulled a manuscript off the pile on the coffee table, and he went back to the football.

After fifteen minutes, he said, not turning his head, "Did you really kick the hedge funder?"

"Um-hmm," I said, also not looking up.

There was a pause. Then, "Hard?"

"Um-hmm."

"Good to know."

I smiled a very, very small smile, my eyes still on my manuscript. He wasn't looking at me, but he saw it. And I knew it.

8

I wasn't running in the mornings, after my bike accident. I told myself I was sorry, even though I was ecstatic to have an excuse. But because I wasn't, Jake and I were eating breakfast earlier than we normally did. When I say breakfast, I'm only indicating the time of day. I drink three very large cups of coffee first thing in the morning, and sometimes, if I'm feeling I need to make a special gesture toward nutrition and health, I eat a banana. Jake does cereal-ish things that I refuse to get involved in: I don't believe in food first thing in the day. Anyway, he was crunching, I was sipping, and we were both reading the paper. Our normal morning conversation consists of fragments. One of us says, "Did you see that—" and names some scandal in the paper. The other one says, "Mmm," and we subside back into silence. A real rouser of a conversation is, "Will you buy milk on your way home?" It sounds antisocial, but it's very friendly.

At 7:30, though, the silence was broken by the doorbell, and we stared at each other. Still unspoken, I decided that it had to be some emergency for Jake, which view I indicated by returning to the paper. He went down the hall, I poured more coffee and began to read again until I heard voices returning. I closed my eyes. Helena. Who else would show up uninvited for breakfast?

"Morning, darling," she trilled, managing to come in, kiss me, check the coffeepot's level, get a cup, and put down her files on the table, immediately marking out her place as the chair of a meeting about to be in session, in an eyeblink. I don't know how she does it. She's not quite five foot two, and exquisitely neatly made. Yet she dominates a room, even as her teeny-tiny feet tap along so daintily you'd think she was an escapee from a Disney movie: one of Cinderella's mice-helpers. Except Helena wouldn't have let Cinderella hang around waiting for a fairy godmother. She'd have had her stepmother up in court for child abuse; the stepsisters, not being bright enough for further education, would have been sent for vocational training—plumber's mates, perhaps; and as for little Cinders, she'd have got a lecture clarifying that while glass-slipper-wearing and hanging out with frog footmen might be fun, an education and a profession would get her further.

None of which altered the fact that I was now forcibly attending a meeting at my kitchen table. "Good morning. To what do we owe this *early* pleasure?"

Sarcasm bounced off Helena. I don't know why I bothered.

"Good morning again, darling. I thought we should discuss the Matt Holder situation with Jake. Until there's an inquest verdict, nothing is final, and I'd like to dot some i's and cross some t's. I have twenty minutes before I need to leave for my first meeting."

There, that was us organized. Jake and I came to order, and I was amused to see him take out his notebook, as if this were a scheduled staff meeting.

Helena didn't wait for us to settle. "The main question is, what is Reichel's interest in you?" she said to me, tapping a list.

"Interest in me? He has no interest in me."

"I don't mean after you assaulted him." Trust Helena to put it in those terms.

"Then what do you mean? He had no interest in me. When we sat down he launched into some long boring story about why he was the . . ." I faltered.

Jake turned his head. "The what?"

I put my head down on the table and spoke to the mat. "Why he was the world's best art collector." I sat up again. "I didn't think about the subject at all. It was some interminable story about how he'd bested some dealer at some sale for some picture. I never thought for a moment . . . But it must have been chance. Why would he talk to me about it? He doesn't know anything about me."

"That," said Helena, "is open to question. When I rang Stella this morning to thank her for a lovely party—and darling, you have written her a note, haven't you?—she said that she hadn't planned for you to sit next to him, but he'd asked her to change things around so he could talk to you."

I felt Jake next to me, quietly not laughing. I assumed it was because in his staff meetings the boss didn't remind her subordinates to write thank-you notes. Then I processed what she'd said. "Reichel asked to sit next to me? Why?"

"It's a question, isn't it? What exactly did he say?"

I closed my eyes. Then opened them, defeated. "I have no idea. He said the Wynfords had a Hockney he wanted to buy from them, but then I stopped listening. He was pompous and he was boring." Jake was still quietly not laughing, so I turned on him. "It's OK for you. When you're interviewing people, first of all they know it. Second of all, they don't try to patronize you." I returned to Helena. "I can't imagine what you wanted me to say: 'Let's have it, buster, why did you hire the man my friends fired? Speak into the microphone, please,' as I held a dessert spoon to his mouth?"

Jake called us to order. "This is unlikely to go anywhere, but let's look at it all the same. Spencer Reichel asked to sit next to you. He had a reason, which from what you say, wasn't an interest in you personally, because he doesn't have much interest in women in your age group." Unpleasant, and also accurate. I nodded. "Or women who talk back." I started to scowl at him, but he went on. "So he wanted to see if you were aware of something. He probably mentioned a name or an event, but you weren't listening. Did he know that?"

"I have no idea. I kept saying, 'No, really?' in a Kewpie-doll voice. That's usually all that's necessary, and it worked for a while. When he got nasty . . ." I considered. "I thought he'd realized I wasn't listening, but could it be that he'd said whatever it was and I hadn't responded, so he was pushing to get a reaction?"

"He got that." He turned to Helena, but whatever he was going to say was cut off by his phone. He looked at the caller's name and was halfway out the room, "Field," he said, grabbing for his notebook.

Helena began to gather her things. The meeting was adjourned. I decided breakfast was, too, and took the cups over to the sink.

"Have you spoken to Aidan about Holder?"

I fumbled one of the cups. "Me?" I couldn't help it, but I squeaked. "No, why would I do that?"

"To find out why they settled. It made no sense at the time. If what Alan said last night was accurate, that Holder had a new job lined up, it makes even less sense in retrospect. And if Reichel was paying Alan's bill, *and* wanted to talk to you . . ." She snapped her briefcase lock shut with a sorrowing, firm-but-fair click. "There's got to be a reason that makes sense of that."

I sighed. "I was planning to drop by Toby's on my way home from work. If Aidan is there, or Anna, I'll see what I can do."

I could see that "I'll see what I can do" wasn't nearly enthusiastic enough for her, but she nodded. She'd conveyed the points she'd planned to make, and allocated the tasks she'd planned to allocate. She left, as briskly and efficiently as she'd appeared.

I was just finishing the dishes when Jake came back, and the look on his face was not a happy one.

"What is it?"

"I've only got five minutes. Did you know a man named Werner Schmidt?"

I started to shake my head, and halfway there turned it into a nod. "I don't know him at all, but I heard his name last week. This is Merriam-Compton's restorer, right?" Jake nodded once, a "go on" nod. "Then he's Frank's ex-boyfriend, the reason Matt Holder was sacked. Why are you asking about him?" Then I played his question back in my head. "Not 'do.' 'Did' I know him? Past tense." I put my arms around myself, false comfort.

Jake nodded. "He's dead. He was found yesterday morning."

"How?" My voice was hoarse.

Jake's wasn't. He was angry. "Still being investigated. Unofficially, industrial accident."

I relaxed a fraction. Accident was good, wasn't it? I looked at Jake's face. No, it wasn't.

"The file only just came through to us. He runs his own company, lots of clients, so it took twenty-four hours to spot the connection to Compton. Two unexplained deaths in the same week. The Compton file has just been reopened, and we've been handed Schmidt, too. I'll know more when I see that." He looked over at me and spoke more gently, but I could see it was to reassure me, not because he believed what he was saying. "It may very well be an accident. We don't know yet, so don't worry."

Oh yes, that was going to work.

His lips thinned. "I've asked for the reports on your hit-and-run. The file will be with me when I get in to work."

"No."

He blinked, back in the kitchen, no longer at work. "No?"

"No. It can't have anything to do with those—with them. That's not fair." I wasn't thinking, it was just coming out.

He tugged me over to his side of the table. "I know, baby. But life's mostly not fair." He stood me away from him and looked at me. "I hate to have to do this, but are you ready to go? I need to get to the office and I want to drop you off first. You can give me the Holder story in more detail as we go. I'm sure you skimmed over it lightly last night."

I had no arguments now.

Tuesday mornings at work are my least favorite. There is a weekly acquisitions and progress meeting, where grievances get aired, interdepartmental hostilities are played out, and a ghastly time is had by all. Tuesday meetings in the summer are a little less painful, because people are away, not just in our office, but also among agents, and authors, so there is less to discuss in general. In some ways, I was sorry, because on this particular Tuesday a few pointless power plays would have kept me focused. I'd tried to reach Helena after Jake dropped me, but she was in a meeting, so I'd e-mailed her the news about Werner Schmidt. Then I sat with another open e-mail in front of me, with Aidan's name in the address bar, but after ten minutes I closed it without writing anything more. What could I say? Helena would have the information, and she was his lawyer. Let her tell him.

I counted to ten and tried to concentrate on work. Jake had said he'd be looking at my cycle accident, but I didn't—I refused—to believe that there was anything more than a pissed-off driver. The rest wasn't my business. Publishing was, and given the rumors sweeping the company, I should occupy my mind with that, or I might not have a business soon.

The morning meeting would be a focal point of those rumors, anyway. Not overtly. David Snaith, who ran it, would give nothing away, even if he knew anything, which was by no means a given. That wouldn't stop us looking for clues in everything he said. If the acquisition of a new book was rejected, we'd read it as, *You can't buy new books because none of us will be here next month.* If an acquisition was agreed, it was, *You can buy it because there'll be an injection of capital next month.* None of this was rational, but it didn't stop us from reading meaning into things that were entirely meaningless.

The meeting was scheduled for ten. Ten in publishing o'clock, which is 10:20-ish in human hours. That would give me plenty of time to wander around the building, checking in with those people I'd sent copies of the three manuscripts I wanted to buy. Had they liked the books, would they share my enthusiasm by saying they could market the hell out of them, or sell lots of copies, or had high hopes that the big chains and supermarkets would like them? I'd done the costings, and if the sales people would back me up by saying they thought my figures were credible, I'd probably win on at least two of the three. The third was more of a long shot. I loved it, but it wasn't the sort of thing I normally did, and it might be difficult to persuade people I could publish it well. That difficulty was welcome today. I could concentrate on that. Otherwise an "industrial accident," with no details, let me imagine every lurid possibility, and many I'm sure weren't at all possible. Profit-and-loss sheets were a welcome anchor in reality.

As it turned out, the mood in the meeting was either surprisingly cheerful, or just completely reckless, a sort of We're-going-down-with-the-*Titanic*-so-let's-have-fun-beforehand. No one stood up and sang "Nearer My God to Thee," but that was probably an oversight. At any rate, my first two books, as I'd hoped, slid through with no trouble. The advances it was agreed I could offer the authors matched what I thought the agents would be looking for, so unless the agents lost their minds, or the competing publishers did, I should at least be in the running. And as I expected, the third book was a problem. In fact, it became the touchpaper for a huge barney. Should we do this kind of book, how would we market it, did we have the expertise to promote it, and on and on. There was also a looping digression that took in a novel that three of us had turned down last year, which had just been shortlisted for the Booker. There was no real point in that kind of after-the-event flagellation, but we flagellated away all the same. Well, the editors who hadn't been offered the book, or hadn't read it, flagellated on our behalf. The three of us who had rejected it all agreed that the book had been bollocks when it was offered, and it continued to be bollocks now. If it won the Booker, it would be Booker-winning and financially rewarding bollocks, but you couldn't acquire books on an I-hate-it-but-maybe-it'll-win-the-Booker basis. Everyone knew that, but it didn't stop us from churning the subject over for a good, or bad, half hour before we finally returned to my potential third acquisition.

And after all that David, who hated and feared dissension with a passion that made pet bunnies look confrontational, decided I should get some marketing plans drawn up, and we'd discuss it again the following week. Which meant, translated out of David-ese, that by then maybe the agent would have sold it to someone else, and David wouldn't have to make a decision that was bound to irritate half his staff.

It was all in a day's work—not the barney, the not being allowed to offer for everything I wanted to buy. No one ever achieved that, and I was pleased about the two that had been okayed. I immediately sent offer e-mails to the two agents, outlining how much I could pay, and for what. Marianne, our rights manager, thought they both had good potential for translation, which meant I could add a bit more money in the expectation that we'd make it back by selling foreign-language rights. All of this was run-of-the-mill, but it still had to be outlined carefully, and the figures juggled so we stayed ahead on the bottom line. The meeting had taken up the entire morning, breaking up in bad-tempered pseudo-agreement only when we got too hungry to continue, and the figures took even longer, so I'd just managed to get the two e-mails off before it was time to go.

I wanted to leave on time, so that I could go and see Toby without it looking as though I was expecting to be asked for dinner. I was sure they wouldn't want me, the night before the funeral, but if I got there later in the evening, they might feel they had to offer, or, even worse, put me in a position where I had to accept. I figured that if I got there by six, I could decently leave at seven, and honor would be satisfied.

The tube would be faster, but I decided to take the bus up to Highgate. First of all, it was a nice evening, and I'd been indoors all day. But that was a polite fiction I made up to fool myself. What I really wanted was something to keep my mind busy so I didn't have to think about this second death. I was sure I would hear the details at Toby's: the man had been the gallery's restorer, and lots of the people there must have known him. But information was one thing. I longed for information. What I didn't want was to have to turn the bare facts that Jake had given me over and over in my head, which I would do if I was straphanging on the tube. If I took the bus, I could busy myself with the day's backlog of e-mails: the meeting, and then rushing to get the two offer letters written, meant that I'd otherwise only dealt with emergencies, or things that looked like they might soon become emergencies. I hear that other cities have this legendary thing called Wi-Fi on their underground systems, but as London had yet to join the twentieth century, much less the twenty-first, we see no reasons to pollute our transport network with such crass modernity. There were a few stations that proudly announced they had a connection, but that was only on the platforms. If our ancestors could fight the Crimean War without Wi-Fi, seemed to be the consensus, then it must be admirable to continue proudly on without it. I think that is the technical explanation.

It was rush hour, and the bus was crowded. I was lucky to get a seat, and it was on the top deck. Since they banned smoking on the buses years ago, the only people who go upstairs if there are seats below are tourists and children. The natural swaying of the bus is magnified; add in bus drivers' union regulations that require them to stomp on the brakes with the strength of a rhino in heat, and doing e-mail becomes complicated. But sitting was better than standing, and e-mail was better than worrying.

I clicked and scrolled busily as we stopped and started up the hill to Highgate, getting through an enormous amount of dull but necessary routine as we went. Two or three stops before we reached Toby's, I looked up to check where we were. I was staring out blankly at the street below, not really paying attention, when something nagged at me. I looked again. That was it, a russet flash. I turned to look back, and sure enough, there was Celia Stein.

Without thinking, without even processing the thought, I leaped across the person sitting next to me and flung myself down the stairs. The bus was already in motion again, but it was one of those new ones, with the old-style back opening. This, too, is a space for tourists, or maybe for government ministers to look at nostalgically as they drive past in their cars, remembering the days of their youth. Whatever, it's not officially for use, and each of the buses boasts a conductor whose sole job is to prevent people entering and exiting this way. But in my mad scramble the momentum I'd gained on the stairs was no match for him. I leaped off the moving bus and was steadying myself on the pavement before he'd even managed to put out a hand to stop me.

I looked in the direction I'd seen Celia. There was no one there now. I looked up and down the street. No one. Had I been mistaken? Was I having Celia Stein hallucinations? For all I knew this was where she lived. It was as likely a place as anywhere.

I was an idiot. That wasn't news, so I turned and headed up the hill to Toby's.

I walked slowly, dreading the evening. I'm not good in social situations—if I were, I'd have become a publicist. But more than that, there was the little job Helena had landed me with. People who have never met Helena tell me "Just say no" when I complain about her making me do things like this. Not about making inquiries linked to sudden death. That hasn't come up much up until now. But more generally. My answer is simply to introduce them to my mother. Then they know better.

The front door was ajar when I arrived. I took this as a sign that lots of people were there, or at least were expected, so the family didn't have to run back and forth. That was hopeful. And so it proved. The sitting room already held maybe thirty people, standing and talking as though it were a drinks party. I slid through, nodding and smiling at the few people I recognized— some gallery staff, whose names I didn't know but I'd seen them over the years and their faces were familiar, and some people I'd met at Aidan and Anna's. But I saw no one I knew and I could see their eyes widen as they saw my injured face, not something I felt like discussing with strangers. So when I saw Lucy, I stopped. At least we'd chatted a bit, and we could talk about Jim, and the show. In these circumstances she was as close as I was going to get to a friend.

She seemed just as pleased to see me. She had, she said, been head of "kitchen operations," feeding the people who had come to visit over the past week. Now there was just the funeral to get through, and then things would return to normal, so she wasn't going to be needed anymore. I apologized for having failed to bring the supplies I'd promised on the weekend. She examined my face with a naïve openness that was much better than the covert looks I'd been getting, and said, peering at the scabs, "If you were making excuses, at least you went to the trouble of making it look authentic."

I smiled. "My mother's a lawyer. I'm a stickler for an alibi."

She jumped and flushed. "I didn't mean to be rude."

"You weren't rude. It was a big improvement on the people who talk around the subject, hoping I'll mention how it happened so they don't have to ask a direct question." Asking direct questions in middle-class, professional England gets you deported, probably to the colonies, where they don't know any better.

She put her head on one side, interested. "Sort of the way we treat death. Poor Toby. I think if one more person puts a hand on his arm and says, 'How *are* you, *really?*' he's going to explode. Except Toby doesn't explode. That was Frank. Toby was the smoother-over afterward. Even for gallery explosions."

"I didn't know Toby had ever had anything to do with the gallery."

She nodded, her eyes scanning the room restlessly. Apparently being head of kitchen operations hadn't quite worn off, and she was checking to make sure everyone was supplied. Which they were, and the noise was rising accordingly. "Officially, Aidan does the selling and Frank was the artist-wrangler." She gave a small smirk, to mark off her cynical assessment that artists needed to be herded like cattle. "But without Toby as social glue, I doubt there would have been an artist left on the gallery's books. Or a staff member."

This was as good a place as any to start the investigation Helena had ordered. "I had no idea. I saw one of the gallery people last night, or at least an ex-gallery person." I looked over her shoulder, as though I wasn't much interested. "Matt Holder."

Her eyes snapped back to me, but she didn't say anything.

I shrugged. "One of those who needed smoothing over, I hear?"

She looked curious, now. "What do you mean?"

"I heard that there was an argument about his seeing an ex of Frank's." Who was now dead.

She closed her eyes and shook her head, a worldly-wise twenty-year-old mourning the foolishness of her elders. "God knows why that was ever a problem, but it was." She stopped, seeming to feel that this discussion was at an end.

I didn't want to barge off, as though I'd only stopped to pry, so I changed the subject. "I also chatted to Jim Reynolds yesterday at the Stevenson press conference. What I saw of the pictures looked great." It wasn't the most original, or interesting, comment I'd ever made, so I wasn't surprised when she just smiled mechanically. I was more surprised that she didn't reply. Maybe Jim liked her more than she liked Jim? At any rate, she wasn't interested. So I might as well push off. "Is Aidan here?"

She didn't even look around. "Last I saw he was in the conservatory, talking to Myra."

I turned. He was still there, and having Myra identified was a bonus: she was definitely one of those faces I was supposed to know.

I started to make those noises you do when you're ready to leave. "This all coming together must be so difficult for you."

Lucy had clearly decided the gathering held more interesting people than me, which I couldn't really argue with. "Will you excuse me?" she said, as though we'd never met. "I think they need more ice over there."

Another dazzling display of social skills on my part. I turned and trudged off to the back of the room, which Lucy had called the conservatory. Aidan had moved off, but Myra was still there. She was the one, I remembered, who had sent the e-mail with the funeral details, so I introduced myself and thanked her for including me. She recognized me, but I had no idea if we'd ever spoken before or not. I cast around for conversation, not easy when I didn't know what she did at the gallery. So I just repeated what I'd said to Lucy—that I'd been at the press conference for the Stevenson exhibition and it looked as though it would be a great show, and added, "It must be taking up enormous amounts of everyone's time at the gallery. And particularly now, without Frank."

She wasn't a chatty type, apparently, because the only answer I got was pursed lips. I bet no one ever said, a party's not a party without Myra.

"Does it all end up with Aidan now?" I tried next. "Frank never struck me as a paperwork type." I considered it for a moment. "Not that Aidan does either."

She huffed. "I do the paperwork. That's what a registrar does."

I had no reason to stay with this grumpy woman, but maybe she had been close to Frank and this was her way of dealing with it. I tried to look sympathetic instead of answering her words. "It must be hard for someone who worked with Frank as closely as you did." And then I made a break for it.

I went into the kitchen and found myself a glass of wine. I also found Aidan, who was listening to Lucy, who was gesticulating furiously, but with tears in her eyes—more upset than angry. Whatever it was it didn't appear to worry Aidan too much, because he just patted her on the shoulder when he saw me and walked away, leaving her there biting her lip.

He couldn't have seen me when I'd arrived, because he was now staring at my face, appalled, not bothering with the sidelong glances others were deploying. I agreed with him. Most of my face was now not only scabbed over, but had turned an elegant sea-green from the bruising. But while I found it mostly embarrassing, Aidan seemed to be personally insulted by it. "Jesus, Sam." It was an accusation.

But not one that was worth responding to. "I fell off my bike. It looks worse than it is." I didn't want to talk about it, and if I talked to him quickly about Holder, I could get the hell out of there. I thought "How are you managing?" was a good opening gambit. He could tell me how he was feeling, or how they were managing at the gallery, or he could just take it as a variant on "How are you?," whichever he liked.

He chose reality. "I've been here every evening for a week. I'm contemplating becoming an alcoholic."

I tried to sound encouraging. "These late career changes can be good. I'm sure there's a call for a professional lush somewhere."

I agree, not funny, but it was the night before his partner's funeral. I don't think any of us were making great jokes.

He wasn't really listening anyway. And I was surprised that he hadn't mentioned Schmidt's death. That no one I'd spoken to so far had. I thought briefly that I might avoid it, and then vetoed that. Aidan had come to me when Frank died.

"I heard about Werner Schmidt this morning. I'm sorry. Was he an old friend?"

Aidan rubbed his eyes, much as he'd done that first day at lunch. It was a bit like one of those nightmares, where every time you go back to sleep it starts all over again. "Everyone else has been too tactful to mention it to me." He smiled an old-friend smile. "Your tact levels never change, do they?"

I was mortified. "I never know whether talking about things or tiptoeing around them is worse."

He patted the air. "Tiptoeing is worse. I'm glad you said something. And yes, he was an old friend. He was at art college with Frank, and they were together for a few years. Frank always knew he wasn't good enough to be a successful artist, and became a dealer almost as soon as he graduated. Werner . . ." He hesitated. "Werner wasn't good enough either, but he didn't accept it for a long time. Never did, really. He started to do bits of restoration for friends, and then ultimately retrained, but he always continued to make his own art. It just isn't very good. And so restoration became a living, and his own art a hobby, although he didn't think of it that way."

"Poor man. To do something you love badly, or at least not well enough, and not love the thing you're good at."

He nodded. "He was very bitter. A great guy, as long as you never discussed art. Or, at least, I didn't, apart from the restoration he did for us. He and Frank had a much tighter relationship." Then he frowned. "How did you hear?" Even as he asked, he knew the answer. "Your policeman?"

"Yes. This morning." I shook my head, preempting his next question. "I don't know anything apart from the fact that he's dead, and it was probably an accident. That's all Jake had when I went to work."

"Then I know more than you. He was found dead in his studio on Monday morning by a courier who was booked to collect a job from him. As far as any of his friends can work out, he was last seen on Friday night. He was invited to a party on the Saturday, and didn't show up, so we're assuming between then sometime."

"Do you know how? Jake said 'industrial accident,' but I don't know what that means."

Aidan's mouth twitched. "A very official phrase. At the moment, we've been told that it looks like it was glue inhalation."

"Glue inhalation? Sniffing glue, you mean?"

"Sam! Spray glue is used for mounting works on paper."

Of course it was. Designers at T&R always had tins of glue lying around, too. But I hadn't known it could kill you. I said so, and Aidan agreed. He hadn't either.

"That's all I know at the moment. No doubt the police will be back in the gallery soon, buzzing around the place." He saw me wince. "I'm sorry. I didn't mean your policeman in particular. Although . . ." he raised an eyebrow. "Will it be him and his colleagues again?"

"I think so. I'm sorry."

We were both apologizing back and forth, like some sort of parody of English people stepping on each other's toes. Aidan recovered first. "So, how is it out there in the real world?"

He didn't want to know about my world just then, and anyway I still had Helena's dirty work to do.

"Same old same old. Timmins & Ross might be taken over. And I disgraced myself at a party last night. I kicked my dinner partner."

He was amused. "On purpose? What did he do?"

"Grabbed my face, the dick. A man named Spencer Reichel. Do you know him?" I kept everything except annoyance with Reichel off my face.

Aidan's face didn't alter either. "Sure. He collects twentieth-century art. He buys from us a bit, although he's not a regular client. And he funds that art charity, the one for reproductions.

We dealt with them in the past for a couple of *catalogues raison-nés* of our artists."

Dear God, this hadn't been where I was going, but I grabbed his arm. "Wait. What?"

He looked at me curiously, and repeated, "He's an art collector, and he funds an art charity. What's wrong with that?"

"The Daylesworth Trust?" I accused him, as though this were information he'd been hiding from me. "Celia Stein works for him?"

"Yes," he said patiently. "And?"

And what indeed? I didn't know why it should matter, but somehow it did. I tucked it away and returned to the fray. "And the man's a dick."

Aidan didn't bother to hide his contempt. "He is, but that's not why I mentioned him. What are you ferreting around for?" It wasn't as if he didn't know me well.

"Matt Holder was at the dinner, too."

Aidan was cross now. "And?"

I might as well be blunt. "I also sat next to Alan Derbyshire— I didn't kick him," I added virtuously.

He smiled briefly. "Well done." The smile vanished almost before it had appeared. "Holder's solicitor. What the hell is this about? If it's just Helena wanting to make sure that there's nothing that's going to come back and bite me, tell her to ask. And then I'll tell her that there isn't." He stomped off.

My, hadn't that gone well.

9

I stopped to fill the sit-by-Toby position for ten minutes, and
then made my escape. It was a gorgeous evening. It would
be light for another couple of hours, and the air had that sense
of elasticity that summer in London does, as though there were
magically more hours in the day.

It made me feel as though I ought to use that extra time, so I
walked instead of taking the bus. It would only take another ten
minutes, and if I went the way I would have come from the market on Saturday, I could collect my bike, which should still be
chained up to the lamp post where I'd fallen.

Should. It wasn't the greatest neighborhood, but then, I didn't
have the greatest bike. In the privacy of my own web browser I
look at what I call bike porn—high-end Dutch and Danish com-
muter bikes, with amazing add-ons and accessories. But back
in the real world, a combination of pragmatism and cheapness
means that, whenever I need a new bike, which has only been

twice in twenty years, I end up with a bog-standard city bike. Nothing anyone would want to steal.

I know this for a fact. One day I had a brainstorm when I was in town, and forgot to chain my cycle up when I went to see a film. Three hours later, right on a main road, it was still there when I came out. I stood there boiling with fury at the insult to my poor cycle—*my bike isn't good enough to steal?*—even as I realized this was not an entirely rational response.

Nonetheless, the odds, I thought, were anything from fair to good that that same cycle would now be where I'd left it on Saturday, and so it proved. Somebody had even reattached the front basket, which had flown off when I'd gone arse over tit. As I bent down to unlock the chain, I saw there was a note taped to the basket's base: "Thank you for the flowers. I hope you're alright. Viv at number 73."

It was written on a piece of paper that had been torn from an exercise book, and the writing looked like the kind that was taught in schools in the thirties and forties. I presumed number 73 meant 73 of the street we were on, or a street name would have been included. I looked around. There was a 73 only yards away. I didn't give myself time to think, or even wonder why I was doing it. I replaced the chain, walked over and rang the bell.

There was a long pause, and I was about to give up, when I heard a step in the hall. "If you're selling something, you can bog right off," called a voice.

I was immediately glad I'd rung. "I'm not selling anything," I called back. "I'm the person who had the cycle accident on Saturday."

The door opened immediately. It was the gray-haired woman

who had suggested I ring a friend, and she must have been standing on the mat. I'd been flat on the pavement when I'd last seen her, and not in any condition to notice anything much, but even so, I was surprised that I hadn't noticed how short she was—she was more than a head shorter than I am, and I'm shorter than almost everyone over the age of eight.

Despite her lack of height, she looked me up and down and made me feel that I was the small one. She didn't say anything, either, just waited.

"I came to collect my cycle, and was so pleased to see you'd left your name in the basket, so I could say thank you for your help."

Her eyes, which had been so vague on Saturday, snapped now. She nodded decisively. I had passed some unknown test. She stood back. "Would you like some tea?"

I loathe tea, and think of it as something that I'm forced to drink when I'm ill, but I realize that only emphasizes my foreignness, which I didn't want to do now. "Very much, thank you." I wiped my feet carefully, even though it was sunny and there was no particular reason for them to be dirty.

She nodded again. Another step up in her estimation.

"Come in," she said over her shoulder, already moving down the passageway.

Most of my part of London is a patchwork. Because of the nearby railway lines, the area had been heavily bombed in the war, and so afterward streets got chopped up, rows of Victorian houses like mine suddenly stopping dead to give way to blocks of flats like Viv's, built in the 1950s to replace flattened neighborhoods. The 1950s was an unbeautiful time for building generally, and these buildings were particularly unbeautiful. It seemed likely, looking at the kitchen, that Viv's parents had been the flat's first residents. The linoleum on the floor was a 1950s-style black-and-white check, the few cupboards were chipped melamine, both the cooker and the fridge were tiny and incredibly ancient. Nothing could have been altered or renewed for at least four decades, and it might well have been longer. But everything was cared for, looked after and valued. There were crisply ironed blue-and-white striped curtains at the windows, and a blue-and-white rag rug was on the floor in front of the sink. A tray of seedlings sat in a patch of later-evening sun on an almost doll's-house-sized white-painted table, with two doll's-house-sized white chairs pushed underneath. Above the seedlings were pots of herbs, and a hanging basket, and—I looked again—pots were on every single flat surface, lining the back of the counter, on top of the fridge, everywhere.

"It's a garden," I said, amazed.

She smiled, the first genuine smile she'd given me. "I'm lucky. This side is south-facing, and so even though I don't have a garden, I've got the next best thing."

"Then the flowers went to a good home, although you might say it was coals to Newcastle."

She speared me with a don't-give-me-any-nonsense look. "I haven't managed to grow peonies in here." Then she gave the sink a considering stare, as though now she'd mentioned it, she might give it a try.

The kettle must have just boiled, because she moved a teapot that had been sitting beside the cooker onto the table. She gave me another look, up and down again, and then turned and took a biscuit tin off a shelf. I don't know what it was that made her decide, but it was plain that I'd passed whatever test it was. Not everyone got biscuits. I was both pleased, and felt silly for being so pleased.

"I'm Sam," I said. "Sam Clair. We didn't have time for introductions last time."

"You're lucky you kept your teeth," she said tartly, then wiped her hand on her skirt before passing it over to me, as you'd pass a parcel over a shop counter. "Viv Thrale."

I sat in the seat she nodded me to, and took the bloody tea. The biscuits were home-baked, and made having to drink it worthwhile.

She sat, too, and stared at me, expectant. I wasn't sure what it was she was waiting for, so I started to thank her again. She waved it away. If someone was bleeding on the pavement, the wave said, you picked them up. End.

I liked the attitude and moved on. I asked her if she knew who'd chained up my bike, and who had chased down my groceries, and if she did, would she thank them for me, too. She nodded with the same bored briskness. Of course she knew them, the nod said, she knew everyone.

I finally stuttered to a halt. She waited a moment, to see if I had anything to add, and then she said, "The police didn't come up with anything."

"No," I agreed. "No one managed to get the car's registration, or even know what make of car it was. I didn't either. Or, rather, I saw the car, but it was too confused. I'm not even sure of the color."

She pursed her lips. Then, as though she wasn't entirely sure she was going to say it, she said, "Blue. Dark blue. A Volvo."

I blinked.

She had decided now. "One of the boys thought it was new, maybe two years old. And definitely a woman driver, although he couldn't say more than that. He's a silly boy. He only got the last two letters of the registration: 'MR.'" Her expression told me what she thought of the poor boy's inadequacies. And that she'd probably listed them out for him.

"But the police . . ." I let the sentence trail away.

Her expression was unyielding. "The boy . . ." I noticed she was careful not to give me his name. "The boy has been in trouble, and he wouldn't volunteer anything. The way the police use stop-and-search around here, I wonder they expect anyone to tell them anything. The only people who will are the oldies." Her sniff said she was not in that category. "And they don't see anything."

"But you do," I prodded.

She took it as a compliment, and also as her due. "But I'm not home much. You were lucky to catch me in on a Saturday." I loved that, as if a cycle accident was the equivalent of dropping by to swap scone recipes.

"And lucky now, too," I ventured. "May I pass the information on? Even if no one is willing to make a statement?"

That's why she'd mentioned it to me, her silence said. Then she snapped the lid back on the biscuit tin. My audience was over. She had places to go and people to see.

Jake had texted to say he'd be late, certainly after dinner, and maybe not even then. While I wanted him at home, so he could tell me that of course Werner Schmidt's death was an accident, and that everything was fine, I doubted that that was the way the conversation would go, so I was sorry he wasn't there, and at the same time I was also glad. And, I told myself, it would give me the evening to work on my sodding Arts Council presentation. Neil had e-mailed me his (now my) ideas, but I needed to merge them with the information I'd collected from the other people I'd spoken to, and make them into a coherent whole. Maybe not coherent. That was too much to ask. But at least somehow give the illusion that I knew what I was talking about, even if no one else did.

I sat down at my desk as soon as I got back from Viv's. If I started to faff around in the kitchen, or picked up a book or a manuscript, I'd persuade myself that I could write the presentation at some mythical "later" time, putting it off either until Jake appeared, which meant I wouldn't do it, or until I was too tired and went to bed, which meant I wouldn't do it. Before I began, though, I e-mailed Jake with Viv's update on the car. I googled car registrations first, and found that the two letters the boy had seen were the least useful part of the number plate. The first letters or numbers would have told the police where the car was registered, and the year. I didn't trouble to include Viv's views on why the police hadn't found the information for themselves. It wasn't news to me, and I presumed it wouldn't be to Jake either.

Once I had my e-mail open, I realized I'd just assumed I would also tell Jake about Celia Stein. But now I paused. If I did that, then it brought Reichel into the picture. Which brought Matt Holder into the picture. Which shone a spotlight back onto the gallery, back to where we didn't want it to be now that Frank's death was being looked at again. Instead, I jotted everything down in an e-mail to Helena. I didn't even know why the Celia Stein/Spencer Reichel connection seemed important to me. Let her decide who should know and what they should know. I had no idea what I was doing, and she always knew what she was doing.

Done. I opened another document and started on the presentation. I'm normally in favor of procrastination, but it was Tuesday, and the panel was on Friday. At some point, procrastination begins to look like a death wish. Tonight, I'd decided, was the tipping point. So I wrote the damn thing. Not happily, but I did it. I included lots of buzzwords—discoverability, inclusivity, cross-platform availability—and while I was on a roll lots more buzzwords that I think I made up but which sounded great—integrated virtual sectionality. I had no idea what they meant, but I didn't think it mattered. The points Neil, Celia, and Emma wanted to make were made. After that, I might as well entertain myself.

It was eleven before I e-mailed the final text to everyone who had given me input, with a covering note asking them to let me know by Thursday lunchtime if I'd misrepresented their ideas. And then I was done. I decided to celebrate with a glass of wine and a rest on the sofa before thinking about dinner. I knew perfectly well that that meant that thinking was as far as dinner was going to get, but it's like throwing leftovers away. If you put the leftovers in the fridge for three days after a meal, throwing them out on the fourth day isn't as wasteful as throwing them away right after supper would have been. So if I thought about making dinner for a while, then drinking, the meal wouldn't be as bad as if I'd just admitted from the outset that it was going to consist of three glasses of wine. Besides, I'd had some crisps at Toby's, and a biscuit with Viv: alcohol, fat, salt, and sugar, the four major food groups, were accounted for. Then I remembered the tea. It had had milk in it, and so dairy was covered, too. Damn, but I was healthy.

I propped myself up against the arm of the sofa in my usual reading position, but I knew it was a lie even as I grabbed a manuscript off the pile. I stared out of the window, thinking about the past few days and drinking my wine. I must have sat like that for, well, at least five minutes.

When I woke up Jake was moving the bottle and glass off the floor and onto the table. He saw me lift my head and bent over me. "Come on, sweetheart. Bed."

"What time is it?"

"Two."

In the morning I'd want to know what was happening that meant he was working until two, but not now. Now I very much wanted to pretend we were back in the days when I didn't know about Jake's work. Instead of getting up, which felt like too much effort, I pulled him down to me. "How tired are you?"

"Not that tired."

By the time the alarm went off, Jake was gone again. It was like going out with—or staying home with, rather—the invisible man. I lay in bed for a while, thinking evil thoughts about vampires who materialized after dark and vanished—poof!—before light. Then I thought evil thoughts about people who had four glasses of wine and only a sandwich to eat all day. Yesterday I'd sworn to myself that even if I couldn't run yet, I'd get up early and go for a walk. I thought more evil thoughts about people who make resolutions. And still more about wimpy types who don't keep them. Then I got up.

I was in no rush. Because of Frank's funeral, I'd told Miranda I wouldn't be in until the afternoon, if then. I was, like my colleagues, working from home. I took my coffee into the spare bedroom, which I call my office, and sent a few gossip-collecting e-mails to friends in other publishing houses, to see if any of them had picked up on our rumors. Were their bosses having early breakfasts with unnamed others, for example? Then I settled down to try and find the information I wasn't brave enough to ask Jake for.

My library has online access to most UK newspapers, and several of the big U.S. ones, so I started there. Werner Schmidt. There were a few reports on his death, most only a few lines long. Art restorers are not big news, and the preliminary conclusion, that he had accidentally inhaled glue, was not of itself newsworthy. A couple of tabloids had used the glue angle to write about the hazards of glue-sniffing, creeping out their readers with addiction horror stories. But even they were forced to acknowledge that, when spray glues had been reformulated nearly two decades ago, it all became increasingly rare. The spray had to be extremely close and extremely dense to cause the convulsions and asphyxiation that they so gloatingly described.

I closed the tabs, feeling sick. What a terrible way to die. I thought of Schmidt sitting alone in his studio, gasping for breath. As a displacement activity, and because it was too horrible to think about, I began to search for information on Celia Stein and Reichel. Reichel didn't lead anywhere much. He was exactly what I'd been told, a hedge funder who collected modern art, which, I noted in passing, many hedge funders did, the way nineteenth-century robber barons had bought truckloads of Gainsboroughs. I didn't read any of the financial-press reports on Reichel's hedge-funding activities because, truth be told, I wasn't entirely sure what a hedge fund did, and the articles never troubled to explain. Were funds hedged, or hedges funded? Either made as much sense to me. On the art front, the reports were no more enlightening, although there I could at least understand the words. Reichel was Great and Good as far as the art world was concerned, a trustee for heritage bodies like the National Trust and English Heritage. He gave liberally to the right charities, went to the right arts venues, had his picture snapped with the right people. Dee-dah-dee-dah. Admirable, but I couldn't see how it was relevant.

Apart from being a prominent man, Reichel also had a usefully unusual name. Searching for Celia Stein together with Stevenson at least got rid of those other Celia Steins I'd been confronted with when I first searched for her, but there still wasn't much that was helpful. Most of the references were to exhibitions where she was quoted as the family representative, and that was bland: she was thrilled to be bringing her father's work to insert-name-of-city-here. If she had interesting or original views on art, or on anything else, she had kept them to herself. I checked Delia Stevenson, too, just to see what there was, and the answer to that was, basically, nothing. She left being the face of the Stevenson estate to Celia.

I stared at the screen. Now what? I checked my e-mail. Nothing from Helena or Jake. Three e-mails about a submission I hadn't begun to read from an agent I particularly disliked. Two from marketing asking for catalog copy I hadn't written. Miranda, listing out meeting requests from our finance people, to go over my next year's budget. All of them needing to be dealt with swiftly. So I decided to google Stevenson himself. I read the newspaper features on him, and on the upcoming show. One of them said that this was Stevenson's first major European retrospective. He was one of the "fathers" of pop art, but had never had the same kind of success, or profile, as many who came after him.

That gave me a new idea—anything, frankly, not to have to write catalog copy. I found a website where, for a tenner, I'd get three days' access to world auction prices, which sounded like a reasonable deal. So I fed my credit card number in and watched the numbers come back. It was like I imagine playing the slot machines at Vegas would be: put some money in and, most of the time, nothing comes back, but the spur of a possible return keeps you upping the ante each time. I wasn't sure if I was ready to put more than a tenner on it, but I was willing to make that my entry stake.

Stevensons didn't fetch nearly as much as Warhol or some of the other big names, although that wasn't a secret. But seeing what was spent on art was weirdly compelling, like looking into the shopping carts of the people behind you in the line at the supermarket—three tins of cat food and a single tomato? Diet soda and two dozen muffins? The auction houses didn't tell you who bought what, so you couldn't try and construct a lifestyle, the way you could with supermarket baskets, but even just the prices were fascinating. Almost involuntarily I signed up to more websites. More credit-card numbers, this time for more than a tenner, and for less than three days. But it was Vegas, and the next pull at the one-armed bandit was going to be the one that produced a jackpot, and answers would tumble out. More auctions, more anonymous sales.

I stared out the window, trying to remember why I was doing this, and what I thought it would achieve. I had no answer, to either question, but the stubborn part pushed in: if I stopped now, then not only would I not have learned anything, but I'd have to admit I'd wasted all that money, as well as—I looked at the clock—three hours. I'd pulled on jeans first thing, and I needed to dig out my dark suit for the funeral. Helena was collecting me so we could go together. Officially she was due in half an hour, but in Helena time that was more likely to be twenty minutes. Maybe fifteen.

I was ready and waiting outside in ten minutes. I wish I could pretend that that was because I had one of those streamlined "capsule" wardrobes I read about in the Sunday supplements. Really it's because I don't have any clothes. But I was in my dark suit, and heels, and I'd put on makeup. Good enough, surely. I stood talking to one of my neighbors, who was complaining about the kids who congregate at the bottom of our street, near the pub. They smoke outside, and make a fair amount of noise in the evenings, but what bothered her were the fast-food containers and the cigarette butts they dumped in her garden. I agreed that it wasn't pleasant, but I had no suggestions apart from cleaning it up in the mornings, which we all did. None of us enjoyed it, but it was just part of city life. She didn't see it that way, and complained regularly to the pub's manager, who promised each time that something would be done, and then did nothing. I'd heard the story before, so I made soothing and sympathetic noises in the right places while not giving it my full attention. Or, to be truthful, any attention at all.

When Helena drew up, therefore, I leaped into the car with an enthusiasm that was entirely misplaced. I didn't want to go to the funeral. I didn't want to see Aidan again after last night. And I really didn't want to discuss my lack of interrogation skills with Helena. Now I was going to be doing all three. Fun.

Helena didn't waste time. I knew she wouldn't. It's only ten minutes to the church from my house. "Aidan rang me last night."

"I imagined he would." It was a block, rather than a parry. I hadn't wanted to talk to Aidan, but Helena had forced it on me, and now she was going to give me grief for having done it badly.

"That was clever, being so blunt," she said approvingly.

I blinked. "Oh. Good."

She laughed. "I know you didn't intend to be blunt," she said, "but Aidan didn't. And it finally got him to tell me what happened with Holder. If he'd done that at the time, I could have saved him a lot of money."

"What happened?" I was less interested in the money.

"According to Aidan, Holder was sacked because he'd been

told that Merriam-Compton were not willing to have Reichel as a client, and he sold him some paintings anyway."

That one sentence created so many questions I didn't even know where to begin. So I asked them almost at random. "Reichel wanted to buy from them and they wouldn't sell to him? Since when do people refuse to do business with rich clients? And how would Holder have the authority to make sales when his bosses said no?"

Helena looked at me approvingly again. This was a good morning for me. Usually I asked questions that she thought "everybody" knew the answers to. "Aidan says that Reichel first started to buy from them five years ago. Not a lot, but he was a regular purchaser. Two years ago, he went to a dinner the gallery gave for one of their artists. Anna was there and she told Aidan the next day that Reichel had . . ."—Helena was choosing her words carefully—"that he had assaulted her. She said he'd groped her in the hallway when she'd gone to get her coat, and pinned her against the wall. That when she said no he hit her. Someone came past, and she managed to move back to where there were people, but she was sure she wouldn't have been able to otherwise."

I remembered the way Reichel had behaved in public, at a dinner party, and could well believe that the private Reichel would be worse.

Helena continued. "Anna refused to go to the police, and Aidan agreed with her. She'd had a couple of glasses of wine, and she also had adolescent children. The way the courts work, they and their classmates would have had the opportunity to read newspaper reports of prosecuting counsel's picture of their mother as a drunken slut." Helena's mouth was pinched tight. "Anna told Aidan she wanted to go on exactly as if it had never happened, and Aidan agreed."

"That's a horrible story." Poor Anna. I'd have to make sure she didn't guess that I knew. I switched back to the present. "Where did Holder come in?"

"They told Frank, and that was it. The gallery just cut Reichel out. When he got in touch to say he wanted to buy something, he was told it was no longer available." Helena pulled into a parking space a few hundred yards from the church. She cut the engine, but neither of us moved, continuing to sit and stare out the window as though we were still driving. "Holder was simply told that Reichel was not welcome in the gallery, that he was not an approved purchaser. But instead, when Aidan and Frank were both away, he promised him two works."

"But if Holder had no authority, then what's a promise from a junior?"

"According to Aidan, an agreement is an agreement in the art world, and Holder was an accredited representative of the gallery. And Aidan and Frank feared that if they withdrew, Reichel would become a problem. As it turned out, he became a problem anyway."

"In what way?" How could a nonclient become a problem?

"In the way we know: Holder sued for constructive dismissal, financially backed by Reichel. The gallery ended up paying out a year's salary and a lot of legal bills to keep Anna's story quiet."

"Two things. First, why would Reichel go to the trouble? I'm sure Merriam-Compton have lovely things to sell, but there are millions of other galleries he could buy from. And two, was Aidan saying that the whole story about Werner Schmidt dating Holder was made up, so Anna's story wouldn't come out?"

"After dinner the other night"—her look froze me; I wasn't going to live down that kick for a very long time—"I asked around, spoke to a friend whose firm has done legal work for Reichel for years." There isn't a lawyer in the western hemisphere that Helena doesn't know well enough that they will tell her things off the record, even ratting out their own clients. I returned idly to the notion that Helena is a Martian. I'd say Superwoman, or one of those other cartoon heroes, but she'd never make such terrible fashion choices. I looked at her gray-green silk suit, and tried to replace it with pants over her tights, or a cut-away bustier and a PVC cape. Never going to happen.

I snapped back to reality. "What did he say?"

She frowned at me. "She." Oops. "She said that for Reichel a two-year-old grudge was nothing. She was quite sure that he was still plotting revenge on the boy who had scribbled in his coloring book when they were in kindergarten."

"That's question one. And Schmidt?"

"Essentially, it was made up. That is, Holder did date Schmidt. Whether Frank cared varied with the day. Sometimes, said Aidan, Frank talked about Schmidt the way anyone would about an old ex. But other times he spoke of it as if it troubled him. Aidan said he never knew if it really mattered, or if it was just one of the many things Frank and Toby found to fight about. But they used the fact that the relationship existed to give color to Holder's sacking."

I thought about that. Then, "I didn't tell Jake anything about my conversation with Aidan."

"Because?" She was giving nothing away.

"Because until Werner Schmidt died, they were content to think that Frank had killed himself, even if they didn't know why. There were the coincidences." I ticked them off on my hands. "Frank's death coming so soon after the discovery of Stevenson's body, and the similarity in their suicides; Celia Stein getting in touch with me for no reason right after Frank died; and, even more, the death of Schmidt. If I told him we'd learned that Celia worked for someone Merriam-Compton had quarreled with, that would add one more level of coincidence, as well as bringing the story back to Holder, and back to Aidan and the gallery." I stared miserably out the window. "So it just seemed easier not to talk about it."

Helena was tart. "One of your best things."

I wasn't sure I was ready for a motherly this-is-what-you-need-to-do-to-fix-your-life chat right now. Or ever. I thought never might be a good time for that chat. Maybe I could get her to schedule it in her diary for never. Because yes, I've always got by on not discussing anything important, while chattering frivolously and amusingly about everything that isn't.

It works for me. I think.

10

There seemed nothing more to say, so by silent agreement we got out of the car and walked up to the church. The flowers were lined up by the door, ready to be taken out after the service and transported to the cemetery. We stopped and look at them on the way in. That seems to be the etiquette. Or everyone is simply doing it because everybody else always has, and none of us really knows what to do. I bent down to read some of the cards. When I send flowers for a funeral I'm always stumped as to what you're supposed to write. Most people write directly to the person who is dead, which I think is either ghoulish, or missing the point. Each time I'm hopeful for tips for the next time, and each time I'm disappointed. Today was no different. There were lots of flowers, at any rate, which I hoped would be some comfort to Toby.

The church itself was still quite empty, but we were very early. We found a pew not too close to the front, and sat on the aisle. People would have to clamber over us to get in, but we'd be in pole position for a fast getaway at the end and we wouldn't be caught by anyone on the way out, and have to stand around gassing on the church porch. We sat, occasionally greeting people we know—Helena, big surprise, knew almost everyone; I, even bigger, knew almost no one—and I chewed over the Reichel-Celia connection once more. There might be a very simple answer: the art world is as small as publishing, everyone ends up working for everyone else, that kind of thing. But I still didn't want to bring it back to Stevenson, and, therefore, to the gallery.

The church was well over half-full now, and Aidan and Anna and their kids were sitting in the second row. Anna looked just as she always did, beautiful, calm, and intelligently observing. Unlike Anna, Aidan didn't look calm. He looked like he hadn't slept for a week, and although his clothes were what he usually wore, they also looked like he'd had them on for a week, too. I looked more closely. There was nothing wrong with them, they weren't wrinkled, or slept-in—Anna wouldn't have let him go out like that at any time, and definitely not to Frank's funeral. It was Aidan inside them, in the end, who just looked like death warmed up and served on toast. Cold toast. Cold, stale toast. Toast made from supermarket bread. That had been bought last week.

I thought about that. Aidan, I mean, not the toast. He hadn't looked that bad last night. He'd looked tired, and unhappy, but that was natural under the circumstances. Yet less than eighteen hours later, he looked like sleep was a concept he had once heard of, but had never experienced personally.

Just as Toby and the family were arriving at the front of the church, I felt someone nudge me. I was cross. There was plenty of space on the other side. I didn't see why latecomers couldn't go that way. I looked up, ready to give my most British stony-faced look. I might even throw in a sigh if they didn't seem abjectly apologetic. Oh. Jake. I scooted down the pew, pushing Helena along one seat farther.

"Really? The police come to funerals, too?" I whispered, even though the service hadn't begun yet.

He sat down and glared at me. "I'm here as your partner."

I was ashamed. I hadn't expected him at all, and definitely hadn't expected him to appear as my other half.

He didn't say anything, he didn't move, but I knew that inside he was shaking his head.

Just as silently, I told him that he may have told himself he was there as moral support for me, but I saw him watching Toby, and Frank's family, arrive all the same. True, everyone else in the church was also watching, but everyone else in the church was not investigating Frank's death. I was watching, too. Toby was with an older couple. His parents, most likely. There was a man who looked just like Frank, and must have been Lucy's father. He was with a much younger woman, so much younger she could not possibly have been Lucy's mother. Second wife, then. And Lucy and another girl, a bit younger, presumably her sister.

Then the coffin was carried in, and we were off. We listened to readings from friends, we recited prayers, we sang hymns. I did the first two, and mouthed the words to the latter as a courtesy to everyone in earshot. No one should have to listen to me sing, certainly not at a funeral. The vicar gave a eulogy that even sounded as if he'd known Frank.

And all the while, I watched people watching. Anna was watching Aidan. Lucy was watching her father. Jake was watching everyone. Only Toby, poor soul, might as well have still been staring at the rug in his sitting room, for all he was aware of his surroundings.

Lucy and her sister stood and sang something. Not a hymn, maybe something from an opera, or possibly something written originally for boy trebles, high and pure. Then the coffin was carried back out, and it was over.

We followed fairly swiftly, but Helena had to stop and say hello to several dozen people on the way. As we reached the pavement, Jake said, "I'm parked on the next street."

I hadn't expected to see him, so I hadn't planned for this. I gestured meaninglessly at the street. "I came with . . . that is—"

Helena interrupted brightly. "You go with Jake, darling, and then I can give the McMasters a lift."

"Great." Or not.

Jake wasn't fooled. He slung an arm around my shoulders as we walked away, and kissed the side of my head. "Good morning. What are you not telling me?"

"So many, many things." I gave him a flat, guarded look.

He grinned. "I expect that. You never tell me anything. But what, specifically, are you not telling me this morning?"

"Have you been talking to Helena?" I was decidedly cranky now.

"Frequently. She tells me far more than you do."

I pressed my lips together and ostentatiously didn't respond. We got into the car and I made a great production about moving my seat back, putting on my seat belt, getting my handbag settled just so. When I couldn't delay any further, "I'm not telling you the same things I never tell you. I am not not-telling you anything else," I enunciated carefully.

Jake was still annoyingly cheerful. "Of course you are. You were talking to me last night, and now you're not."

I didn't remember much conversation the night before, but now didn't seem the right time to mention that. Happily, we were only a few minutes from Kenwood, where the after-funeral-thingie was being held. "What's the proper word for an after-funeral-thingie?" I asked instead.

Jake looked startled. "That's what you're not telling me?"

I smiled at that. "No, I'm still not telling you what I'm not telling you. It's just that I realized I don't know what you call an after-funeral-thingie. A reception? It can't be a party, can it?"

"That's what you're thinking about?"

I tried to look inscrutable. "Everybody's got to think of something."

Jake didn't reply. That was sensible.

Kenwood is a lovely place to go on a summer Sunday afternoon. It was summer, but the rest did not apply. There was nowhere to park nearby—the last parking spot near the Heath was taken sometime in 1957—so we walked along the hot pavement in the sun, with me bitching the whole way.

"Imagine it's Sunday and we're going for a walk." Jake was still chipper.

I wasn't. "If it were Sunday, we would be heading for a drink, or for coffee and a cake, or sitting out on the lawn. I wouldn't be wearing this bloody awful hot suit, and my shoes would be comfortable."

"Imagine that they are. You'll get the drink, and possibly the cake, too."

"And I'll have to talk to people I don't know, and who don't know me, and we're happy to keep it that way. Or, worse, I'll have to talk to people who know me and I haven't got a clue who they are."

Jake wasn't daunted. He rarely was, which really didn't seem fair. "Always the little ray of sunshine, aren't you, sunshine?"

Put that way, I guess I was. I smiled apologetically, and we walked the rest of the way in more amicable silence.

At Kenwood we walked around the main building, where the art gallery is, to the old stables block and kitchen garden. There's a café there, which is what I'd been thinking of when I mentioned coffee and cake—it was always the focal point of a walk on the Heath, or always my focal point. Next door, it turned out, were two rooms that could be hired for parties, or even after-funeral-thingies. They were a bit gloomy. The front wall of the café had been replaced by glass, giving a spectacular view of the Heath, with London dropping away dramatically below, while the hire-room walls were, well, walls. But the stone floors kept them pleasantly cool, and the period features stopped them feeling as if you'd been teleported to a Holiday Inn while your back was turned.

The family and closest friends hadn't returned from the cemetery, so the people who were there already were more uninhibitedly party-like than they would have been if Frank and Toby's families had been present. I looked around. Helena wasn't there yet. Not surprising, as she'd been deep in conversation in front of the church when we left. I didn't immediately see anyone I knew. I'm not very good at walking up to people at parties and introducing myself. (Translation: I'm terrible at it. More accurate translation: I don't even try.) So I sidled round to the table where the drinks were. There was wine, and something greenish. I took a greenish glass and sipped: lemon and mint. Nice. I picked up another one. Jake would most likely be going back to work, so he wouldn't want wine either. And it was only just noon, which felt a bit early. Although that was a minority view: the noise level was rising.

I returned to where Jake was standing near the entrance, hands in his pockets. If you didn't know he was a policeman, you wouldn't have known. He was looking at the crowd with the level of interest anyone walking into a party would show. But I knew he was checking things out, cataloguing faces. I wasn't. I had no idea what he was looking for, and I wouldn't have recognized it if it had jumped up and hit me with a wet fish. Instead I watched a toddler who had left his parents somewhere in the crush and was exploring. He wiped his nose on the tablecloth holding the drinks and then set off for a glass door behind the bar, which probably led to the catering area. Peek-a-boo with his reflection kept him quiet for a while, but then that got old. He wiped his finger across the glass. At first I thought, given the runny-nose scenario, he was finger-painting with what was left. But he wasn't enjoying it; he was puzzled. He did it again. It wasn't puzzlement anymore, it was despair. Something had gone terribly wrong. Of course. He wasn't wiping, he was swiping. Phones, computers, iPads—you swipe, you get dancing penguins. Here was a perfectly good, very large screen, and yet, however much he swiped, no singing, no dancing, no animals playing counting games, just a bunch of smears. The world was not a good place, and he was going to share that view with us. Loudly. Then his mother came out of the crowd and gave him her phone to play with. Existential crisis averted.

I turned and saw Jake had stopped watching the crowd and had been watching me. "Don't even think about it." The words were out of my mouth before I'd considered them, startling both of us.

"You like Bim." He was tentative, but it was something he'd apparently been thinking about.

"I do like him. And when he gets cranky and snotty I like handing him back to Kay."

He shrugged. "Just wondering."

"Stop wondering. I'm forty-three, for God's sake. I'm too old. And I'm not a hen. I don't do broody." I paused and re-grouped. "A little early for this conversation, isn't it?" I looked around. "And an ideal place to have it, too, at a funeral."

"You never want to have any conversations anywhere, at any time, so here and now seems as good a place as any for you to avoid one. And it's not a funeral. It's an after-funeral-thingie. I have it on the best authority." He smiled, but he wasn't happy. He was angry.

I couldn't blame him, and I hadn't meant to start a quarrel. "You're right. We do need to talk, and I have been avoiding it. If we can coordinate so that we're awake at the same time . . ." I trailed away. We hadn't been, much, recently. "Are you working this weekend?"

"According to the rota, no, although it depends a bit on this." He nodded toward the crowd. Having a we-need-to-talk talk, or having my friends investigated. Life was filled with such wonderful choices.

"We'll find time then. I promise."

"It won't be so terrible. You don't have to look like you're about to have your wisdom teeth extracted." He bent down and kissed me benevolently on the forehead, as though he were my Great-Uncle Hugo returning me to boarding school. Except that I didn't have a Great-Uncle Hugo, and I hadn't gone to boarding school.

By now those who had been to the cemetery had arrived, as had the latecomers from the church, Helena among them. I wiped away my wisdom-teeth-extraction face and plastered on a social smile instead. "We should talk to some of the others. And say hello to Toby and the family, do the formal regrets thing."

I started to head off and then stopped. "Do you want another one?"

"No. You're safe."

I wasn't going anywhere near that line.

As we headed toward Helena I saw a silvery glint of hair by the bar. I looked over and, sure enough, it was Delia Stevenson. It made sense. The gallery had looked after the estate for more than twenty years, and Frank had been his dealer before that. She must have known him well, and she was in London anyway for the opening of the exhibition. It would have been strange if she hadn't come. I steered Jake over, telling him who she was as we went.

We swapped our empty glasses for full ones, using the maneuver as a passport to dropping into conversation with her. I introduced myself, saying I'd seen her at the press conference, and allowing her to assume I'd been there for a reason. As I was now at Frank's funeral, she probably thought I was something to do with the art world, and I let that slide past, introducing Jake as my partner.

She was in a different elegant silver outfit—maybe she always dressed to coordinate with her hair. If my hair were that good, I would, too. But while the outfit, and her surface, were both polished, she immediately revealed herself to be less so, being very obviously relieved that someone had come up to speak to her, so she neither had to brave the crowd herself, nor stand alone on its edge. We made the usual chit-chat: the funeral, how terrible Frank's death was, who the family members were. In the guise of idle small talk I asked her about her trip, and she said she'd arrived from the States two weeks ago, which I saw Jake noting was before Frank died. She rambled on, with the blithe disregard for the conventional give-and-take of party conversation of someone who lived alone and rarely had company: she hardly went to shows of her husband's work, leaving most of the PR side to Celia, and in fact rarely left Vermont. She was only here for this show because it was much bigger, and therefore more important, and besides, she liked London. She was thinking of moving here, because Celia was here, and she was hoping for grandchildren, yadda-yadda, but even though Celia had that huge house, they both liked their privacy, dee-dah-dee-dah, but maybe they'd build an annex in the garden, and so on and so forth.

I steered her back to the main points from this blizzard of information, shocked to find I had no trouble with the idea of facilitating a covert interview in a place where the interviewee had every right to believe she was among friends. I told myself it was because she wasn't a suspect, but I knew if it had been Celia, not Delia (and really, who did that when they named their child?), I would have done it with redoubled enthusiasm. I not only would have, but I was about to, because Celia walked over before we'd had five minutes with her mother. We smiled and filled Delia in on how we knew each other, and I introduced Jake again as my partner.

Celia was in no-nonsense form, though. She smiled her killer smile, like a basking shark, and then said, straightforwardly, "You've been popping up everywhere this past week."

She wanted to overlook the reality, that she'd approached me in the first place? "So have you," I said, also smiling, but aware I couldn't match her basking shark danger. I was more a come-in-the-water's-fine dolphin, maybe. No, I wasn't that clever. A seahorse. Cute, but dumb enough to get washed up by every tide.

Her shark smile never wavered. "Yes, but they've been Stevenson events, and I'm a Stevenson."

Which pushed me into justifying my presence, even as, dumb seahorse, I knew I didn't need to answer to her. "Aidan and I are old friends. And I was at the press conference because your exhibition designer is on an Arts Council panel with me—the one you helped me with."

"I must try and make a point of being there," she said. It may have been my imagination, but she made it sound as if she'd be sure to pack her handy travel-sized stiletto.

"That would be great." I sounded so enthusiastic anyone

listening would have thought I was a contestant on a game show. I leaned toward Jake in what ostensibly looked like comfortable friendship, but was really a silent either-join-in-or-get-me-the-hell-out-of-here appeal. Luckily he speaks gesture fluently, and he leaped in.

Given that he couldn't say, Where were you at 6:57 on the morning of the eleventy-seventh of December, and what was the purpose of your initial conversation with Ms. Clair? Or even, Can you confirm your whereabouts on the evening of the insert-date-here, and what business took you to Chiltern Villas, Highgate at approximately 5:48 P.M.?, which were the questions I wanted to ask, I waited to see where he would go.

He began with a meandering discussion of the upcoming exhibition, offering sympathy on how much work it must have been for her.

She looked frosty. "It's my job." Then, with a sideways look at Delia, she backtracked. "It's both of our jobs."

Delia broke in. "Celia's modest, but really she does all the work. I mostly refuse to travel, so she goes everywhere, whether it's for exhibitions, or to meet collectors. She and Frank never thought twice before jetting off to São Paulo, or Stuttgart"— the two places appeared to be equally inaccessible to Delia— "although since the pieces started arriving last month for the exhibition, they were both stuck in London. Since I was coming, I suggested we have a holiday, go to the country somewhere, the week before, but Celia insisted she couldn't leave the city, that it was too good an opportunity to miss seeing Eddie's pictures that were in private collections, arranging for them to be photographed and recorded." Delia shook her head at her daughter's

dedication. Her daughter smiled tightly at her mother's chattering flow of information, but she didn't try and stop it.

I jumped back in. "I hadn't realized that the works owned by
private collectors are as inaccessible to you as they are to the
general public."

She nodded. "Celia, Frank, and their gallery technician have
been working like maniacs to get everything recorded as they
came in this past month. They even set up a little studio at
the house," she ran on, admiringly. "When I think of the way
Eddie used to work, cutting photographs out of magazines, or
using the bathroom as his darkroom." She turned to her daughter.
"Do you remember that time he was doing the flower pictures,
and we couldn't have a bath for weeks because he had the
prints drying over the shower rail?"

Celia smiled without humor. Whether about her bathless
childhood, or sharing the information with us, I had no idea.

I encouraged Delia. "It must all be so different now, when
everyone can take photos on their phones."

She looked wistful. "Eddie would have loved it." And for the
first time, I felt badly. This wasn't some abstract idea, this was
her husband, and she missed him. Then she smiled, determined
to remain positive. "Celia's house last week was a bit like having
Eddie back, photos, papers, magazines everywhere. When I think
what his studio was like." She became confidential. "I couldn't
bear it after he left. I had everything packed up. Everything. I
couldn't look at it, so I put it in storage. And then"—she smiled
again, a guilelessly sunny 1960s flower-child smile—"once I ar-
ranged for Frank to take on the estate, everything was ready for
shipping off. It worked out for the best."

Poor woman. Her husband had, she thought, abandoned her, and even so, she packed up his work not because she was furious with him, but because it hurt too much to look at it. Twenty years later, and she had only just found out he hadn't abandoned her, or at least not in the way she'd thought for all those years. And yet, here she was, assuring everyone, and herself, that it had all been "for the best."

Someone came up to talk to Celia, and we took it as an opportunity to excuse ourselves—we had to offer our condolences to the family, I told Delia, we looked forward to seeing her at the exhibition, I had to get back to work. Now I was the one who was rambling, overcome with pity for this not very bright, but very brave woman.

As we walked away, Jake said, "You're worryingly good at this."

"At letting my partner interrogate witnesses without them knowing it?"

"She knew it."

I stopped. "Celia? She knows you're a detective?" I ran the conversation back in my head. He was right. She had. I don't know how he had known, and I don't know how I did, but I was sure of it.

He nudged me forward again. "It's not surprising. She approached you in the first place, and so she knew who you were. And I'm not a secret."

"True. Although we still don't know *why* she approached me."

"Also true." But he appeared unworried by how much we didn't know. "And anyway, I didn't mean you were worryingly good at letting me interview. You were doing the interviewing, and you are worryingly good at it."

I stopped again, ready to deny it. But he was right. I shook my head in disapproval, whether of my interviewing, his noticing, or his finding it worrying, I didn't say. Mostly because I had no idea.

We went and offered our condolences to the various family members—I was right, Frank's sister-in-law was barely older than Lucy; I bet that had gone down a treat—and to Anna and Aidan. Aidan was looking better. Maybe it had just been the funeral, and now it was over, he felt he could move on. The way Frank had died, and the investigation, had made me forget that Aidan had lost his closest friend.

I also talked to some of the gallery staff. You don't have to remember people's names to offer condolences. Myra was one of the few whose name I did know, so I stopped when I saw her. She had a red nose, which I charitably ascribed to the funeral, although the death-grip she had on her wineglass and her slightly fixed stare suggested another source. I introduced Jake, and although she must have seen him before—he'd been the lead investigator, and had spent time at the gallery—she either didn't remember him, didn't remember anyone in her present condition, or didn't care.

"That's that," she said, as though she'd just taken the rubbish bins out on collection day.

I couldn't remember Debrett's recommended response to that. So I aimed for neutral. "I'm sure Toby will be relieved it's over."

She tsk-ed, as though Toby were a schoolboy who'd forgotten his homework. "And it's not over." She stared morosely into her glass, which had emptied substantially in the few minutes we'd been standing there.

"No?" A few minutes ago I'd balked when Jake had said I'd been interviewing. Now I was doing it again, and I was entirely unashamed. Jake didn't move, but I knew he was mentally rolling his hand at me: keep her talking. "What happens next?"

"Probably nothing." She drank again. "Depends."

"On what?" I looked around and flagged down a passing waiter with a bottle. *Interested, me?* said my body language.

Myra brightened as her glass was refilled. "On who replaces Frank."

I aimed for noncommittal. "It must be very difficult for you at the moment." I had no idea what that meant, I was just hoping that it was bland enough to keep her moving. Nope. The glassy look faded and a sharpness came into her face. "Who are you?" she said to Jake. "I've seen you before."

He moved toward me slightly. "I'm Sam's boyfriend."

She was not appeased, and continued to stare at him, her eyes appraising now.

"It was so nice to meet Delia Stevenson. I'd heard Frank speak of her so often," I put in, reaffirming my bona fides as long-term friend of the family. She turned and stared at me, too, as if I'd said something important.

Then a polite smile appeared on her face, click, like a slide had changed. "It was good of her to come over for the retrospective. We're thrilled. Will you excuse me?" She turned toward a group behind us and said, "Tom! I've been hoping to catch up with you." Short of adding, *Don't let the door hit you on the way out*, she couldn't have made her feelings more plain.

Lucy, who had been standing with Tom, whoever he was,

must have seen Myra cut us dead, and she came over, kissing me like an old friend, introducing herself to Jake. I was surprised she hadn't met him when he'd been investigating Frank's death. He saw me thinking that, and shook his head infinitesimally. So instead I complimented her on her singing at the funeral, about which she was charmingly bashful. We discussed the choir she and her sister had belonged to, and how she no longer did now she was at university, because she missed too many rehearsals. Desperately searching for conversation, I asked how her plans for the summer exhibition were going. In exchange, she made polite noises again about my face.

"Are you still cycling?" she asked. "I don't have the courage to do it at all. I don't know how you could get back on the road."

"I haven't yet," I admitted, and then, "Oh. Yes, I have. I collected my cycle from where I'd left it when I fell off"—whatever Jake said, I was going to call it that to my dying day—"and I just cycled home without even thinking." I smiled as broadly as the scabs allowed. "Thank you for pointing that out. I've been dreading starting again, and you've made me realize I already have."

The chill that Myra's personality change had created dissipated in the relief I felt.

But when we were back outside, and had almost reached the car, "Oof." I wriggled my shoulders, as if a weight had been pressing on them. "You have a strange job."

He knew that, so he didn't bother to answer.

"Did you get what you wanted?"

"That's not why I was there, remember?"

"I know you weren't. And did you get what you wanted?" I may have felt a little guilty about not expecting him to show up, but I wasn't deluding myself that he hadn't been working, either.

"At the moment I don't know what I want. The file was closed. Now we're looking at Schmidt." His eyes flickered over to me. "Do you want an update?"

Did I? "Maybe." That seemed like a good compromise.

His lips quirked. "Maybe?"

"If you're going to say Frank's file is still closed, and Werner Schmidt died in an accident, then yes, I'm ready for an update."

He put his hand on mine briefly, a touch that said, *Yes, wouldn't it be nice if the world worked that way.* And then he went on, as if I'd acknowledged that it didn't, "The probable time of death for Schmidt is late on Saturday night. He doesn't seem to have eaten in the previous twenty-four hours, so there was nothing to go on there. Just a measurement of blood alcohol, and the level should have made him barely functional, but with alcoholics it's often surprising how much they can consume. We're waiting for more detailed toxicology reports. In the meantime I've had a look at the report on your hit-and-run." He felt me tense, but kept talking, his voice steady and low, the way you talk to a shy animal—*See, I'm not paying any attention, so you can come out of from under the bed now.* "There's nothing to go on. The statements don't agree even on the make of the car. That corner is just out of CCTV coverage." He shrugged. "Not unusual. Someone is looking at downloads for adjacent streets, but there's no information yet."

Fine with me. I didn't believe it was real, and I was going to go on not believing it. I turned the conversation away from what I was refusing to look at. "Why didn't Lucy recognize you?"

"One of my colleagues interviewed her. She's at university at the moment, not working in the gallery." He wasn't interested. "Come on, I'll drop you on my way to work."

I'd moved on from my earlier feeling that he was a custody sergeant escorting me, and was now enjoying being ferried to and from the office. It was like being taken to school as a child by my father. Perhaps not a comparison Jake would enjoy. Maybe it was more like a 1960s novel of suburban angst, and I'd have martinis ready when Jake got home, over which we could passive-aggressively destroy our failing marriage. OK, that wasn't great either. I'd never got into trouble by keeping my mouth shut. Maybe I'd do that.

11

By the time I got to work, the mass exodus for lunch was over, and the building was almost empty. Miranda was still at her desk, however, with a sandwich in front of her. She looked up. "I wasn't expecting you till later."

"It doesn't take very long." That sounded unnecessarily bleak, but I couldn't work out how to soften it, so I just kept going.

But Miranda's voice followed me. "Have you got a moment?"

Just the perfect day. First Jake and his we-need-to-talk, now Miranda and a have-you-got-a-moment. Neither is ever followed by good news.

I smiled, pretending I didn't know that. "Sure, come in. Or"—I eyed her half-eaten lunch—"is it very private?"

She looked taken aback.

"It's a nice day. If I grab a sandwich, too, we could go to the square."

"That would be great."

By unspoken agreement we walked up to Malet Street Gardens, stopping at the deli to pick up something for me. We were lucky to find an empty bench, and we sat and busied ourselves with unwrapping and eating. After a couple of minutes, though, it was time to give Miranda a nudge. "Whatever it is, it can't be that bad. Just tell me."

She laughed. "It's not bad. Or not for me. I've been offered another job."

"Shit." She blinked, I shrugged. "I'd like to keep you, but I knew that couldn't happen for much longer. You deserve to be promoted, but if we are going to be taken over, or whatever is happening, I know that even if a vacancy comes up, we're unlikely to be allowed to fill it." I summarized. "What I'm saying is, I let it slide, because I didn't want to lose you."

"Really?" She was surprisingly surprised.

"Of course. Tell me what you've been offered, and where."

She did. It was a nice enough job, but nothing spectacular. A better job title—junior editor instead of editorial assistant. Probably, although she didn't say, very little more money. In publishing, where the money is never great except at the very top, we accept job titles in lieu of salary. In an ideal world, Miranda would be promoted internally, to the same junior editor job she'd just been offered at Apollo. T&R published a wider range of books than they did, and she'd get more experience, and have more options when she was ready to be promoted again, which I fully believed would be soon. She'd shown a lot of ability in the work she'd done for me. Editorially she could see where a book was weak, and make good suggestions about how to strengthen it; administratively, she was efficient and organized.

The administration side is rarely mentioned, but those skills are almost more important than editorial intelligence.

I chewed more slowly.

"Sam?" She was waving her hand in front of my face.

I came back to earth. "I was trying to work out a way of keeping you at T&R, even if I can't keep you myself. If I could get you something similar, would you want to stay?"

"Want to? Yes, I'd want to. Could you—that is, would you?"

"Would, yes; could, that's what I don't know." I got down to practicalities. "How much leeway do you have in terms of time? When do you have to accept by? Or have you already accepted?"

"I haven't." She was clearly not only thrilled, but astonished that we'd make an effort to keep her. Mental note: give more positive reinforcement to the next good assistant. "And yes, there's a bit of time. The person who interviewed me"—she tactfully omitted who it was, although I was sure I knew from the job description; the publishing world is small—"she's just gone on holiday, and won't be back until the week after next."

"That works. Let's think about what you want, and what might be feasible." I put my sandwich down. This was serious. There was no point, though, in holding out false hopes. "Probably the best we can do is an interim solution until a vacancy comes up. I could try to get David to agree that you'd work as my assistant for most of the time, and you could acquire a couple of books on your own. And I can hand over a couple of my authors to you to look after. What do you think?" It wasn't much of a counter-offer.

Miranda was shrewd. "It's worth a try. At Apollo I'd have my own books, but the advances I'd be able to offer would be so low

I couldn't compete. Anything I bought would be because people like you had already passed on them. And if you didn't want them, what was wrong with them?"

"You want to do my kind of books?" I was ridiculously pleased. Most people in publishing want to do literary fiction, or, if their interest is in commercial publishing, it's often in genre—science fiction, or fantasy, or crime. Apart from anything else, those are more easily defined than my beat, which is vaguely referred to as commercial women's fiction, whatever that means. The negative side of my kind of books is that people in publishing often look down on them; the positive is that since no one knows what it means, I can make of it what I want. Oh, and my kind of books tend to make money. Even the sneerers like that part.

"Absolutely." She nodded so vehemently her nose piercing strobed wildly in the sun.

"Then if you'll be happy, for a while at least, to work in a half-and-half job, I'll do my best. And I'll see if I can extort a salary increase as well." I was hesitant. "Do you want to tell me what they've offered? You don't have to, but I might be able to use it as a lever to pry out a bit more money for you."

She was carefree. "The increase is so small I don't see why I shouldn't tell you."

She did, and I flinched. If that was the going rate for new editors, we were all doomed. I gathered my thoughts. "Here's what I'll do. I'll tell David you've been offered more than that, and then maybe we'll be able to match what you have really been offered." We smiled at each other: editorial solidarity against The Man. That made me realize it was the man who was going to be the problem. "It's David. He'll haver over this for weeks. I'll try and prod him along by saying you need to confirm one way or the other next week, but you know what he's like. There's no real way to know if, much less when, he'll ever reach a decision."

"And he's on holiday next week, too. There's no time." She plunged straight down to gloom.

But the news moved me in the opposite direction. "That's the best we could have hoped for. If he's away, I'll have to go over his head to Olive, because you need a decision right away. Olive at least will say either yes or not, not, *I'd like to, but let's talk again soon, maybe just before the death of the solar system.*"

"But what if she says no?"

"Then you have a bright shiny new job at Apollo. And we can keep our eyes open for something else, either at T&R or elsewhere, to move to after a year or so. You won't become invisible. But that's if it's no. We're not there yet. I'll see Olive first thing on Monday, when you'll 'just' have told me your news."

She gave a little skip as we walked back to the office. "Office maneuvering. I'll have to learn some of that, as well as editing."

I gave her an I-am-a-modern-Machiavelli smile, but she wasn't fooled. She was young, she wasn't a moron.

I spent the afternoon prepping for the Arts Council panel. I'd decided it would be good if people had some pictures to look at while I droned on. Finding images that related to the various points I was making on behalf of Neil and Emma was straight-forward. They were talking about current books, so I could just lift the jacket covers off Amazon and use them, and I raided the T&R archives for some twentieth-century examples to compare them to. For Celia's part of the talk, she'd mentioned a few books on artists that the trust had subsidized, and I easily found examples for them, too, if you didn't mind the fact that they were nicked off the Internet without paying a copyright fee, and I didn't. Celia probably would, though, since it was her job to stop people like me doing things like that. I hesitated. Could I really give a quasi-government-funded talk on how to protect artists' and writers' copyrights, while using stolen reproductions to illustrate said talk? I moved the JPEGS to the recycle bin and rang her office.

Denise-with-the-sexy-voice said that Celia was away, so I explained the problem to her and she promised to hunt around in Celia's files and see if she could find me something. She was as good as her word, e-mailing me just before five. But she'd only located a few images. Not enough. I eyed my recycle bin, but the moral case hadn't got any better in the intervening hour. Then I had a bright idea, and e-mailed Jim. Sorry to trouble him and all that, went the gist of it, but could I use some of the Stevenson pictures? Twenty minutes later, and I was done. As far as I was concerned, the CultCo panel, and my contribution to it, were over. I'd make the presentation in the morning, and after that, if anyone said the words "arts council" to me ever again, I would stand up on my chair and howl like a wolf until they stopped. Or I got locked up. Whichever came first.

Jake hadn't said anything to me about how I was supposed to get home. I'd noticed that he worried about me getting to work, but not back again, which didn't make any sense. I had had the wisdom, however, not to point this out to him, although I thought about it again as I left the shelter of the office. As I walked from the Tube station to my flat I gave only a single backward look over my shoulder. I hadn't looked even once between the office and the Tube, the West End being much too crowded even for a person who knows what they're doing to spot anyone who wants to follow them discreetly. While I probably would have noticed a bare-chested Turkish janissary in full Ottoman Empire rig if one had materialized beside me, that was the outside limit of my sleuthing abilities. No janissaries, bare-chested or otherwise, appeared between the Tube and home, though, so things were definitely looking up.

When I got in, there was a postcard taped to the door of my flat. I knew even before I pulled it off to read it that it was from Mr. Rudiger. He not only didn't do texting or e-mail, he wasn't a fan of voice mail, either. Or maybe he thought leaving a phone message for someone you share a house with is rude. Anyway, when he wanted to be in touch, I got a postcard. This one was longer than usual, saying he hoped that the funeral hadn't been too stressful. The important point was in the P.S., as is so often the case, even in business letters: would "you"—whether this was just me, or Jake and me, was left courteously vague—like to come up for a drink, "if you have time." Mr. Rudiger always included an opt-out, to allow me to decline without feeling I was being rude.

I rarely did decline. I liked him, and right then, more specifi-cally, I wanted to talk to someone who knew what was happen-ing, but was not involved. Helena was no good. She would list out, in bullet points and subsections, what I ought to have done, what I ought now to be doing, and what I ought to do in future. Everything she said would be right, and sensible, but I didn't want to be set right sensibly. I just wanted a listener.

I dumped my bag, added a line for Jake in case he got home early, saying, "Invitation accepted, I'm upstairs," and stuck the card back on the door frame. I knew Mr. Rudiger would have heard me come in, so I went straight up. And it was exactly the right thing to do. We sat on his tiny terrace, which he tended as carefully as a baby. It was filled with herbs and flowering plants in pots, and even tomatoes and courgettes in grow bags. I told him about Viv, and suggested they start a neighborhood plant-swap. I hadn't seen him since I'd fallen off my cycle, so we went through all of that, but I was getting used to it by now, and it helped that he didn't make the kind of noises of gratified horror that most people did, half shock, half a told-you-so triumph that I think is mostly relief that it didn't happen to them. Instead he told me about the Vespa he'd had in Rome in the 1950s. I've only seen him outside the house once, and that was an extreme emergency. So I was especially taken with the idea of him dashing about, and I immediately dressed him in my mind as Gregory Peck in *Roman Holiday*, with Audrey Hepburn riding pillion behind him. He smiled at me quietly, a smile that said, *I know exactly what you're thinking.* I smiled back at him, and we moved on to the funeral.

I told him, in a faintly scandalized tone, about my enabling Jake's interviewing techniques with Delia, and then I moved on to Celia. "They look a lot alike," I finished, "but they couldn't be more different. You know that a Vermont hippie-chick still lurks under Delia's silver suits. Celia, well, she wouldn't faint if you suggested that she had a hippie vibe, but that's only because I can't imagine her doing anything as spur of the moment as fainting. She'd probably . . ." I frowned, trying to work out how

Celia would show her disapproval. "She'd probably look at you *very* severely."

He smiled again, but the personalities of the women didn't engage him the way Stevenson's had. He merely said, "It's getting cool now the sun is off the terrace. Shall we go inside?" We did, and by the time we'd sat down again, the subject was somehow closed. I moved on to the CultCo presentation.

And that was a revelation. I'd known Mr. Rudiger had been an architect, but I'd never thought of architecture as having anything to do with subsidy, which is imbecilic of me. Museums, libraries, any civic building, really, is entirely subsidized if that's what you call government funding. And so are private houses, if they're built by the very rich. The rich don't think they're subsidising the architect, they think they're buying what they want. But according to Mr. Rudiger, a commission from a rich client, if you can make them sympathize with, or even share, your aims, is the very best kind of subsidy there is.

After only five minutes I called time—"Wait a minute, wait a minute"—and rushed downstairs to grab my laptop. I raced back up, opened it up to the presentation and thumped myself down on the sofa next to him. "Start at the beginning," I demanded.

And, God bless him, he did. He tore apart my presentation, made me really think about what I had previously only been parroting. He asked sensible questions, and made me come up with sensible, not fashionable, answers. His fastidious avoidance of comment made me shamefacedly remove the jargon I'd so snidely put in. It was like having a private tutorial with your own resident genius. It was thrilling, and what had been a chore had turned into something that was worth doing.

I showed him the images I had chosen. He liked the 1950s and 1960s typographical covers I'd pulled from the T&R files to use as examples of the way publishing houses could make brands out of their books—the way publishing houses *had* made brands out of their books, long before anyone had thought to call books "brands"—and he suggested good ways to carry that idea through with products from other arts. Architecture was his area of expertise, but he made suggestions for theater design, film, and television, about all of which he had an encyclopedic knowledge.

I went onto WikiCommons and pulled out some pictures to illustrate his new points. He'd never seen that before, but within four minutes he had the hang of it and was mousing about, suggesting more and more material.

"I only have twenty minutes," I finally said. "We need to stop."

I was saving the new material when he lifted his head. "Jake's home."

I listened, too. Nothing. Really, the government should give my neighbor security clearance and then they could decommission GCHQ. A huge budget saving.

"He's on his way up." And Mr. Rudiger, ever polite, was already on the way to let him in.

I watched the two greet each other, talking quietly by the door. Jake had taken to Mr. Rudiger right away, even before I had got to know him properly. He kept his distance, respecting Mr. Rudiger's fierce privacy, yet from the beginning they had also acted as . . . I considered. As colleagues, I thought, although I wasn't entirely sure what I meant by the word when applied to the two of them. Allies, maybe. And their alliance was about me: how to take care of me.

I pressed my lips tightly together. I didn't need taking care of. But I didn't doubt what I was seeing, either.

As they walked back into the sitting room, I shook it off. What was I going to do, shout "I'm not feeble-minded, you know" at them? That would make me sound feeble-minded, if anything did.

Jake saw my laptop and raised an eyebrow. "Picking up editorial tips?"

I grinned. "Much better. Mr. Rudiger just rewrote my CultCo presentation. It makes sense now. It might even be interesting."

That merited a double-eyebrow raise. "A government-sponsored event, interesting? You'd better watch out. They'll either run you out of town, or make you do it again."

"Oh dear God, don't say that." I closed my eyes in terror. I knew he was joking, and so was I, but even a joke about having to do another committee made me want to lie on the floor and scream like Violet Elizabeth Bott.

It was too horrific, so I changed the subject. "Did you bring any supper home? Because we're almost at the end of whatever food was salvaged when I had my accident on Saturday. I don't think there's anything except some pasta sauce in the freezer."

"Pasta it is, then. I didn't stop because I didn't know we needed anything. And we have to eat soon-ish, so pasta works. I'm due back at the office."

I looked inquiring. He looked put-upon. "You know I can't

talk about work, Sam." He turned to Mr. Rudiger for some male solidarity, but Mr. Rudiger smiled benevolently at both of us. Not getting involved, said the smile.

I didn't smile benevolently. I scowled fiercely. I also thought, *You couldn't talk about Frank's death to me, but you did. Or Schmidt's. Or have me run interference at the funeral. And while we're on the subject, you aren't supposed to fuck your interviewees, either, but you did that when you met me. So don't piss me off, buster.*

Luckily Jake was adept at thought-reading. He grinned at me, and said, "I know," as if I'd handed him the whole list on an inscribed tablet of stone. Mr. Rudiger looked amused again.

I wasn't going to leave it there, though. "And?"

He scrubbed his hands over his face. "Not a lot. We started late, so we've only just finished most of the interviews. They're being collated now, and I want to go through them with the team, plot out a timeline. We're still trying to track down the source of the glue. Although, I went to look at Schmidt's studio this afternoon, after the technicians finished, and it looks like he never threw anything out. It could have been there forever." He sighed. "It was like he was two people. On one side, his life was shambolic. Everyone said he drank, and was getting worse. He was a good restorer, but he didn't deliver on time, so galleries were beginning to fight shy. His bank accounts look all right: he was keeping his head above water, and he paid his bills, mostly. He had no system of bookkeeping, and payments came in irregularly. On the other side his studio—" he smiled, "I had this idea that an artist's studio would be chaotic, with old dirty rags and paintbrushes all over the place. Instead Schmidt's life was chaos, but the studio was like a chemistry lab. Everything was slotted into a specific place, and labeled. Not just 'paint,' but 'acrylic resin 1960s,' or 'oil, no titanium dioxide 1980s.' Even the damn glue that killed him had its own slot: 'polymer resin, 1992.' "

Mr. Rudiger cleared his throat. Both our heads swiveled round. He looked apologetic for chipping in, but this was a field he knew. "He was a restorer. The chemical makeup of the materials he used mattered. Paint degenerates, or discolors, as it ages. He needed to know that the layers he added to a painting would age in sympathy with the original material."

Jake considered that for a moment. "So a tidy professional existence and a chaotic private life. Not exactly unheard of. If it weren't for the connection with Compton, we wouldn't be looking at this twice. He was drunk and using a dangerous, banned substance, however carefully labeled. And he died from it."

On that cheerful note we went downstairs. Supper was a quiet meal. We were both preoccupied. The day had been busy enough that I'd managed to push thoughts of Reichel and Celia out of my head. Now, if Jake was going back to work, I'd have time to look further; and if he wasn't home, I wouldn't have to decide whether to tell him or not.

We did the dishes—he was remarkably housebroken, and I'd often silently thanked his mother, or his ex-wife, or maybe just years of living alone—and after we finished Jake apologized for his preoccupation, not having noticed mine. "I'll be very late. Should I go back to Hammersmith tonight?"

"As you like. You don't wake me when you come in. Or at least, I don't mind being woken when you do."

He was barely listening. I got a fast kiss, and "I'll see how late it is," and that was it.

There was nothing to stop me returning to that morning's computer searches. Instead I watered the plants. I made a shopping list. I even thought I might do some ironing. For some reason, I didn't want to find any answers. But I didn't want to do the ironing even more, and that would have been next on my list. So I made some coffee and settled down in front of the computer. Delaying further, I went through the new material Mr. Rudiger had suggested for CultCo, like a small girl with a new pile of Barbie clothes, taking them out one by one and admiring them. That could only last so long. Sooner rather than later I'd gone through the fun, sparkly stuff, and was staring at the rest, more Ken's safari suit than Barbie's sequinned disco mini.

I reminded myself that I had no idea what I was looking for, and that there was nothing to say that what I had already found would be considered unusual by anyone who knew what they were talking about. Bolstered by this reiteration of my own incompetence, I opened up the websites I'd bookmarked that morning.

I returned to Reichel, this time putting him in a search with Celia Stein. A few random photos came up of the two of them at the same art world parties. That wasn't incriminating, I already knew that Reichel moved in art world circles, and as he funded the trust Celia worked for, it wasn't a hot newsflash that they knew each other, either. I noodled around the auction websites, which told me exactly nothing. Then I tried to narrow my search on Reichel to his connection to collecting. Most of the articles just said he "collected," without saying what it was he collected, as though the act of purchase was the only part that was interesting. I checked the sources. Financial newspapers. For them it was only the act of purchase that was interesting.

I started again, going back and searching each of the articles for references to artists. This was so boring that the ironing actually began to look enticing. And then, suddenly, there it was. A feature on Reichel in the *Financial Times* had a photograph of him in his office. And behind him was a Stevenson collage. And next to it was another. And another above. Three.

I sat staring at the picture. Reichel collected twentieth-century art. I knew that before—hell, he'd told me so himself, before I assaulted him. Stevenson was an important twentieth-century artist. So was it surprising that Reichel owned a Stevenson? Not really. Was it surprising he owned more than one? Define "surprising," I mocked myself. Major Collector Owns Several Pictures by Major Artist = Not Surprising. And if it *was* surprising, which it obviously was, because I was surprised, where did that get me?

I was cranky. I'd drunk far too much coffee, and had found far too much information that meant nothing. But whatever it meant, it had to do with Merriam-Compton. The thought made me feel sick. I thought about how Aidan had looked before the funeral, and how, finally, afterward he began to look like the person I'd known for so long. Was I going to direct my current lover toward my ex-lover's business?

I tried to find reasons to do no such thing. I couldn't see any role for Werner Schmidt. He'd been killed by an old tin of glue, not an old Russian handgun. I might not know about guns, but I could tell those two apart.

I brooded on the difference between what I did and what Jake did. Superficially, looking at documents was more my field than his. He liked action, not reactions. I liked dealing with paper, but only, I now realized, because books are magic. A book works if it means something to the reader. It doesn't matter if what it means to the reader isn't what the author intended, or even if it directly contradicts what the author intended. If it speaks to the reader, then it works; if it doesn't, it's dead.

These documents might speak to a financial expert, but they were saying nothing to me. And therefore, in literary terms, they were dead.

I ever so gently put my head on the desk and moaned. Frank's death couldn't be resolved because the material had no narrative arc. That would work for Scotland Yard.

12

When i woke up I found that Jake had come in some time during the night. I had sworn to myself the night before that I would get up first thing and go for a run. Instead I found myself spooning around Jake's sleeping back. If he woke up, it might be too late to go.

I smothered a shocked laugh into his back. Really? I was thinking of initiating early-morning sex so that I'd have a reason not to go running?

The laugh woke him. "What's funny?"

Being caught out was even funnier. "Nothing."

He rolled over. "Nothing?" He smiled sleepily. "Nothing is awfully funny at—" he squinted at the clock. "Jesus, Sam, at six o'clock? This better be really funny."

I told him. I wasn't sure now if I was appalled or amused. He wasn't sleepy anymore. And he wasn't laughing. "You are going to be *very* sorry for that."

An hour later, I was feeling smug rather than sorry, but I was also extremely late. Jake had gone back to sleep, but I needed to be at the office by eight, because that was the only time I was going to have before the CultCo panel.

I put on my posh suit in honor of the event and whizzed around getting my things together—laptop, manuscript, e-reader. Christ, there was more to carry now that everything was electronic than there had been in the old manuscript days. I dumped a cup of coffee beside Jake and kissed the back of his head, which was all that was showing.

"Go *away*," he whined into the pillow, which I took to mean, *Have a good day, dear, and I hope the panel goes well.* It was now either safe for me to go into work on my own, or he was too tired to care.

To my amazement, Miranda was already at her desk when I got in. Most publishing people aren't early, and she had fit neatly into that category from her first day in the job, usually appearing around ten. That was fine with me: she worked long past her contractual hours—I'm not sure if anyone in publishing even knows we have contractual hours—and she was happy to stay as late as necessary to finish whatever it was that needed to be done. And I always like the quiet first thing, time I usually spend doing the tedious jobs I put off if I leave them until later in the day, and can plead that more urgent things prevent me from getting to them.

I stopped in front of her desk. "I'm going to speak to Olive, I promise. You don't have to earn that gold star."

She laughed. "I hadn't thought of that. I just came in so I could get through last night's e-mails before we need to leave for your Arts Council thing."

We? I was touched. It hadn't occurred to me that she'd want to come, just as, apparently, it hadn't occurred to her she wouldn't automatically go. Had I not had the session with Mr. Rudiger, I would have hated for her to have been there. I don't mind doing a half-assed job if no one I know is watching, but I would have died of shame if she'd been in the audience for my original presentation. Now, though, I was quite pleased with my contribution.

The earlier meetings had been in the Arts Council offices, around the back of Parliament, which was a nuisance to get to. It wasn't far, half an hour whether I walked or took the bus. But whatever time I saved by the meetings not being far from work, I lost as I hit Parliament Square, being stopped on average ninety-seven times in five minutes by tourists all desperately searching for Westminster Abbey, and having to give directions in International Mime, signaling "right" and "left" with the bored panache of an airport worker flagging in a jet.

Today's seminar was in the same building, but, as Miranda and I discovered, in a conference room reached via an entrance around the corner. Only in England does 14 Great Peter Street mean, *Don't go to Great Peter Street at all, but the next street along, the name of which we won't tell you, and look for a door with a completely different number on it, which we're also keeping secret, for reasons best known to ourselves.* Neither of us was surprised. If this kind of thing bothers you, you'd best move to New York.

We registered, and got our little folders of agendas, and I got a badge, while the woman behind the desk hastily made up a temporary one for Miranda, which was just a sticky label with her name on it. Those are fine for men's suits, but when women have to put them on their blouses, the sticky backing destroys anything that isn't cotton. Still, the real badges were even worse, with those little clips designed to snap on to men's ties. They physically reinforce that neither badge-makers nor conference organizers have looked around in the previous half century and thought, *Yes, my goodness, some of those strange creatures called "women" do actually attend conferences.* Or maybe the badge makers and conference organizers had wives who wore ties. The idea of a row of middle-management, tie-wearing men going out to dinner with their tie-wearing wives, trailed by a line of small, tie-wearing children, with a tie-wearing dog guarding the tie-wearing baby at home, allowed me to repress my outraged feminist sensibilities.

Meanwhile, Miranda was flicking through her folder, checking out the schedule, and I swallowed my momentary snit. I didn't want to be a downer, just because I'd done this kind of thing too often. "If there's anything you want to go to, do. The office is quiet, and I'll hold the fort if you want to spend the day here."

She looked up, doubtful. "Would that be OK?"

"Why not? I'm going to leave after I've done my stuff, but you don't have to. I promise not to sign anything off at work without leaving you a note. I won't mess up your nice systems."

She looked severe. "See that you don't," she said with dignity, before giggling.

CultCo was up first, the five of us, plus a Q&A session. The event was scheduled to last two hours. "I'm going to check the AV is set up, and give them my memory stick."

I set off in search of Jim. I'd meant to e-mail him, to sort out the order we would speak in, but with the other things going on, I'd kept forgetting. Serve me right if I ended up speaking last, and therefore having to incorporate or delete material on the fly, depending on what the others were saying. Which would also mean I'd have to listen to their talks. Sensible man, Jim was standing by the biscuit plate in the coffee room. And, I was pleased to see, the biscuit plate didn't hold biscuits, but miniature croissants. I'd laid down enough caffeine by now, I was ready for some saturated fats. Janey, the video producer, was there, too, and Amelia Wilson, the curator from Glasgow who so far hadn't been at any of the meetings. She and Jim were old friends, and so after I brushed off their horrified questions about the state of my face, we easily agreed the running order, presenting it to Willa when she finally stopped smarming the senior Arts Council people and joined us. She was miffed, but that was her problem. If she'd headed for the people she was supposed to be collaborating with instead of doing career promotion, she'd have had some say in the matter.

The other three wanted to talk one after the other, because their work overlapped. Fine with me. That put me up first, and then I could more or less zone out until the questions. Which is what I did. I did listen to bits of the others. Jim's presentation was about museum shops, which was interesting. Willa's was about Willa, and how, if I understood her correctly, the arts world would be a blighted, withered shoot instead of the fine, flowering plant it was, had it not been for her stalwart work. I may have paraphrased that slightly.

The Q&A was smooth sailing, too. One of the great benefits of going first is that the next hour tends to blur everything in people's minds, and they focus more on the last things they've heard. So I emerged relatively unscathed. There's always a moment in conferences when you can feel people thinking, *That's enough now,* and beginning to pick up their bags. We had, with unspoken unanimity, reached that stage.

I began to collect my things, too. My plan was to head for yet more coffee, have a quick cup and briefly be sociable, and then head out. But as I stood up, a slip of paper was shuffled down the line of panelists and stopped in front of me. "Can I have a quick word while we've still got the AV going?" And Jim, at the far end of the table, nodded first at the paper, and then at the now-blank screen.

So I waved at Miranda, a see-you-in-a-bit wave, and waited for Jim.

"Great talk," he said, walking down to my end of the table.

"Thanks. Yours, too. Very interesting." What on earth?

"I didn't want to say . . ." he looked embarrassed. "That is, I wanted to say . . ."

"Maybe you should just 'say?'"

"Your talk was great."

So he'd said. And there was a "but" coming. So I prompted. "But?"

"But." He nodded. "But." Then it came out in a rush. "But did you know your dates were wrong?"

I was taken aback. "They were? Show me."

He thought I was arguing. "I don't want to be rude. But I just thought, when you give this talk again . . ."

"If I do this again, you have my full permission to shoot me, on the grounds that I will have lost my mind."

He laughed, relieved I wasn't angry, or even insulted.

I wasn't, but, "Tell me anyway. I'm interested." I joggled the mouse of the laptop to activate the screen, and then clicked back till I found my images. "Which ones?"

"The Tetrarch jackets." I went to them and brought them all up on the screen together.

"Show me."

"The ones you say are from the 1990s are from the 1960s."

"No." I didn't mind being wrong, but in this case I wasn't. Jim was a designer, and had a better eye than I did, but I'd worked for that company for nearly a decade. I knew the material inside out.

"They are." He was just as certain. It was like children in a sandbox: no they're not, yes they are. Any minute he'd call my mother to tell her that I'd hit him with my spade. I liked him, but hitting him with a spade didn't seem like a terrible idea.

I decided to hold it in reserve, and in the meantime present myself as a rational human being. "Why do you think so?" Subtext: I *don't* think so.

He reached out for the mouse. "Do you mind?" I moved over and he clicked forward. He brought up two Stevensons, one that I had got from Denise, and the one he'd sent me, the one he'd wanted to use for notepads. I'd included it as a little joke for him.

He clicked again, and zoomed in on both. "Look," he said. I

looked. He'd zoomed in on the jackets of the books in both collages.

"OK," I said, in a tone that meant, I'm not seeing whatever it
is you're seeing.

He clicked over to my 1990s examples of Tetrarch jackets.

"Oh. Damn. You're right." The colophons on the Tetrarch
book jackets from the 1990s were identical to the ones on the
jackets Stevenson had included in his collages. In the 1960s.
Thirty years before they had been created. I tried to think
it through. "So. The colophons that were used in the 1990s
must have been drawn earlier, in the 1960s. But I'm sure they
weren't in regular use." Quite sure. This had been part of my job.
"I guess they were drawn, used a bit, a design director decided
he didn't like them and they were dropped until they were re-
located thirty years later, and revived for a while as 'heritage'
branding." It was possible. Maybe plausible. "Stranger things have
happened. But thank you very much for not pointing out that
I'm an idiot in front of the entire conference. That was kind
of you."

"It's not often anyone else is interested in this kind of design.
We logo-nerds have to stick together."

"Then thanks for not having me expelled from the logo-nerd
club."

I left Miranda to the joys of discussions on subsidy in the arts,
and bailed out of the rest of the day, planning to walk back to
the office and enjoy the sunshine.

But I didn't even notice it. Now that the conference was over, everything I'd pushed to the back of my mind reasserted its prominence. I was withholding information from Jake. I hadn't told him about Matt Holder, nor about the Reichel-Celia connection. I'd been telling myself I just didn't like bringing attention back to the gallery. I stopped dead in the middle of crossing Parliament Square. That was foolish, but no more foolish than walking through Parliament Square in the first place. Between self-important police stopping pedestrians and cars so self-important MPs could flash by, or newbie cyclists wobbling off on their freshly rented hire bikes smack into flocks of tourists who had forgotten everything they'd been told about looking right, not left, when they crossed, it is likely that aliens have pinpointed this patch of London as the place to land and atomize a healthy chunk of the human race without being noticed. Or perhaps they already have. Hard to say.

I continued across to the relative safety of Whitehall before I returned to the very unsafe thought I'd just had. Without giving myself time to consider it further, I pulled out my phone.

"Merriam."

"Ade, it's me."

We both paused. I hadn't called him Ade in twenty years. And I'd stopped assuming he'd know who "me" was almost as long ago. I sidestepped that. "Can we talk? Are you in town?"

"I'm here." He didn't sound worried, or angry. Just tired. "Lunch?"

Things were bad if he was free for lunch not just on the same day, but an hour ahead. Trying to fit into Aidan's schedule normally was like trying to see the pope. But with fewer assistants, so more rescheduling. "Sure. Usual place?"

"See you in half an hour."

I dropped my phone into my bag and stood staring at the pavement. I knew I should call Jake. I looked for a cab instead.

This time I was there before Aidan, and I spent ten minutes figuring out what I was going to say. But when he arrived I postponed. "How's Anna? The kids? Toby?"

Before he could answer, our usual waitress came over, and this time she was a little happier with us, as we both ordered, and interacted with her. Some change, then, in a fortnight. She left, and Aidan stared down at his mat. He didn't bother with my questions, knowing I was stalling. "Officially, we're in limbo. The inquest on Frank was adjourned, pending new inquiries after Schmidt's death; the inquest on Schmidt is next week. I've been told that it's likely that will be adjourned, too. So, unofficially, we're moving on. I've made Lucy an offer to come and work for us when she finishes university, which is what would have happened if Frank had been alive. Now, I'm thinking that in a few years, if it works out, she can replace him as a partner—she and Sarah inherited his share. We're acting as if everything's fine, as if things will just go back to normal, but they aren't, and they won't."

"What do you think happened?"

He was startled. Apparently it had never occurred to him to ask himself what he'd thought. He considered it now. Finally, "I don't know about Schmidt. I barely saw him except in a professional capacity. But I don't think Frank killed himself for some private reason—that he was ill, or depressed, or that Toby

213

was going to leave him." He was still staring at his mat, and now he drew lines on it with his fork. Then he blurted out, as if he hated himself for it, "I think it was something to do with the gallery."

I did, too. "Do you have any idea what? You told me the police said the books were clean." He hadn't told me that, Helena and Jake had, but this sounded more polite.

"They are clean. The accountant Helena found for us says so, as well as Scotland Yard's people. And they would have found something if it had been there, because they wanted to find it. Which means that there's something that we aren't seeing. And I don't know what." He was genuinely frustrated.

I stared at him, waiting until he looked up. "Forgery." It seemed the only possible answer to me.

He stared back at me, completely blank. If what I was thinking had happened, he knew nothing about it. I would stake my life on that.

"You're serious." It started out as a statement, but by the time he'd finished the second word, it had turned into, not a question, but a plea.

"I'm serious that it's a possibility that has occurred to me, yes. That it seems likely, even. It starts with Stevenson." He nodded. "I gave a presentation this morning, on publishers and branding. I used a bunch of book jackets to show how publishers had used logos and typography over the past half century. I also used a Stevenson, one of the ones that incorporates a book jacket. The one that has a puppy in the corner, with a picture of Kafka."

He shrugged and shook his head.

I was hesitant. "You don't know the one I mean?" How could he not know what his gallery was selling?

"I've probably seen it." He saw he was going to have to give me a lesson in art dealing. "Everything we own isn't just sitting around the office, Sam. Some is in the building, but most is at a couple of specialist art-storage sites."

I'd never thought of the mechanics before.

"And if I haven't seen something we've sold, that's normal, too. Frank would have said the same about some of our Eastern European artists. We both have—" He grimaced. "We *had* areas of expertise. I mostly handle European artists, and some South American ones. Frank did the States for the most part, although for some reason he was also interested in new Chinese artists. God knows why." He stopped, realizing that he was digressing. "If a collector one of us normally dealt with was interested in the other partner's area, we just passed them on. It was the only practical way to work."

I thought. "Then what you need to know is that this Stevenson is a collage of an interior, and the back wall is made out of a book jacket. The picture is from the late 1960s, and I was using it in a discussion of how publishers had branded their books, how they'd used typography and design to create an . . ."—I waved my hands—"it sounds pretentious, but an aura. Not just for the author, but for the publisher, too. After the talk, a designer came up to say I'd misdated some of the colophons. A nerd thing, he phrased it." I half-nodded, half-shook my head, acknowledging the truth of that. "Except I hadn't made a mistake about the date. The differences are small, but once you're aware of them, you can't make a mistake like that. And if I didn't make a mistake, then that Stevenson, from 1968, has a book jacket in it that was printed in the 1990s."

I sat back. I hadn't said it out loud before, and now it sounded preposterous.

Aidan believed none of it. "A book from the 1990s? How could that be? Someone would have noticed it."

"The book itself, the novel, doesn't date from the 1990s. It's an old book, Jack Kerouac's *On the Road*. There's probably an even earlier edition, because it was first published in the 1950s, I think. But when books are reprinted, at least at Tetrarch, where this book jacket was from, the colophon on the spine is automatically replaced with the one the company is using at the date of the reprint, not the one that was on the previous edition, even if the cover isn't otherwise redesigned. And I know those colophons inside out. I know which ones were used in the 1960s, and I know which ones were used in the 1990s."

"Go back a bit. A colophon is . . ."

"It's the little symbol on a book's spine. It's the company's logo. Penguin uses a stylized drawing of a penguin, other companies use their initials or some other illustration."

He nodded. Now he knew what I meant.

"Tetrarch uses the outline of the heads of four Roman emperors. And like all logos, it gets redrawn, updated every now and again. When I was at Tetrarch, I sorted out a new version, so I spent a lot of time looking at the old ones." I shrugged. "It's not much of a claim to fame, but I can date most of them within a decade."

"You're suggesting that someone is forging collages, and

they've slipped up by using what appeared to be an old book cover? But that any publishing person could date the jacket from the logo."

I waved my hand in dismissal. "No. Even most publishing people wouldn't be able to. As I say, it's a nerd thing. Some would. Me. Most people, even publishers, wouldn't notice unless a book from each decade was put in front of them, to compare. The differences become obvious once they're laid out side by side."

Aidan sat turning his knife over and over, staring at it as though it had the answer etched onto the blade. "I have almost nothing to do with the Stevensons. Frank brought him to the gallery originally, and bought up the estate later. There was never any reason for me to be involved." He thought for a moment. "Of the collectors I deal with, only two, I think, have ever bought a Stevenson, so I've hardly looked at them. That is, if we're talking about the big pieces."

I thought we probably were, so I nodded for him to go on.

"If we take as the starting point, that we've been selling forgeries . . ." He looked as if he'd bitten into a rotten egg, and I couldn't blame him. This was his life's work, and now someone was coming along and telling him that it was most likely built on fraud. "If we allow for the moment that the gallery has been selling forgeries, then the question has to be how."

Of course it did. "Schmidt is the answer, isn't he?"

Aidan wasn't rejecting the idea. "He had the technical ability. He was a good artist, just not one with anything original to say. And he would have worked on our Stevensons over the years, without doubt. Collages are fragile: newsprint and other cheap paper of the kind Stevenson used degrades quickly. They need a lot of looking after." He thought about that for a moment. "And Stevenson was prolific. That would be a good reason to choose him. No one except Frank and Myra knew the holdings well."

"Myra? She told me the other day that she was the registrar, but I didn't—don't—have any idea what that means, or what she does."

"What doesn't she do? A gallery registrar is its paperwork queen, the admin center. Myra organizes the movement of all our art—shipping it out to art fairs, or to buyers, or lending it to exhibitions—as well as generating the documents that moving art around the world requires: tax, customs, loan agreements, insurance, you name it. She catalogues what comes in, what goes out, what is sold, what is bought. Whenever a piece moves in or out, she checks it and makes a condition report."

Too much information. I made a get-back-to-business gesture, and he smiled, admitting he'd been glad to get sidetracked. "So, yes, if I were going to forge, Stevenson would be a logical artist to forge. Lots of pieces. And, until Celia took over, the executor who lived in Vermont and never traveled. And wasn't an art expert, or a lawyer."

"Celia does seem to come into this, doesn't she?"

"Are you seeing her involved?"

"I can't figure out how it could have been done, otherwise. Werner Schmidt might have the technical ability to forge dozens of artists, but if he worked with Celia, then he had the"—I waved my hands—"well, the ingredients, for lack of a better word. To produce the kind of collages that Stevenson made, he'd need lots of 1960s and 1970s print materials: photos, newspapers, magazines, old photocopies. Of course you can buy old newspapers and magazines. But if you're working with the artist's daughter, isn't it even better? Then you have access to the artist's own files, the cuttings and clippings that must have been in his studio when he vanished." I thought some more about how collages were made. "Not only that, you even have the damn glue. Jake was telling me about Schmidt. He said he filed and dated all the materials he used, the way you'd expect a restorer to. But don't restorers use *different* materials than the ones the artists use? On purpose, so that experts can tell which areas are original and which the restorer has repainted?" I waited until Aidan nodded: yes, that was true. "Someone restoring Stevensons would use *different* glue, not the glue Stevenson used, so experts could identify which areas had been restored, and which were original." Aidan nodded again. He could see where I was going, but he didn't want to get there himself. "A forger of Stevensons, however, would need to have the kind of glue dating from Stevenson's day. The kind that's been illegal for twenty years. The kind that was somehow sitting in his studio, courtesy of his daughter."

We stared at each other. I felt like a dog that has found a bone, and was now waiting for the nice human to make a decision. Was it "Good dog!" and a scratch behind my ears, or "Bad dog! Take that dirty bone out of the house?"

"What does your policeman say?"

If he called him "my" policeman one more time, I was going to kick him, too. Maybe I'd start to kick everyone I had a meal with. "I haven't mentioned it." I was looking anywhere but at Aidan.

So much so that he had to bend down to break into my line of sight. "Sam? Why not?"

"Why not? Because my loyalties are all over the place. Am I just supposed to mention, as pillow talk, that I think my friend's gallery has been selling forgeries?" He flinched at that. Good. I stared at him accusingly. It was down to him now.

Aidan reached for his phone, dialed, and asked for Helena.

13

Helena was in a meeting that was scheduled to run all afternoon, so we assembled at her house that evening. I'd stopped and bought cold meat and salads on the way over, but I might as well have paid for Styrofoam, for all any of us ate. I repeated what I'd told Aidan, only this time I used Helena's computer. I had the memory stick with my illustrations, so it was easy to show them the details. And once you looked for it, you had to wonder how it had been missed. Helena made notes, impassive, as though it were any other meeting with a client. Which it would have been, if it weren't for my being involved.

When we'd both finished she sat thinking for a moment. Then, "It's out of our hands, now." Aidan and I had both known that, but we had somehow hoped she would make it go away. Not happening. "As an officer of the court, I will report what my client has told me. In the morning." She looked calmly at me. "If you want to talk to your partner, I have no control over that."

Wasn't that just hotsy-totsy.

As I made my way home, I went back and forth, trying out scenarios and then discarding them, practicing conversations I knew wouldn't go the way I was scripting them in my head. Which might be fortunate, because even the scripts that I was writing sucked.

Happily, I didn't have to try any of them out. Jake was still at work when I got home. I decided on early bed, and then with luck I'd be asleep by the time he got home.

It half-worked. I was in bed, and I switched off the light as soon as I heard his key in the door. The bedroom faces the back of the house, and he couldn't possibly see the light from the street.

He got undressed and slid into bed without speaking. Just as I was congratulating myself on a nifty maneuver, however, he reached out and mussed my hair. "Your I-am-asleep breathing needs work. It wouldn't fool a two-year-old. What are you avoiding?"

I turned over to look at him. "You. Otherwise I wouldn't be doing my avoiding in bed. Or not in a bed where I expected to find you."

There was a startled pause. "Have you been spending much time in beds where you don't expect to find me?"

That wasn't what I'd meant, but it was a good diversion. When in doubt, try wild exaggeration. "Yes, of course. Dozens. Daily. Didn't I mention it?" I waited to see if he'd chase off down this rabbit hole.

No such luck. "Well if it's only dozens every day, then I don't need to worry. But that's not why you were pretending to be asleep."

I think I snarled. "I was pretending to be asleep because I need to talk to you and I don't much want to. Can we do it in the morning? Are you working this weekend?"

"Yes, we can do it in the morning, no, I'm not working."

"Good. Now I'm really going to sleep." I turned over again. I'm a terrible liar. There wasn't a chance I'd sleep, and I didn't. Instead I lay awake for hours trying to think of a way to avoid the coming conversation. The only halfway feasible solution I could come up with was emigration, and only if I could find a country that kept its visa office open after midnight.

There was one small side benefit to my feeling of impending doom. At six I realized that if I went for a run, it would give me an extra hour before I had to face the firing squad. So I did. My running is inept at the best of times, and after a week off, it was even more so. But I was getting fresh air and I was puce with effort, and those, I told myself as I pulled up at the front door, gasping for breath, were the main things.

Jake was waiting for me in the kitchen. He didn't bother with any soft soap, for which I was grateful. He did smile, though, and I was grateful for that, too, although I suspected he wouldn't be smiling much longer. "Out with it."

This was the third time I was telling the story, so at least I was now telling it efficiently. I ran through the colophon evidence, and added in Aidan and Helena's views.

"Forgery." He sat thinking about it. "Compton finds out what is going on, kills himself rather than admit it to his partner. The forger . . ." he frowned. "The forger is no longer threatened with exposure, and so he kills himself?"

I'd already stumbled over that. "The forger, who used to go

out with the man who has just committed suicide because of his actions, and is also an alcoholic, feels terrible, gets drunk, or drunker, and uses toxic chemicals without taking precautions."

He seemed to think that was possible. "And Celia Stein?"

"She's the source of the material, she's the way the forgeries get back into the estate, to be sold as originals. And she got in touch with me when she shouldn't have ever heard of me. She wants something, and hasn't said what it is, which makes me think it's something she's not willing to have known."

"Why would she get in touch with you, though? Nothing could have drawn attention to her more."

"Maybe she thought approaching me through the trust would give her cover. If Lucy hadn't mentioned the Stevenson exhibition that first evening at Toby's, we would never have looked twice at her."

Jake was noncommittal.

"It also makes sense of her income."

"Her income? How would you know what that was?"

"I don't, but I can't see a charitable trust salary even covering the cost of her shoes."

Jake stared pointedly at my T-shirt. "Yes, I know." I brushed that aside. "I'm not interested in shopping, but I am interested in clothes in the abstract, on other people. And I'm telling you, she wears Armani. And very expensive shoes and handbags. If she receives a share of the Stevenson estate earnings, or the estate pays her a salary for the work she does for it, then maybe, but think about her house. It's in Highgate. Expensive area.

According to Delia, it's big enough to build an annex in the garden. I live on a publishing salary, and I can't imagine being able to afford that. Maybe she got a good settlement from her ex-husband, but isn't it worth looking at?"

Jake didn't respond directly. "I'm going to have to go in. We need to get the Specialist Crime unit in." He saw my blank response and translated. "The art fraud people."

I tried not to look as nauseous as I felt. "Helena told Aidan to put together a list of the Stevenson sales over the last ten years. I agreed to look at any that include book jackets. Obviously they're going to have to get experts in, but I can at least see if any of the others have the same problem."

He nodded his thanks. He and Helena both had a tendency to treat me as clerical staff during an investigation. I always felt I ought to resent it, but I never did. I was quite sure they knew what they were doing, and I was quite sure I didn't.

"I won't be long. They'll get their own people on to it, and they won't need me after the briefing."

Our weekend together had turned into a weekend with Jake working. I mentally shrugged. He'd told me from the first it would be like that, and I was happy enough most of the time. I just hadn't expected our game of Happy Families to involve me being Mrs. Dick, the Detective's Wife. I gritted my teeth and got on with those thrilling activities that make weekends such a bower of earthly delights. I started a load of laundry, and changed the sheets and towels. I gave the kitchen and bathroom a quick clean. Any more excitement and I'd explode with happiness. Whoom. It would be like *The Muppet Show* when the musicians self-destruct. Maybe "happy" wasn't quite the word I was searching for to describe my mood.

The phone rang as I began to make lunch. Jake.

"Are you on your way home, or is it turning into an all-day deal?"

"I'm on my way home, but I have a question. When we spoke to Celia Stein at the funeral, did you get the impression she was planning to go anywhere?"

"No." I thought for a moment. "The opposite. Delia said she was always traveling, but with the Tate show she was stuck in London."

"You're right. I'd forgotten that. Thanks." He was planning to hang up.

"Not so fast, sunshine. Why do you want to know?"

He wanted to tell me it was police business, but since he'd just co-opted my memory as his interview partner, based on a whole pile of information I'd dumped in his lap that morning, it was harder than usual. His voice was grudging. "We're waiting to hear if she's drawing an income from the estate once the U.S. office opens. But otherwise you were right. Big house in the most expensive part of Highgate, bought three years ago, no mortgage. Moved from a small, mortgaged flat. Husband gone long before that, no alimony. Jobs in various arts organizations, nothing with a big salary."

Told you so would have been vulgar, so I contented myself with, "And the trip?"

"We decided it warranted an interview—not formal questioning, just an interview. She's not at home, which isn't suspicious in itself, but we managed to get hold of the receptionist who works for the Trust, and she says Stein took sudden leave last week. We were just wondering where she might be."

I was interested to note that she'd become "Stein," not "Celia." "We know where she was for part of that leave of absence. On Wednesday she was at Frank's funeral."

"I know, it's a precaution, nothing more." But his voice was tight. He was irritated with himself for not having looked into her earlier.

I went back to the salad I'd been making, but I turned the information over as much as the leaves, maybe more. Denise's reported conversation implied Celia hadn't been scheduled to go on holiday, that on Friday she hadn't said anything, just rung in on Monday to say she wouldn't be in. She'd been at the funeral, but that was after, and nothing had happened on the weekend.

My hands stilled. I'd been knocked off my bike at the weekend. By someone who didn't stop, which might happen at any time. In what several bystanders thought was a deliberate sideswipe, which I didn't. It's true that I'm bolshie, and I have a bad habit of saying what I think without filtering it through my brain first, but up to now, no one's tried to kill me.

I texted Jake. *Did you ask neighbors/Denise/whoever if Celia drives a dark blue Volvo?*

The answer was unhelpful. *How do you know Denise?*

Missing the point, you fool, I shouted at the phone. Then I politely and quietly tapped in, *I met her when I went to interview Celia for the panel. Voice to bring grown men to their knees.*

Yes. Married her this morning.

I obviously wasn't going to get an answer. Jake had said he was on his way back. It would keep. I returned to the lettuce. Then I dried my hands. If I waited, I'd decide it was stupid. And Jake would be home, and he wouldn't let me.

I narrowed my eyes. I didn't like being "let" do anything, and the fact that Jake had tried to prevent me only in my imagination was irrelevant. I grabbed my laptop off my desk, added my keys and wallet, and threw everything into my bicycle basket. If pressed, I could say that I was going to the market.

I went halfway, which was all I'd intended. Without even thinking about it, I passed the crossing where I'd been sideswiped and was off and had the bike chained up before I remembered and had time to be afraid. It didn't matter if I couldn't recognize Viv's door again. Clutter accumulates at the bottom of my basket, and her note would still be there somewhere. If she was in, I'd ask my question. If not, I'd head for the market and try on the way back.

No problem on either front. I recognized her door, and she was in. As soon as I heard her footsteps I didn't wait for her to tell me to bog off again, but called out, "Good morning, Viv! It's Sam Clair. The one who got knocked off her cycle."

She opened the door, but wasn't prepared to let me in yet. I did the How-are-you-yes-my-goodness-my-face-still-looks-terrible-but-much-better-now-the-bruising-is-going-down first, and then the how-was-your-week in return.

There was no need to belabor it, though. Her manner made clear that if I said whatever it was I'd come to say and then let her get on with her day, it wouldn't break her heart.

"I have a question for the boy who saw the car registration."

The shutters came down.

I put up a hand, Boy-Scout-oath style. "I promise that he won't be asked by anyone except me. I will pass the information on, if it's what I think it might be, but I won't say how I know or where it came from. I promise," I repeated, radiating sincerity so hard I nearly buzzed.

She still didn't say anything, but this time she was thinking, not rejecting the request out of hand.

"There might be a possibility that I know who was driving. If it turns out that this is the person the boy saw, she will be wanted for much more than a hit-and-run where no one was badly hurt. If she's not the person, then there's no harm done, and I won't mention it."

Decision made. "I'll see if the boy is about. And if he's willing to talk to you. I don't promise, but come back in half an hour."

I was going to the market after all. Sometimes I turn out to be telling the truth even when I don't have any plans to.

I was back in half an hour on the dot. And so was Viv, waiting for me on her doorstep with what she had called the "boy": late teens, hangdog look, trousers down around his bum—all the signs of a boy who had been in what Viv called "a bit of trouble," and also all the signs of a boy who hadn't. Basically, just the signs of being a teenaged boy.

I held out my hand. "Hi, I'm Sam. Thank you for agreeing to talk to me."

He looked at my hand as if no one had ever offered to shake hands with him before. And maybe they hadn't. He was young. But he took it and grinned. Terrific smile. "Hi, Sam. I'm Sam, too." Viv clicked her tongue and he subsided. He wasn't supposed to have told me that.

I grinned back. "So if I need to, I'll say I was talking to my-self." Even Viv smiled. I opened my laptop. I'd found some pic-tures of Celia and Delia at the press conference, and now I pulled up the page, with the first ten or so photos showing them and a dozen other people. "Do you recognize any of these people?"

He took the laptop and held it close. He had light-brown eyes surrounded by eyelashes of an indecent, giraffe-like length. I followed them as they moved carefully from one picture to the next. Then he handed the laptop back. He didn't even say any-thing, just shrugged.

I was stunned. I was so sure he was going to say yes, I hadn't prepared for the possibility of his saying no.

The hell with police procedure, or at least the hell with what I imagined police procedure to be, based on my extensive read-ing of crime fiction. I clicked on a picture of Celia by herself. "Her?" I said bluntly.

He looked, and shook his head. "No." Not even "I don't think so." Just "No."

"Fuck." I said it without thinking. It made Sam laugh, but Viv glared. *No more biscuits for you,* her look said.

Story of my life.

"So if that's not her, what *did* she look like?" He stared at me blankly. She looked like a woman.

"Red-headed? Brown hair? Blonde? Pink?"

He grinned again, hangdog look entirely gone. "Not pink. The others?" He shrugged. No idea.

"Age?"

Nothing. He knew she was female, he didn't know how he knew, and that was it. I pulled a couple of business cards from my wallet and scribbled on the backs. "This is my mobile. If you think of anything, will you give me a call?"

Both took one, Viv with the enthusiasm of an angler who, at the end of a long day's fishing, has hooked up a tin can. Sam's response was more curiosity than enthusiasm. It was like shaking hands with adults. Not something that had happened to him before, but not unpleasant now he'd tried it.

Jake was home by the time I got back, and was staring dubiously at the salad. "Lunch?" he whined.

I waved my basket. "Saved by the market. I got you tough-guy grub to water down the wussiness of a salad."

All the same, he ate his share of salad, too. Talk is cheap.

He waited until we were washing up before he said casually, "You went to the market OK?"

"OK? As in, you're such a lunatic you might forget where the market is, and then how to get home? Or OK as in, I still think a madman will zoom out of a crossing and try to murder you if you venture out, even though I've stopped insisting on driving you to work?" I stood with my hands on my hips. It was a savage reply to a fairly unloaded question—well, a fairly loaded question, but a fairly fair one, too. I couldn't help it, though. I hated being reminded that someone might want to hurt me, and it made me want to hurt whoever reminded me of it. I rubbed my hands over my eyes. "Sorry. Yes, I went to the market with no problem. And then, on the way home . . ."

Jake's back was to me, and he waited, standing with one arm raised halfway to putting the dishes in the cupboard. Finally, when I didn't continue, he prompted, "And on the way back, what?"

"I stopped to chat to the woman who'd helped me last week. When I fell?"

He didn't move. "And?"

"And the boy who said the car was a blue Volvo."

He finished putting the plates away and turned around, rolling down his sleeves. "And he couldn't identify Celia Stein."

"What? How did you—?" I felt like a lab rat in a cage, my movements monitored, even predicted. "Being with you is creepy." I saw the look on his face. "No! That's not what I meant. Being with you isn't creepy, but what you just *did* is creepy. How did you do that?"

He pointed to my laptop, still at the bottom of my bicycle basket. "You don't take your laptop anywhere much, and never to the market. So you wanted it for something, and if you spoke to the boy, that must have been what you wanted it for." He held up his hands, palms out—*See, nothing up my sleeves.*

Most men don't notice anything ever. Which can be infuriating to live with. But I wasn't sure that men—or a man—who noticed everything were any easier to live with. Maybe I'd give up on men and get a dog. They only noticed dog food and other dogs' bottoms. Neither of which mattered to me. I went back to what Jake had said. "All right, that was how you knew that I'd been asking. How did you know that he said it wasn't her?"

He started to answer the question, then was diverted. "He was sure it wasn't her? That's interesting." Then he went back. "There are always three possibilities." He pointed, lecturing. "The witness positively identifies the person of interest; the witness says it was definitely not the person of interest; or the witness is not certain." He left the textbook behind and returned to Celia. "If I'd guessed, I would have said he wouldn't be able to say one way or the other."

"He was sure. It wasn't her."

"Were the photographs good? What did you show him?"

I pulled up the page again. And then I also admitted to pointing out Celia when the boy hadn't recognized any of the photos on his own. Jake looked disapproving, but I could see he was trying not to laugh. What I'd done was probably what the police wanted to do all the time, jabbing at a photo and shouting, "Her! Her, for God's sake."

He agreed that the photos were good enough for identification, just adding mildly that it was lucky the boy hadn't recognized anybody, as my pointing her out would have made his evidence inadmissible. I shrugged. He hadn't recognized anybody, so it was moot, and anyway, I'd promised not to identify him, so at least that was a battle I now wouldn't have to have.

But I still didn't know how Jake had known that the boy hadn't recognized her. He was dismissive. "Nothing very clever. You wanted it to be her. If he'd said yes, you would have told me first thing."

That simple. I closed down the page. Behind it, I saw a new batch of e-mails had appeared, including one from Lucy. I clicked on it. Aidan had asked her to send me photos of the Stevensons with book jackets in them. And she attached eleven JPEGS. I turned the screen toward Jake. "Do you want to send this on to your office?"

He looked at it and nodded, forwarding it on.

"Is that it, then? Are you finished for the weekend?"

He looked smugly pleased. "Barring emergencies, yes. And just in time. The football begins in half an hour."

Be still, my fast-beating heart.

14

I like to imagine that I subscribe to the never-do-today-what-you-can-put-off-until-tomorrow school of thought. In reality, I'm methodical and plodding. So while Jake watched the match, I opened up the JPEGS Lucy had sent, zoomed in on the colophons and printed them off. The pictures were all dated, three in a cluster from the late 1960s, which included the puppy/Kafka one I'd already got. Then there was another series of four that had been made in the early 1970s. After that, Stevenson must have stopped using book jackets until the 1990s. The final four were from just before he vanished.

I stood in front of my bookshelves, scanning for Tetrarch spines, then checking each one for a date. I pulled examples from the 1950s through to this year, and then carefully went through each one, checking the reprint dates inside, setting them down spine upward on the floor, in groups for each decade, with smaller groups within the decades, whenever the publisher had had the colophons redesigned. This was why cop shows always got an audience, right? The glamor.

Jake kept his eyes on the television, but he was watching me all the same.

I was working at a glacial pace. This wasn't the kind of situation where "close enough" was going to fly. It took me nearly an hour to find enough examples from each date. I wanted at least one example for every five-year span, but the early years, before I had been buying books, were thin on my shelves. In two cases, however, I had copies of the books Stevenson had used—he was not exactly a literary maverick, and his taste ran to counterculture-mainstream, if such a category exists, and I think it does. One was the Kerouac. Mine was a later reprinting, from 2000, so I moved that to the 2000s decade group. The other was a William Burroughs novel.

Only when I'd chosen all the books did I let myself pick up the copies from the printer in the next room. I had cropped each image so that only the colophon showed, not the title above it on the spine, with no other identifying features visible. I didn't want to be guided by what I thought the dates ought to be, based on when I knew the books were published, or the collages created.

Then I sat on the floor moving the photocopies from group to group. Small children can be kept quiet for hours with a pack of cards turned face down on the carpet: turn up two that match, you encourage them. The level of difficulty was the same with this task. The answers were as immediately and screamingly obvious as two aces would be to a six-year-old. Anyone who had ever worked in publishing or design could have seen what I saw right away. But I pretended I didn't, and went through each one slowly and carefully.

When I'd paired up each photocopied colophon to a book with a matching colophon, I got my laptop out and opened up the JPEGS again. Then I went back to the photocopies, checking the collages' titles and dates, copying them down onto their respective photocopies.

I sat back.

Jake had given up all pretense of television half an hour before. "Well?"

"Two." I said, talking to the floorboards in front of me. I'd just proved that my ex-lover's gallery had been selling forgeries. "The one that I knew about, with Kafka and the puppy—which is, by the way, with dazzling originality entitled *Kafka's Puppy*. And one more, a late one, from 1992."

He whistled. "Two out of eleven."

"That's what it looks like." I didn't look up. "What now?"

"May I take the books?"

What did he think, I was going to withhold the evidence? At this stage? I got up wearily, and started to re-shelve all the books except the eleven from the dates of the pictures. It was good to have something mechanical to do. I stared at the title of each book carefully, as if the alphabet were a new concept that had only just been explained to me, and I didn't want to jump to any conclusions about whether Dostoyevsky came before or after Asimov.

Finally nothing but the eleven books and their photocopies sat accusingly on the floor. I tucked each photocopy into the book whose colophon it matched, and piled them up on the table by the door.

Jake looked at me sympathetically as he stood and picked up his phone. "Mark each sheet, and its partner book 1a, 1b; 2a, 2b; and so on. Then sign and date both the books and the sheets under the numbers. Someone will come and collect them." He stopped. "I'm sorry, you won't get the books back."

My voice sounded swollen, as if I had a cold. "I never want to see the bloody things ever again."

And I went into the bedroom and closed the door behind me firmly. It wasn't Jake's fault, but I didn't want to talk to him, and I didn't want to listen to him explain to whoever he spoke to on the phone, or see the person who came to get the books. I wanted to go to bed and pull the duvet over my head. But that was stupid and melodramatic, so I sorted the laundry I'd done that morning. At least Sam Spade regretted losing Brigid O'Shaughnessy, I thought. I was sitting on the bed trying not to cry over a lost sock. And my poor lost friend Aidan.

After half an hour I'd heard the front door open and close, and I went back to the sitting room. The football had ended, and some sort of historical adaptation was on, the kind television companies think are improving. Cultural Weetabix. But Jake wasn't watching, he was staring out the window, waiting for me. I went and sat down beside him, leaning into him.

"I hate this a lot," I confided.

"Me, too."

I knew he hated it only because it touched my life. That made me feel better. So I scrubbed at my face and sat up. "Can we forget it for the rest of the weekend?"

"We can try."

And so we did. I sent Helena an e-mail telling her about the colophons, but that was as far as I thought I needed to go. She would tell Aidan. Jake's office didn't call him in, I didn't have anything terribly urgent to read, and instead we spent the time together without any of the scratchiness that had been hovering around so many of our conversations in the past weeks. So much so that we silently decided not to break the harmony by discussing any of those things we'd postponed to "later." Later was, by mutual agreement, not now.

The only episode remotely connected to the case, therefore, was an e-mail from Aidan on Sunday, sent to both Helena and me. "The installation is almost finished, and tomorrow evening a few journalists are coming in. It's not the main press view, but just for the broadsheet reviewers whose deadlines are early. Do you want to come? I'll be there around five, and I'll leave your names. Ask for Esther Wolff in the press office, and she'll bring you in."

By this time we were sitting in the garden after dinner. It was just starting to get dark, not enough that we needed to turn the lights on inside, but not light enough to see each other properly, either. The phone's glow cast a little sodium firefly on Jake's face as I handed it over to him to read.

I resolutely didn't look at him as I said, casually, "What do you think?"

He grunted. Then, "I don't know what the specialists will have got up to on the weekend, but if you want to go, go. Why not?"

"I doubt Helena will. She thinks leaving the office early is for lightweights. I might, though. Although I need to try and set up an appointment about Miranda. It'll depend on when Olive can see me. And five means I'd have to leave at four. I am, theoretically, in full-time employment. I can't just wander off whenever the fancy takes me. I was out all day Friday." I have no idea who I was trying to convince. No one in the garden was fooled. We both knew that the first "I might" meant "I will," while the torrent of reasons why not that had followed was nothing more than window dressing.

We sat on for a while longer. Then, "Are they looking for Celia?" My voice was much smaller than I intended it to be.

Jake didn't answer, but he took my hand until it got too cold, and then we went in and went to bed.

On Monday, Jake dropped me at work again. I didn't tease him anymore. He thought there was some danger, but not enough to warrant full-out precautions. If he could watch over me he would, and when he couldn't, he would trust to my good sense. Whatever he thought that might mean.

I hadn't tried to set up a meeting with Olive the previous week, since I needed David to be on holiday before I could legitimately go over his head. When I got in it was early, only just eight, but I thought I'd get my foot in the door for an appointment today if that were possible.

Publishing office etiquette is informal, but there are ways we shape that informality that we unconsciously adhere to. Most conversations are conducted by e-mail along the corridors, unless it's serious gossip, in which case the kitchen is the place for conversations that begin "You have to promise that you won't tell anyone." Some of us, though, are still old-fashioned enough to like talking face-to-face. Whoever wants to do that just puts their head around an office door, or wanders into an open-plan area. An open door means any gossip, or even idle chit-chat, is welcome. A closed door says "Knock and come in, but only if its work. Oh, all right, but the gossip better be *really* good."

Olive nominally subscribes to this code, but as she's the publishing director few people take her up on her open door. Instead, I e-mailed Evie. "If Olive has time this week, can you slot me in for five mins? Won't take more, I promise. Sam." In tacit acknowledgment that this was a formal request for a formal appointment, I didn't add the "x" that most publishing people—all publishing women, and far more publishing men than would care to admit it—add beside their names automatically. I suspect many of us e-mailing the bank to sort out a missing direct-debit payment have absent-mindedly blown cyber kisses to bemused data processors.

Less than two minutes after I'd hit Send, a reply pinged back from Olive directly. "Now is fine if you're in. O." I hadn't known she read Evie's e-mail account, and there were no kisses for me. Still, there was an appointment.

The downside of this up-and-at-'em early-morning maneuvering was that Miranda had yet to appear. I was going to have a little trouble saying she'd "just" told me when she wasn't there to tell me anything. I headed down the hall. I'd burn that bridge when I came to it.

Olive is great. I think everyone at T&R knows how lucky we are to have her. She's a couple of years younger than me, probably just turned forty or so, and came up through editorial, which means she knows about books, and reading. It sounds unnecessary to say that, but more and more publishing houses are run by accountants, or sales people, or people who love marketing brands. Even sales and marketing people are a lesser evil. At least they worked with books before being elevated to the money end. One or two companies are now run by people who have never had any connection to books. To them books are just another commodity. Like Cheddar.

None of this should matter. What we sell is imagination, the possibility of being somewhere else, talking to people who never existed, or died a millennium ago. How you do it, by words on paper, or on an e-reader, or carried through your window by phosphorescent pixies driving chocolate sleighs, shouldn't matter. But it does. Which is why we have been so fearful for the past fortnight. The big fear is that we'll lose our jobs. The lesser fear is that we'll keep our jobs. Just in a corporate gulag.

Of course, when I went into Olive's office I hadn't officially heard anything about her meetings, or any takeover rumors, so I just plonked myself down with my coffee and thanked her for squeezing me in. "I wouldn't have bothered Evie so early if I'd known you were picking up her e-mails."

"Not a problem. If I hadn't had the time, I would have left it for her."

Fair enough. "It's a smallish thing, and normally I'd speak to David." If I'd ever wanted proof that God didn't exist, I had it right then, because if he did exist, and he was as passionately devoted to micromanaging our lives as most religions suggest, he'd definitely have struck me dead for that lie. "But unfortunately, it needs to be sorted right away, and he's on holiday this week." I filled her in on Miranda's job offer, which she'd notified me of by e-mail on the weekend, I now discovered as the lie tripped fluently out of my mouth. "There's no immediate slot for her to move into here, but I'd hate to let her go without at least trying to find something. She's terrific. She did most of the work on Breda's last book." Breda is my starriest author, and a major contributor to T&R's bottom line. "And not just editorial. The authors like her personally, and she's made really good contacts." I summed up. "She's great, and she'd be an asset to T&R." So what about it, lady?

Olive was direct. "If you want her, we should try and keep her. But if there isn't a vacancy, or likely to be one soon"—she raised an eyebrow, asking if I'd heard anything on the office grapevine that she hadn't, and I shook my head in reply—"we can't create one. There is no possibility of adding another salary at the moment." That was final, her expression said. Don't go there.

So I didn't. "I thought that would be the case, but maybe half-and-half? If I have her three days a week, and she does junior editorial two days?"

"Are you willing to give up your assistant?" Her tone was a warning: don't come crying to me later, saying you have too much work and you need a full-time assistant.

"*Half* my assistant. And when we find a vacancy for her to move into, I get the other half back." Olive smiled at how fast I'd corrected her, and how vehemently. Miranda was terrific, but I wasn't willing to lose all my backup to keep her. I went on more moderately. "It goes without saying that I'd like not to have to give her up. But it's, well, it's just unkind for her to miss a chance because I'm not willing to take on a bit more. And anyway, she does more than my last three assistants combined. If we go out of our way for her, she'll pay it back. She does."

Olive considered that. "I've spoken to her to say hello to, but no more." My lips twitched, and Olive nodded as if I'd spoken. "Yes, the Goth thing isn't great."

I agreed, it wasn't. "But it's part of the reason that says we should keep her. Some of my oldest, most traditional authors love her. If she can make them see past her hair and the piercings . . . I keep thinking she'll outgrow it. Which makes me sound like her mother."

Olive laughed. "As long as you don't tell her she's just going through a phase." I liked watching Olive laugh. Her skin was dark, like her name, and she had deep crow's feet around her eyes, as if she'd spent a lot of time laughing.

She continued smiling even after she'd had her laugh, although now it was turned on me. "You look like the child now. One who's just brought a stray kitten home. 'Can we keep him, Mum? I'll feed him myself, and clean out his litter every day, I promise.' When does the decision need to be made?"

This was much better than I'd hoped. "The end of the week." It was the end of the week. Just not this week. But if I admitted that, then there would have been no reason not to wait until David got back next Monday. And then we'd grow old and die while he failed to make a decision.

I'd done what I could for the moment. I stood up. "Thanks." And escaped. A decent start, with a possible maybe in less time than it took for me to drink a cup of coffee. Take that, David

Snaith, I mentally toasted as I walked past his office. And then hastily lowered my cup as Olive put her head out of her door.

The lines around her eyes deepened again, but she pretended she hadn't seen anything. "Will you ask for Miranda's personnel file to be sent up?"

And she shut the door before I laughed.

It was good that I'd got that meeting in early, because the rest of the day might not have existed for all the attention I paid to it. Miranda came in around ten, and I told her to come in and shut the door, which meant I had news for her. She was too experienced to think it meant gossip, because what gossip could I have possibly heard at the weekend?

She looked worried, which was touching. I knew that we worked well together, and I knew that she'd rather stay at T&R than go to a smaller house, but I hadn't realized quite how much she wanted it.

First the bad news, that Olive had confirmed that she wouldn't let us create a job for Miranda. "But we knew that. And she sounded quite positive about the half-and-half job: that if you agree to be a half-assistant, half-junior editor for the moment, when a full editorial vacancy comes up you'll be in line for it. Although until she jumps one way or the other, I didn't discuss salary."

I expected her to have to weigh up the option. She had been offered a full-time job that got her more firmly on the editorial ladder, and although she'd still be doing the admin work there that she was doing for me now, she'd be doing it for herself, not for someone else. And there'd be more money. So when she said, "You'd do that for me?" I wasn't sure what she meant.

"Do what? We agreed that this is what I'd suggest to Olive last week. Didn't we?"

"You didn't say you'd lose half your assistant. Or if you did say it, I didn't understand. I thought you'd be allowed to hire someone else."

"I told you, they aren't going to let us make new hires or add salaries."

"But are you willing to do that?"

Clearly we were both speaking foreign languages. "Of course I'm willing. I've done it." I amended. "If Olive agrees, I've done it."

Miranda's eyes filled with tears. "I don't know what to say. You're making your job harder, to help me."

I qualified that overstatement. "I'm making my job a *little* harder, and no one except you helped you. You've done far more than your job description, and you've done it really well." I like to get brownie points when they're due, and a lot of the time even when they're not due, but this really wasn't a case for making me out to be a saint. I don't think I could even have got beatified for this morning's contribution. "We don't have to worry right now. It hasn't happened yet. Olive might say no."

"You're right. Chickens. Counting. Don't." She nodded and stood up to go back to her desk. At the door, though, she stopped, turned and came back, and gave me a fierce hug. And at lunchtime a huge bunch of cornflowers and poppies silently appeared on my desk.

I remember that part, but otherwise, while I know I went to

meetings, sent and received e-mails—I even participated in an auction for a book—I only know it because I have the e-mails, and T&R is now the proud publisher of a new author. I have no memory of any of it. As far as I'm aware, I spent the day staring out the window and worrying away at the Stevenson question.

I'm not even sure how, or when, it became "the Stevenson question." Two weeks ago, Aidan had told me that his partner Frank had died. Only fourteen days, and yet that dark figure in the dark room had vanished as though he'd never been. Werner Schmidt's death had never been very real to me, in part, I think, because I didn't know what he'd looked like, or anything about him except that he shelved his oil paints by date and drank too much. Instead it was the equally dead Edward Stevenson, and Celia Stein, who had taken over their space, and everyone's attention.

By the time four o'clock rolled around, therefore, of course I was going to the preview at the Tate. I stopped by Miranda's desk and dropped some things off: a list of proofs to be sent out to authors who might give us quotes to use for promotion; some sales material to be proofread; a reminder to nag at the design department to return the family photographs an author had lent us to use in her book. It was routine, mechanical work that I should have done myself, but that had sat, untouched, on my desk all day.

"I'm out for the rest of the day. I'm going to a press view at the Tate, for a show by the woman from the Daylesworth Trust's father." It was a convoluted explanation, but since there was no real explanation for why I was going, it would have to do.

"Get you," said Miranda cheerfully.

"Living the high life. Is there anything before I go?"

She shook her head, then reconsidered and changed it to a nod. "You've been sent a new novel by the scout from Jansen's, who says it's the newest thing in Scan-noir crime. Except that it's not really Scan, because it's Finnish. Shall I try and find us a Finnish reader somewhere? I've checked, and no one here uses one, but I can e-mail a few friends at other publishers. Oh, and I've done the permissions and copyright forms for Carol Dennison's book. I'll leave them on your desk. I checked them, and they're fine, but you need to authorize the payments."

And she wondered why I thought she deserved promotion?

When I got to the Tate, the guard at the front door tried to stop me. The gallery was closing in half an hour, and admissions had just ended. But I said the secret passwords, "Esther Wolff" and "press," and he immediately stood back.

"Go down to the bronze sculpture at the end of the hall," he said, pointing through the central foyer to the rear of the museum. "The entrance to the exhibition is on your right, and the warder there will find Esther for you."

Open sesame.

Even half an hour before closing, the museum was filled with people getting their final thirty minutes' worth of culture. But the school groups had long gone, and so had the people who had come up to London for the day. And the mothers with small children. The visitors now were, on average, older and quieter than the first and the last groups, and younger and more mobile than the middle ones. I stood and watched idly for a few minutes, wondering about these people assiduously art-ing around the place at five o'clock on a weekday afternoon. Didn't they have jobs? Could they all be self-employed? Or had they, too, just cut out of their offices early on a summer afternoon? I'd certainly left work early on summer afternoons, but I'd never thought to go to a museum. It was an enticing idea, but even as I played with the idea I realized that these were not office-skivers. They were tourists. London without tourists is as unimaginable as boiled eggs without toast soldiers. If you remove one half, is there any point to the other? At least, that's the official view. On tourists and London, I mean. I don't think there's an official view on toast soldiers.

I stopped daydreaming and turned right as directed. Facing me was a temporary barrier with a poster for the Stevenson exhibition on it, and a pasted streamer over one corner: "Exhibition opens 16 June." I stopped to look at the painting they had chosen. I was expecting *Poppity Princess*, as the most famous, but it wasn't that one. It was only a detail, a close-up of an eye and a nose made up of photographic negatives. Clever. It felt familiar, yet at the same time, you didn't think you'd know everything, which you might have with *Poppity Princess*. I slid behind the roped-off section, with an entirely unreasonable feeling of being an insider.

The guard by the door did not share my delusion, and he kept a beady eye on me as he checked his list of names. But Aidan and Esther Wolff had done their work, and he was forced to let me enter, although his manner suggested that when he ran the museum, things would not be so slipshod. I squinted quickly down at my skirt. It was clean. Farther down. My shoes were a pair. Was there more I was supposed to be doing? I consoled myself that it was my scraped face that made the whites of his eyes show, not that I looked generally un-private-view-worthy. So when he handed me a folder marked "Press," I took it as though I expected it. As soon as I'd walked through the foyer, though, I checked it out. Nothing exciting: thumbnails of illustrations that were available for the newspapers' picture desks; a list of the pieces on show; a page of welcome blah from the gallery's director, most of which was taken up by begging the journalists to mention the show's sponsors as frequently as possible. Dull. I shoved it in my bag.

Earlier in the day Aidan had sent Helena a list of all the Stevensons the gallery had sold over the last ten years, as he'd promised, and had copied me in. I hadn't looked at it. The titles meant nothing to me, and it was only my specialist geekery that had meant I'd been able to spot the problem with the collage at the Arts Council panel. I'd look again at the ones with the book jackets, but it wouldn't add anything to what I'd done yesterday. In fact, I had no real reason to be here, so I decided to just go through as though it were any other show, only with fewer people about.

I started off with good intentions. I looked around the room I was standing in. A wall panel introduced Stevenson, and outlined the early part of his career after he got to art college in London, and before he moved to the States. The walls were hung with a handful of early works, oils rather than collage, and mostly muddy brown, probably chosen to make viewers grateful that he'd given up painting. I moved quickly on to the next room, which was a long, top-lit gallery holding more than twenty pictures, and some ceramic-and-iron assemblages from the 1960s. It was also holding Aidan and Jim, who were in a heated discussion with a man wearing a suit and a pair of white gloves. He was pointing at one wall with a spirit level, so I assumed they were discussing the arrangement of the pictures, and didn't interrupt, just waving furtively to Lucy as I passed.

I moved slowly through the next rooms, enjoying the show with the front of my brain. Colophons aren't my only area of nerdiness. I also classify exhibitions. It's not something I mention in public, but privately, the Sam Clair Theory of Retrospectives sums up all shows in just three categories: 1) Wow, I had no idea s/he was so great!; or 2) Wow! I had no idea (s)he was so terrible; or, the killer, 3) Yep, I knew that s/he was great/terrible/meh. (Select one only. Do not write on both sides of the paper.) This is not the world's most thrilling insight, but I put it out there, because the Stevenson show was falling into the second category. I'd gone in admiring Stevenson's work, and some of the pictures I was looking at I still thought were terrific. But they were few and far between. And between the in-between were endless variations on a theme. Aidan had said the prices of Stevensons had never risen the way his pop contemporaries had. Maybe it was because, although at his best he was very good, his best didn't come along very often.

I'd been there more than an hour, and I hadn't seen even half the show yet. And in all that space, I'd passed maybe six people. A few of them had the press packs open and were scribbling industriously, breaking off only to take photographs with their phones. Others were guards, although they weren't in every room. We had been invited, vetted, and were known by name. We weren't a threat to the art.

I was beginning to flag. I walked into the next room, and

looked around. I know it makes me a philistine, but all I could think was, "More?" I was about to skip ahead to the next room when I saw Aidan again, still with Jim and Mr. White Gloves. If he saw me, I'd have to be polite about the show, and I was tired and cranky. So instead I moved back to the room I'd just left, fixing my eyes on whatever was nearest the door. As soon as Aidan headed off, I'd zip quickly through the next few rooms. He did and so I did.

Three rooms on, I paused to look back and make sure he couldn't see me skimming past his livelihood. And there, at the end of the next room, stood Celia Stein. My heart did a peculiar leap, as though something extraordinary had occurred. I spoke to myself severely. *She represents the estate, you fool. Where else would she be?* I peeked back. *See?* I went on. *She's talking to Myra and Lucy. It's gallery business. Now just stop this silliness.*

My body parts were not listening. By the time I'd formulated the thought, I found I'd taken three giant steps into the next room, removing myself from her sight line, and I was staring blindly at a painting. *Well,* I told myself snarkily, *you can either stand here forever, becoming the world expert on*—I peered at the label—*on Untitled #38, or you can act like an adult and move.* Apparently my body parts were still not on speaking terms with my brain. *World expert sounds good,* my feet said. They weren't going anywhere.

Someone else's were. Brisk footsteps sounded in the room I'd just left. A woman in heels, not a man. And the steps were moving steadily, not stopping to look at paintings. Which meant that she wasn't a journalist. They were more purposeful than a guard doing her rounds, and anyway, did guards wear heels? The reality, that I was standing in the middle of a national art collection, with guards wandering through regularly, with Aidan around the corner, with other Merriam-Compton staff, even Jim, coming and going, had no effect. I was in a blind panic.

There was the outline of a door next to the painting I was looking at. It had a doorknob painted the same color as the wall, and only a thin edge of light behind it made it noticeable, that and a "Staff Only" sign. I looked around. No one was in view. I turned the knob cautiously and pulled. No bells rang, no sirens sounded. I slid through it, and closed it softly behind me.

I was giddy with rebellion. In my mind, I am devil-may-care and do whatever I want whenever I want to. In real life, I am cautious to the point of being mistaken for street furniture. The height of rebellion for me is to toss aside an unopened utilities bill marked "Open Immediately." And now here I was trespassing. I didn't know what happened to people who were found with no authorization in the private areas of museums, but I suspected it was frowned upon. Possibly using the police, and the courts. I shook my head. What had I been thinking? I'd slide back into the room and pretend nothing had happened.

I could still hear the heels as they tap-tapped into the gallery I'd been in. I waited for them to move off so I could emerge without embarrassing myself. But they didn't. And instead of me turning the knob, I felt it turn in my hand. Without thinking, I leaned my full weight against the door. It gave fractionally, but I held it shut, as though it were locked. There was a pause, and then the knob was released, every bit as slowly and cautiously as it had turned a moment before. Which made me think it hadn't been a gallery employee. The person on the other side did not want to be heard. Then nothing. Including no footsteps. I couldn't now return the way I had come.

I took stock. How to find my way to the public parts of the museum without drawing attention to myself was the question. I was on a staircase landing. I knew that there were no galleries on the floor above, so the stairs up probably led to offices, or other spaces where I also didn't belong. Downstairs there were galleries, and a second entrance hall. With luck, I could find my way to that.

I walked down without trying to be particularly quiet. I didn't sing and dance and play the ukulele, but I decided it was better not to creep about, either. If the worst came to the worst and somebody saw me, I'd say I'd been to the press view and had got lost.

The stairs ended in a vestibule, with three doors. One said "Education," which didn't look promising. The second was a loo. By default, Door Number Three, then. I took a breath. Despite my best intentions, I opened it like a burglar in the night. An amateur burglar, on her first expedition. No one could remotely mistake me for a lost visitor.

It turned out not to matter. This wasn't a public part of the gallery, because, apart from anything else, it was dark. I stepped forward and the door shut behind me, reducing the light to just a small rectangle from the landing. I waited for a moment for my eyes to become accustomed to the gloom. There was a faint smell of metal and damp. Nothing unpleasant, but these weren't offices, or even rooms that were used regularly.

I reached out to see what was beside me. A light switch, which I didn't use. I couldn't counterfeit that much confidence. Beside that, wood. What felt like bookcases, higher than my head. I stepped forward cautiously. Only a few feet ahead, the way was blocked by a wall. Was I in a corridor? I felt with my hands. No, not a wall. Smooth and cold, like a filing cabinet. And not much wider. Then a crack, then another smooth and cold section. And again. I ran my hand up higher, and felt a raised metal rectangle. Paper inside, like an old-fashioned label on an office door, telling you who worked there. I ran my hand down. A wheel. And I understood.

I was in an archive. These were rolling metal stacks, shelving that, to save space, runs on a track. The shelves look like ordinary library bookshelves, but if you turn the wheel at the end of each set of shelves, the whole unit rolls along, and one by one the sections close up against each other, giving double the quantity of shelving in half the space of conventional storage. Lots of libraries have them. T&R didn't, but Tetrarch, being bigger, stored its archive copies that way.

If this was an archive, then I could assume a standard layout for it, and if I walked along beside the stacks, at some point the odds were there would be another exit. I kept one hand lightly on the units. The gloom wasn't absolute now I'd been there a few minutes, but it was gloom all the same. If there was anything on the floor—a kick stool to help researchers reach the top shelves, or files or boxes—I wasn't going to see it.

The shelving ended. I reached out to feel if I'd got to the end of the room, but I hadn't. It was just a gap between two stacks, where someone must have been working earlier and hadn't rolled the two units back together. I was about to continue when I heard—I don't know what I heard. What I knew, however, was that someone else had entered the archive. Without even think-ing about it, I slid my shoes off and stepped silently into the gap between the stacks. In hindsight I know I can't have held my breath for the next ten minutes, but that's what it felt like. There was nothing I could do. I had no idea where in the room the other person was, so going back to find the door I'd come in by was as impossible as going forward.

I waited. I made, and discarded, plans. I had my phone with me, but even if I kept it shielded in my bag, the light would tell the watcher where I was. And it was a watcher, not someone willing to turn on the light and move about looking for a file. I imagined a 999 call. "I'm in an archive in the Tate without au-thorization, and a Bad Person, whom I cannot identify, is threat-ening me with harm. How are they threatening me? She—or possibly he—is breathing."

Jake would take me seriously, and so would Helena or Aidan, but to call them I would have the same problem with light from my phone, and no guarantee I'd get anything except their voice mail. There was also no guarantee that I would even get that far. I was in a basement and there might not be a phone signal. I might give away my location and not be able to make a call.

I berated myself: *Where is Lassie when you really need her?* I call myself organized, but a really organized person would have bought a collie years ago, just in case she fell into a river and needed the townspeople to rescue her as she washed toward the rapids. *Get help, Lassie. Go on, girl!*

I have no idea how long I stood there thinking these entirely un-useful thoughts. My watch was old, and not luminous, while my phone was unusable because it was luminous. It paralleled my situation: crap, whatever I did. If this had been in a novel and not real life, I would have written in the margin, "Symbolism too heavy-handed?"

My only hope was that a Tate employee would appear. But before that could happen, whoever was following me made up their mind. There was a flurry of steps—not walking anymore, but running—and then something heavy shrieked as it was dragged across the floor. Before I could begin to unravel the sounds, there was a huge crash, and what little light there had been was blocked out, as if by an eclipse.

I had retreated to the far end of the shelves, away from the entrance, where I'd entered the stacks. Now I waited, but still nothing happened. I moved, cautiously, toward the opening. As I got near, my feet scuffed across something that had not been on the floor before. I bent. Books.

I ventured another step. Nothing. Another, and I walked into what felt like a wall. I put up my hand. Wooden. A shelf. Another above it. I reached higher. Shelves as far as I could feel. And I understood. The watcher had decided I must be in the single open stack, but feared that I was lying in wait. And so they had pulled out the bookshelf on the opposite wall, tipping it over so that it fell against the entrance and trapped me.

I listened some more. Had the watcher trapped me and gone to get someone? I hadn't heard a door open or close, although I probably wouldn't have over the noise of the shelves falling, and the books crashing onto the floor. But if they hadn't, what was the point? If I couldn't get out anymore, they couldn't get to me, either.

And then I heard a rumble. A rumble I knew well. Fear

clutched me. It was one of the stacks starting to roll. I'd done it myself, often, one by one when I wanted to get at a book in the library. The watcher didn't want a book, though. They wanted me. And they were rolling all the stacks, slowly but surely toward me.

15

I bit back a scream, even though it no longer mattered if anyone heard me. There was no point in screaming now. No one would get to me in time. And if I let myself scream, I might never stop. I tried to calm myself. Because panic was going to make me slow, and it was going to make me stupid. And if I was either of those things, much less both, I was going to die.

I would probably die anyway, but I didn't have to die berating myself for being a panicky idiot.

My phone. The watcher knew where I was, so that no longer mattered. I'd dropped my bag at some point, I didn't know when or where. I was fairly sure I'd still had it when I slid into the stacks, so it had to be there somewhere. I scuffed my feet along, and then, as I reached the bag, I gave a grunt of triumph: there it was.

I scrabbled through it, searching for the phone even as I listened to the stacks banging, one against the other as they came closer. Stay calm, I told myself. Concentrate. The stacks don't matter. The phone does. I dug it out and clicked it on. I nearly wept when I saw no signal bars. I clicked again. Yes. The hum that said I had a line. I dialed Jake. Nothing. No connection. Again. Nothing. Did emergency calls connect better? *Just do what you're supposed to, you crappy piece of technology*, I told it grimly. 999. "What service?" Thank God.

"Police." I tried to keep my voice calm, but I was a nanosecond away from wailing. "Emergency. Police!"

The connection was made, even as the rolling noise came closer. There was no time. I wedged the phone between my shoulder and my ear, 1960s suburban-housewife style, and knelt down and hooked my hand in flat behind the first book on the shelf nearest the floor. Using my arm like a paddle, I shoveled as many books as I could in one sweep onto the floor, and went back for more.

"Police."

"Please. I'm at the Tate. I need—" I kept shoveling, moving along the floor on my knees.

"Your name and phone number, please."

"There's no time. Someone is trying to kill me. I'm in the basement of the Tate Gallery. The Tate. Pimlico. In an archive. I don't know what it's called but—"

"I need your name and number, please."

"There's *no time*. Call Jake Field. Detective-Inspector Jacob Field, CID. He knows about this. Tell him it's Sam Clair. *He knows.*"

"I'll do that. It's going through." The voice was calm and soothing, although I was neither calmed nor soothed by it. I continued to hook books out. "Give me your number so I can call you back."

I was defeated. There was no time for telephone tag, and no signal for it. The books were more important. I dropped the phone and started putting the books I'd pulled out onto the floor into rows, but across the floor, perpendicular to the shelves, reaching across from one of the stacks to the other. It was a reference archive and the books were mostly thick, maybe encyclopedias of some kind. If there were enough of them, and I packed them in tightly enough, they might block the rolling mechanism for a while. Scoop, stack, scoop, stack.

And all the while, the rolling sound continued. The whir of the wheel, and the clank as one stack hit the next and the growing wall of metal shelving got heavier each time, moving onward. Toward me.

I scooted on my knees up to the other end, the blocked end, feeling around on the floor for the tracks. I started to stack more books along their line. Scoop, stack.

If I had any brains, I told myself as my hands kept stacking, I would have hung up and redialled 999 and called in a fire. But I'd dropped the phone. It was somewhere on the floor back where I'd built the first row of books. I couldn't waste time looking for it.

It didn't matter. It was too late. Rolling stacks are popular because they are easy to use. It didn't take much time or effort to roll an entire row of stacks across a room. And I could hear that these ones weren't more than a couple of units away from me now. I paused, crouched over and waiting, my ear cocked, as though

I needed to hear what was going to happen. As though I wasn't going to feel it.

Long before I thought they'd get to me, when I thought I still had a few more seconds, maybe even a minute, before, most likely I'd be—I couldn't let myself think the word. Before I'd *be hurt* were the only words my mind was willing to accept. Long before that, the shelf beside me bulged out with a clang. The great mass of rolling stacks had got to me.

I concentrated on the rows of books I'd built, even as I knew that they had as much chance of slowing down the stacks as a sand drawbridge protects a castle on the beach. I kept my hands hovering over them nonetheless. It gave me something to do, which stopped me lying on the floor and screaming in fear.

The stacks beside me bulged again, and a few of the books in my makeshift buttresses popped up. I pushed them back, and scrambled back to the other end. The same. My God. They were holding.

The shelf moved back. The pressure had been taken off. I stayed crouched on the floor. Waiting. I didn't have to wait long. I heard the rolling move in the opposite direction, but I had no time to hope. Bang. The stacks were sent back as hard as the watcher could roll them. They crashed into my unit. Books poured out, a great cataract spray of them. I covered my head with my hands. At any other time, hundreds of books being flung onto my back and head would have been painful. These barely registered.

I scuttled back to the front row and felt along the floor again. If anything, the falling books had helped, adding their weight to keep my rows in place.

I could hear the shelves rolling back again. With fewer books on them, they'd probably move more easily the next time. I braced myself, waiting.

But nothing came. Instead, the lights went on, and a voice said, "Who is there? What's going on?"

I shouted, "Stop that person by the stacks. *Stop her!*" But even as I shouted, I heard footsteps running, and a door swing shut.

The voice was from the other end. "What? Who is there?"

I was resigned. "I think there's only me now," I called. "I'm in the stacks, behind the bookshelf." With the light on I could see it, and it was exactly what I'd thought, a tipped-over book-shelf blocking my exit. "Someone attacked me."

"*What?*" The voice was incredulous. So this wasn't a result of my 999 call, but a museum employee who had heard the noise. Well, even if they hadn't caught Celia—I had said "the watcher" to myself the whole time, but I knew it was Celia—even if they hadn't seen her, I'd been rescued.

I started to say it again, when another voice cut in. "Police. All entrances are blocked. Stay where you are, and identify yourselves."

I was bitter. "It's too late for blocking. She's gone. It's just me. She tried to kill me." I admit, in retrospect, that it might be possible to make a more comprehensive, and comprehensible, statement to the police, but that was the most I could manage.

I leaned, one hand against the emptied shelves, my head down. I was breathing shallowly, unable to get enough air, and only now did I realize that I was also crying. When I thought about it, my mind moving slowly and hazily, I knew I'd been cry-ing ever since the bookcase fell. In fact, I was a mass of tears, and snot, and dirt. My hair was stuck to my forehead, and was liberally smeared with the mixture. The nails on both my hands were torn from pulling down the books, and my arms almost to my shoulders were black with archive dust untouched for decades. And I was barefoot. It took a real effort of concentration to work out why that might be, but that's what I was trying to figure out when the bookcase was pulled back enough to let me out.

Or let someone in. Two policemen slid through the gap on either side, both wearing protective vests and carrying guns. And the guns were pointed at me.

We've become slightly more used to having armed police in London in the last few years, but it has never seemed normal to me when I see them at railway stations, or in front of embassies. It did not seem normal now, at close quarters, and in a museum. What had happened had happened so fast that I had had no time to think about the reality of it. Two men in bulletproof vests aiming firearms at me removed all doubt.

I looked at the man nearest me, and said, in a wondering tone, "She tried to kill me." And then, in case he hadn't understood, I turned to his partner and added, "She tried to *kill* me." And then I sat down on the floor, put my head in my hands, and cried.

I don't think it went on for very long. Even as I wailed—and this was not the kind of movie glamor crying, where the heroine gives a few sniffles as her eyes well up photogenically, this was great, horrible, mouth-open sobbing—even as I did it, I was aware of the noise around me. Voices. The stamp of feet going back and forth, of doors opening and closing. And the crackle and static of radios as it was confirmed that the emergency had been contained and apparently comprised one hysterical middle-aged woman.

Finally I looked up. The same two policemen, but their weapons were no longer pointing at me. An improvement. I said, wearily, "I'm sorry." I think that even if I were about to be executed, that reflex would kick in, that English middle-class female need to apologize for having inconvenienced other people, or even just made them uncomfortable. *I'm so sorry, will the blood be troublesome? It does stain, terribly, of course. Shall I move so you can decapitate me over the lino? That would make it so much easier for you to clean up afterward.*

One of the men shifted his weight, but neither said anything. It was up to me to make this social event go with a swing.

I wiped my face with my sleeve. "I got lost. I went through the wrong door. Someone followed me in the dark and trapped me in here. Then she tried to roll the stacks along, to crush me." My voice began to quaver again as I got to the end. Saying it made me realize I'd nearly died.

Their faces didn't change, and they didn't move. I wasn't sure if it was because I sounded deranged, or they were just waiting for more information.

Then one said, "She?"

I nodded. "A woman's footsteps. Heels. I didn't see her."

He didn't respond. I started to stand up, and he tensed. "I'm going to stand up," I said carefully.

He nodded. His job was just to keep an eye on me.

I stood, and wiped my face with my sleeve again. Stylish. "My bag is by the wall. Can I get it?"

He looked undecided. He wasn't senior enough to have undergone intensive handbag training.

"There are tissues in it. I want to blow my nose."

No tissue training, either.

I kept my eyes on him, attempting to convey my utter harmlessness. He didn't appear to be convinced, so I spoke carefully. "If I get the bag and hand it to you, will you get the tissues out for me?" No dice. I tried not to sound aggrieved, or as if I thought I was auditioning for a part in a police procedural, but I'm sure I sounded like both when I modified it further. "If I don't pick it up, just kick it down toward you?"

That was better. He agreed, and we did that. Tissue-transfer safely achieved without incident, I wiped my face. Not that it was going to do much good, but making a gesture toward normalcy made me feel better.

By now there were more voices, and lots of movement. Then, as swiftly as it had fallen, the bookshelf was moved back entirely, and for the first time I could see the space I was standing in. As I'd thought, it was an archive: a narrow passageway down one side of a room, the rest filled with rolling stacks. The door I'd come through was at the far end, and almost entirely blocked by police. There was another door, nearer to me, with another cluster of police, and, peering over their shoulders, a few people not in uniform.

A man in a dark suit with a tie that looked as if it had been knotted the day before yesterday stepped toward me. He was clearly in charge. Thirty-ish, short, wiry, and very, very peeved. Possibly with me. I rolled my eyes at myself. Definitely with me.

I didn't wait for him to speak. I'd had a few minutes as I'd mopped up to think what I was going to say. "My name is Samantha Clair. I was at the press view of a new exhibition upstairs, and I got lost and someone followed me. I panicked and stepped into this space. They blocked it with the bookcase, and then tried to roll the other cases down, to crush me." There was no doubt about it, "crush me" were words to avoid, because my voice wavered again. Stop being a baby, I told myself. It didn't happen. "There are people upstairs who will tell you I am who I say I am. And there's ID in my bag." I gestured toward the policeman who still held it in the hand that wasn't holding a gun. What the well-dressed copper is wearing this season.

The man waited. He wasn't accepting what I'd said, but he wasn't rejecting it, either.

I cleared my throat, the nice-girl preamble to a request. "May I come out?" I looked at my hands. "I need to wash."

"Not yet. How did you get in here? And give me the names of the people who will vouch for you."

"That door over there." I pointed. "There are stairs. I came down from the floor above, a room in the exhibition space. I don't know anyone who works here, but a woman named Esther something—Wolff, Esther Wolff—is the press officer, and she put my name on a list of visitors. A man named Jim Reynolds, who is a freelancer, but is working for the Tate, is also here. He knows me."

He nodded again, still an acknowledgment that I'd spoken, no more. "Why did Esther Wolff put you on a list if she doesn't know you?"

"She was asked to by the art dealer who represents the artist being shown. He's upstairs, too, or was. Aidan Merriam." I wasn't sure how much time had passed. Maybe they'd gone home? I was so tired it could have been midnight. I rubbed at my face.

"You said 'she' attacked you, but you also said it was dark."

"The footsteps were a woman's. Heels."

"Are you certain?"

"I'm certain in my own mind, yes. But I didn't see anyone." I realized exactly how little I could prove—not even that I was followed from upstairs. My eyes and nose began to clog again. I closed my eyes, willing myself not to cry. It wasn't going to work. "Please. I need to wash." I have no idea why it was so important, but it was. I was shaking, and it occurred to me that I might have been shaking all along.

He made a beckoning gesture with his head to someone behind the trio of men boxing me in. A woman in uniform came forward with a water cooler plastic cup of water as my questioner turned aside and began to speak to three men in plain clothes. I took the water, but the shaking got worse, and most of it went down my front. That I couldn't possibly look worse was not a comforting thought.

Once I'd drunk what was left, she took me by the elbow in a gesture that was only partly supportive. She was also escorting me.

"Where?" I'd run out of manners.

"You wanted to wash." She was as brief.

We went. I wasn't allowed my bag, but I washed my hands and face, and I combed back my hair with my wet hands. The cold water helped, and after a while I stopped crying. The woman put her head around the door and spoke to a colleague. Another cup of water was passed in, most of which I managed to drink this time without spilling. Progress.

I straightened what was left of my shirt. One shoulder had torn at the seam, and was only half-attached. I considered ripping it off, but was too tired to complete the thought. The rest was just dirty, and some buttons were gone. I tucked it tightly into my skirt to deal with the missing button issue. I was still barefoot, but I was a little more together.

That illusion shattered when the door slammed open so hard it crashed against the wall. It wasn't just me. The policewoman jumped, too, and the voices outside broke off. I looked up. Jake. And the angriest Jake I had ever seen. Rage vibrated off him.

I didn't move, and I didn't speak. I said before, rather lightly, that I suspected that our relationship, which had begun while he was investigating a murder that involved one of my authors, was probably against police regulations. As he stood silently staring at me, it was brought home that there was no "probably." I couldn't think of anything that I might do that wouldn't make things worse, so I did nothing. He looked me over, from filthy hair, slowly down past red eyes and a runny nose, to torn shirt and skirt, to bare feet. Without turning his head, he said to the policewoman, "Get her some tea. Four sugars."

I still didn't move, or speak. Partly because he was so angry, and partly because the door was open and other people were within earshot. Mostly the former.

His voice was thin with suppressed rage. "Our people are on their way now. These"—he twitched a shoulder backward—"are the armed-response unit; they'll be handing over. I want you to go with the policewoman when she comes back. I want you to sit where she puts you. I want you to drink your fucking tea and I want you to not fucking move. *Do you understand?*"

I nodded mutely. The policewoman had come back in time to hear the last sentence. Even that, her carefully blank expression said, was shocking.

He turned and walked away.

I was taken to someone's office nearby, and we were left there. I drank my fucking tea. I didn't fucking move. After a while, I asked if I could have my bag. No. My shoes? Those appeared at some point. I borrowed a comb from the policewoman, who I think by now felt sorry for me. Finally, I gave up. The adrenaline that had made me act when I had to had drained away in one swoop, like taking out a bath plug. I put my head down on the desk and went to sleep.

When I woke up, I could tell from the metal taste in my mouth that I had been asleep for a while. In the basement there was no change in the light, and no change in the sounds outside—mostly men's rumbling voices, with a few women, phones, and tramping back and forth. I sat up and looked at my watch. Just after seven, but I had no idea what time the police had arrived, or how long I'd been in the stacks.

My escort was still with me. "Boring job," I said.

She looked as blank as she had since she'd heard Jake talking to me. "I've had worse."

That was the sum total of our conversation, except when someone brought yet more tea, which I also drank. So much for sisterly bonding. We sat. I can't remember ever just sitting, not reading, or looking at something, or even thinking. But I didn't do any of those things. I didn't pick up the newspaper that was lying on the desk. I didn't try to work out what had happened, or why. I just sat.

It was nine before anyone came back again. The door opened, and Jake walked in, with two uniformed men, and two more in street clothes. The policewoman left and they shuffled around the suddenly very small space. The two in uniform found chairs that they moved as far away as possible and sat. One of the other men leaned on the door, the second stood next to him. Jake leaned against a bookshelf, arms crossed. I stayed where I'd been sitting, behind the desk. It looked like I was interviewing them. Except that there were five of them and one of me. And I felt very small.

"We'd like you to make an initial statement, which will be recorded," Jake said.

I nodded. I felt hemmed in. Before he could say anything further, heels clicked along the hallway. I stiffened. They stopped at the door and there was a tap. The plain-clothes man moved aside slightly and looked out. I couldn't see anything, but I could hear.

The door opened wider, and Helena appeared. She looked at me calmly. She had probably been warned I was not a pretty sight, although I imagine her expression would have been the same even without the warning. Nothing surprised her. She didn't kiss me, although whether that was because she was in legal mode, or because she didn't want my dirt near her was a toss-up. "I've brought you some clean clothes. You can change as soon as this is over," was all she said, as one of the uniforms gave her his chair.

I stared fixedly at the wall. *You are not going to cry again*, I told myself. "Tell me where you want me to start." I spoke to the air beside Jake's head.

One of the men by the door replied, and I was relieved to turn to him. "We know that you were signed in at 5:15. Several people saw you in the first rooms, and have identified you. Go from there."

So I did. I told them everything that had happened. I saw no reason not to, and if Helena had wanted me not to say something, she would have told me so.

After I finished there was a brief pause. Then one of the two men by the door, whom I assumed were Jake's colleagues, said, "You keep saying 'she.' What makes you think it was a woman?"

"I said before. I have no evidence. The footsteps were short and sharp, like a not very tall person wearing heels. That, and if someone did try to run me over last week, that was a woman, too."

"But you don't know."

"No." I saw no point in reminding him that I'd just said I didn't know.

The questioning went on. Had I heard anyone follow me down the stairs? Had I heard an outer door close? How long between going through the door upstairs and the knob turning did I estimate it had been? Had I seen an outside light go on? And all the while, Jake never said a word. He hadn't said anything since he asked me to make a statement. I looked only at the two men asking the questions.

Finally, when I had said everything at least three times, Helena called a halt. "If there's nothing further that can't wait? She will be available when you need her."

The two men conferred briefly, then looked over at Jake

before agreeing that no, there was probably nothing further for the day.

"Come," said Helena. And I did. It was that easy.

We drove back to her house without talking. I began to think I might never talk to anyone ever again. I wasn't tired now, just in a state of suspended animation. When we got inside Helena handed me a bag and said, "Clean clothes. Have a bath and change."

By the time I got downstairs, I was feeling better; it's amazing what being clean can do. I was almost ready to say something when I stepped into the kitchen. Jake was leaning on the counter, waiting.

He didn't look any chattier than I felt. No hello, just, "Are you ready to go home?"

I looked over to Helena. She was entirely neutral. *As you like,* said her face.

Maybe I wasn't ready to say something. I nodded halfway between them, to the air, and headed for the door. Jake fell in behind and we walked out to the car.

I waited, head down, for him to unlock the door. Instead, his arms came around me and pulled me close. I leaned against him, so his voice was more a vibration than a sound. "If you ever do that again, I think I'll kill you myself."

"If it happens again, you'll have to get in line. I'll kill myself first, and I think Helena's got dibs on second."

16

I fell asleep in the five minutes it takes to drive from Helena's to my flat. Jake woke me, and I walked indoors and got straight into bed without undressing. At some point in the night I woke, and realized that Jake was not there; at another, that he was, and I felt comforted by the knowledge. When he woke me again just before seven, I reconsidered the comfort level. If I'd slept alone, no one would have been able to wake me. I opened one eye and waited.

"I know," he said, as if I'd voiced the thought. "But we need to talk, and I have to leave for work." He smiled sweetly.

We hadn't been doing a lot of sweetness lately. I nodded into the pillow. "Give me ten minutes."

I waited until he left the room before I stripped off. I wanted to take stock of my injuries by myself first. I was bruised where the books had fallen on me—my back was particularly bad, with one or two places where the edges had broken the skin. But the benefit of having had a cycle accident was that my face was no more frightening than it had been the day before. Always a silver lining.

I got myself to the kitchen only five minutes later than I'd promised, and Jake slid a mug of coffee toward me. There were case notes, files, and documents all over the table: he had to have been working for hours, maybe all night. I looked to see if he'd changed his clothes, but realized I had no idea what he'd been wearing the day before.

He was moving papers around, thinking how to begin, and I understood why when he spoke. "It wasn't Celia Stein. She was with Merriam and the show's curator the entire time. When your 999 call was logged, the three of them, and Jim Reynolds, were talking to four members of"—he checked his notes for the term "the working party, which seems to be what the people who hang the pictures are called. There was a problem with a painting in one room, and the whole room had to be rehung. She was taking photos with her phone. We've looked at the time stamps. There isn't even a five-minute gap, and everyone agrees that no one else had her phone."

I started to speak and found I had no voice. I tried again. "Are you saying that *two people hate me that much?*"

All of Jake's formal manner vanished. He was around the table, and I was on his lap before I'd finished the sentence. He hugged me tight. "Sweetheart, no one hates you." He waited until I took a breath. "People kill out of hatred. But that's not what this is. It's not." He stared at me, to make sure I understood. "Someone is afraid. There is no reason to attack you except fear, and the only fear they can have is of exposure. We need to work out what it is you know."

I took another breath. I don't know why someone wanting me dead because they were afraid of me was better than someone wanting me dead because they hated me, but it was. Fear I could deal with. I gave a small nod. *I'm OK*, it said.

Jake moved back to his files. "The most obvious thing you know is the colophons, although how anyone knows that, I don't know. There's something else we're missing. I'm going to go over everything once more, and then I'll need to interview you officially again. I don't know when. The office will call Helena." He looked shamefaced. "I don't know who it will be. You realized, last night . . ."

He didn't finish, so I did it for him, as bluntly as it would be said if his superiors found out about our relationship. Right before they sacked him. ". . . that you should have withdrawn the moment you discovered the case concerned your girlfriend's ex-boyfriend? Yes. I didn't before, which was stupid of me. We can keep it like this for the moment. But you need to straighten it out afterward. I don't want to be your dirty little secret."

He gave me that same sweet smile. "That talk we're going to have 'later?'"

"That one." I smiled back. "Not to change the subject, but I need to go and get my things together." I raised my hands pacifically, stopping the words I saw coming. "You can drop me on your way to work, and I promise I won't leave the building unless you need me to be interviewed. And then I'll order a cab. Or if you don't need to talk to me again, I'll do the same to come home. Believe me, I'm frightened enough to listen to you now." He still looked as if he wanted to argue, so I went for the jugular. "I'm too afraid to stay at home alone."

There wasn't an answer to that, so we went.

It didn't really matter where I was, as it turned out, because I wasn't capable of doing any work. I told Miranda I was diverting my calls to her, and she should only put through Helena or Jake's office. She looked deathly curious, but didn't ask any questions.

I closed my office door, and tried to move in logical steps. I may not be smart, but I'm stubborn. Frank and Werner Schmidt were dead because of something to do with the Stevenson estate. That had to be the start. That there were forgeries in the estate also had to be a starting point. That Celia had something to do with it, ditto. Spencer Reichel's connection to Celia, and to Matt Holder, came into the mix, although how or why was not clear.

In truth, I'm not stubborn. I'm pig-headed. And going over and over the same facts was really pig-headed. It wasn't helping, I was just too stupid to know when to stop. When Miranda put her head around the door, it was almost a relief. "Sam, I know you said you didn't want any phone calls, but there's someone downstairs for you."

I reached for my diary. Had I forgotten to cancel an appointment? I looked. No.

"Who?" I was mystified. Publishing doesn't do drop-ins.

"He says his name is Sam, but he won't give a last name." Sam? I didn't know a Sam. "When I told Bernie that you weren't seeing anyone, he said you'd see him. I went down, because he wouldn't say where he was from, or what it was about. He's . . ." her teeth worried at her lips. She wasn't sure how to phrase the next part. "He's young. Not old enough to be working."

My eyes opened wide. Sam. Viv's Sam. "Seventeen or so? South-East Asian, dyed blonde hair, trousers around his bum?"

Now Miranda's eyes popped wide, too. Her "not old enough to be working," I realized, had been a euphemism for, *Isn't he a bit young for you but what else could he be?* She recovered quickly. "That's him."

I picked up the phone. "Hi, Bernie. Is Sam still there for me? Ask him to come up to the first floor." And I was off down the corridor like a shot, Miranda pretending, very discreetly, that she was going to the loo, and following hard behind.

I got to the head of the stairs as Sam was coming into sight. "Hey, Sam. Thanks for coming." I wasn't going to say more there. Seventeen-year-olds were not part of our daily lives. Everyone at every desk we passed was watching.

He was a quick study. He nodded, as though he dropped by publishing offices every day of the week, and then he put out his hand. Grown-ups shook hands. So we did.

As we walked past the kitchen I paused. Office manners. "Do you want something to drink? Coffee? Tea? Water?"

A very quick study. "I don't suppose you have a beer?"

"No beer. That's why this is called 'work,' not 'fun.'"

"Damn." And we smiled. For some reason, we understood each other.

When we got to my office I closed the door and sat, waving him to the visitor seat. He took his time, looking at the wall of books, the files. "This is what you do?"

"I work for a publisher. We make books."

"My sister reads." In the same tone you'd say, *My sister likes Mongolian throat-singing.*

"It happens. There's no shame in it. Not even a Twelve-Step Program that I know of."

"Girl stuff. Romance."

He wasn't ready to sit down yet. I poured myself coffee from my coffeemaker, waving the pot at him in question, giving him time. Then I sipped quietly. He'd tell me whatever it was when he was ready.

"I saw her."

I sat forward so fast I sloshed hot coffee all over my hand. "Shit." I wiped it quickly, never taking my eyes off him. "Where? When?"

He sat down now. My desk faced the wall, so that when I had a visitor I swiveled round and there was nothing between us. I hitched my chair forward, and we sat knee to knee.

"Yesterday. Around nine o'clock. On the High Street. I was going to the kebab shop. You know, the good one?" He paused questioningly. I didn't, but I nodded. "She was going into the res-taurant next door. It's Italian. Expensive, my mum says."

I sat back, crushed. This wasn't going to help. Someone in a restaurant. How did that identify her the next day?

"I tried to ring you on the number you gave me." He looked at me accusingly.

I started to reach for my phone—had I even checked my messages?—and then I remembered. I had no handbag, so no phone. The armed response unit had decided it was essential to hold onto my tampax to make sure I didn't detonate them and destroy democracy as we know it. I can't say I exactly followed their reasoning, but when I had been on my own I was too trau-matized to argue; by the time Helena arrived, I'd forgotten. All

I had now was twenty quid I'd borrowed from Jake that morning. Everything else, phone, credit cards, money, was in the death-grip of the police.

"There was a problem last night. The police have my bag, and it has my phone."

"You were arrested?" I'd gone up in his estimation.

I grinned. "Nah. Questioning. My mum's a lawyer. She was there to see fair play." Then I sobered up. "Thank you for coming and telling me. That's really kind of you. I guess we can keep an eye out for the woman there. Or maybe the police can ask at the restaurant."

He was insulted. "I didn't let her go."

"You followed her?"

Now he thought I was just plain stupid. "Course I did. Me 'n' my mates." He shrugged. "We went to the kebab place and had something to eat while we waited for her to come out."

I didn't know how to put this diplomatically. "Didn't anyone notice you?"

He grinned again. "Everyone. But no one. Everyone hates kids hanging about, and no one pays any attention to us except to say we're a nuisance."

He was right. People walking past, or looking at them through the restaurant window, would have thought, *Bloody kids, drinking and eating and making noise on the street.* Not a single one would have been able to say what any of them looked like.

I stared up at him, puppy-dog eyes. "Tell me you saw where she went."

He was regretful. "They drove off, so we couldn't follow her.

But . . ." He held out his hand. Written in biro on the palm was a registration number.

I pumped my fist. "Yes." I wanted to kiss him but I thought he'd faint.

"It wasn't her car, though: she wasn't driving."

"Doesn't matter. This is a huge help." I copied the number down. "You are my hero, Sam. Thank you. And thank you for coming all the way here to tell me." I paused. "How do I get in touch with you? I want to pass this on to the police. I'll say again, if it's connected the way I think it is, I don't think the hit-and-run will matter much. But if they need to speak to you—um, my boyfriend is at Scotland Yard."

He considered that. "A copper's missus."

I laughed out loud. "I've never thought of myself that way. And we're not married so I'm nobody's missus. What I meant was, it won't be the local PC Plod who will be looking at this." I suspected that this would make it better, not worse, but I wasn't sure. It did.

He nodded, and picked up the pen and wrote his mobile number beside the registration number.

He looked around, as if he'd suddenly realized he was in a small, enclosed, and very unfamiliar space with a woman old enough to be his mother, but he couldn't work out the mechanics of getting away. I stood. "Thank you again," I said, and moved to the door.

As we passed the assistants' desks in the space outside, I said, "Hold on a minute." Publicity was just around the corner, and I went and scanned their shelves, grabbing half a dozen titles.

"I'll order you up some new ones," I called to the intern looking daggers at me. These were advance copies to send out to newspapers for reviewing, and no one was supposed to take them, although everyone did. She wasn't appeased, but she didn't have the seniority to challenge me outright, either. While I was at it, I filched a T&R bag and dumped everything in, returning to Sam. In the thirty seconds I'd been gone, Miranda had befriended him. He was leaning against her filing cabinet, chatting and entirely at ease.

"Here," I said, handing the bag over. "For your sister. I don't do anything I think you'd like."

He put his head on one side. "Motocross?"

"You're just saying that because of the way I dress." It took him ten seconds to work out that that was a joke, and by that time, he and I and Miranda had got to the front door.

"See you," he said, slinging the bag on his shoulder. Job done.

"And I'm taking early lunch, if that's OK," said Miranda.

I'd said "Sure," and was halfway up the stairs before I looked at my watch. Eleven o'clock, Miranda? I hoped to God he was eighteen. A young-looking twenty would be even better.

Back in my office, I rang Jake. Voice mail. I hung up, and e-mailed instead. "The boy who saw the hit-and-run came through. He saw the woman again on the High Street. She got into a car, not hers," and I added the registration number. Then I thunked myself on the forehead and added. "Also, I'm never going to make inspector. I have no idea what the boy's last name is, and forgot to ask. First name Sam, and I have his phone number. According to neighborhood gossip he's been 'in trouble' with the police. He says he'll talk to you, though. Let me know."

Then I thought about last night again, and sent him another e-mail. "Dear DI Field, Yesterday evening a neighbor who witnessed the hit-and-run I was involved in on Castleton Street last Saturday saw a woman he recognized as the driver. He saw her get into a car in Camden, and although she wasn't driving, he took down the registration number (attached), in the hope that it will help to identify her. I'm afraid that for the moment he isn't willing to give a statement. Yours, Samantha Clair." If the hit-and-run ever became part of a case, Jake was going to need to show how he got the information that led to an arrest. Paperwork. Registration numbers. Phone numbers. All documented. Documentation was good. I admired my own neat and tidy files. And then I sat up again. Documentation.

Miranda was at "lunch," so I rang down to Bernie. "Will you order me a cab on the company account, to come as soon as possible? I'm going to Aldermanbury, and it will need to wait for me afterward and take me on." I'd pay T&R back, but I didn't have enough cash to get me to the City in a cab, and I'd promised Jake I wouldn't use public transport.

Then I called Helena. She was in a meeting. I left a voice mail, and e-mailed her as well, to drive the point home: "I'm on my way over now. We NEED to talk. Get Aidan." I e-mailed Jake again too. "On my way to Helena (yes, by cab, from T&R's regular company, don't worry). Have turned something up. No phone/access to texts or e-mails, so let H. know when you want us. Sooner would be better than later. For you. P.S. If you wrestled my handbag away from your fellow plods you would have my lifelong devotion. And I would have a way to contact you."

And I went downstairs to wait for the cab from the safety of the reception desk.

Helena was still in her meeting when I got to her office, but her assistant told me she'd said she'd be as quick as she could, and I was to wait in her office. That suited me. I took one of her legal pads and had roughed out a summary of my ideas by the time she appeared.

She had also done as I'd asked and got in touch with Aidan. Despite what must have been a frantic day at the Tate, my urgency had been conveyed, and he was there within the half hour. Helena's meeting ended only minutes later. She was her usual calm self; Aidan was not. He was angry and frightened. Two weeks ago, he'd found his partner dead. Now the gallery was up to its neck in forgery. I'd seen him the day after Frank had died. I'd spotted the first forgery. Someone had attacked me twice. This, said his look, is your fault.

I barely waited until they'd sat down. "We've been looking at this from the wrong end," I said. "As soon as the forgery surfaced, the death of Werner Schmidt meant that we looked at him as the most likely source." They nodded. "But we left out a more important element of forgery." I turned to Aidan. "Why aren't there more forgeries than there are?"

He looked blank.

I shook my head at myself. I wasn't being clear. "Not Stevensons. In the world. Why don't more people forge paintings? It's not that difficult, is it? Particularly with contemporary art, which is often factory made. Why doesn't someone produce, I don't know"—I waved my hand, as though it would help me grasp a name from the air "Donald Judds by the score? They're just boxes.

If you had the measurements of one, and some plywood, you could probably knock one up in your garden shed."

He looked contemptuous: *You pulled me out of meetings for this?* "And then what do you do? Stand on the street corner and say, 'Oi, mate, I've got a luvverly Judd for you here. Usually a tenner, but I'll do it for you for £7.50?' Sam, you know perfectly well, you can't sell a painting without d—"

He was exactly where I wanted him to be. "Without documentation. Werner Schmidt could turn out the most beautiful Stevensons in the world. But without the paperwork, they were worth no more than a poster from the Tate's shop." I turned to Helena. "I hadn't realized until Aidan explained last week, how much documentation each artwork needs. Not just the provenance, the sales' records, but valuations, customs and transport dockets, duty paid, and so on. You can track a picture forever with paperwork. And if those papers are in order, there is nothing to it: the artwork is, by definition, legitimate."

Aidan was now seeing where I was going, and looked as though he was going to lose his breakfast. Helena was impassive. Lawyer face. I went on. "Myra James is Merriam-Compton's registrar. She is, as Aidan phrased it, the 'paperwork queen.' She could produce any paperwork that was needed. And," I suddenly remembered, "she and Frank were also the two who knew the Stevenson holdings the best. She was ideally placed to let Schmidt know what was selling well, what would fetch a good price, and then make sure the pictures he produced were backed up by the appropriate documents. In fact, I can't imagine how it could have been done without her."

Aidan crumpled. I can't explain it, but when I said Myra's

name, he just—got smaller. "No," he said now. But it wasn't denial. It was, Please, make this not be true.

Helena continued to look attentive, as if I'd told her that I would be going to the beach for my holiday that year, instead of my usual city-break: an interesting idea. "Yes." She looked at Aidan. "She was with you at the Tate yesterday, Sam said. Was she with you the whole time?"

Aidan pulled himself together and thought. "No. There was a problem with a picture that was supposed to come from Germany. Because of the new government indemnity scheme . . ." he waved it away; too much detail. "There was a problem with a loan, and the picture's not coming. That's why we were rehanging that room. The Irish Museum of Modern Art stepped in and offered us a replacement from their collection. Myra stayed while we hung a dummy, for size, to see if it would work, and when it did she went back to the gallery to sort out the paperwork while we redid the rest of the room." He realized what that meant, and looked over at me. "I don't know the timings exactly, but—"

"But she could possibly have had time to follow me down to the archive."

He nodded. Helena brought us back to order. "If, as Jake tells me, Celia Stein was taking pictures that are time-stamped, they'll be able to say when the dummy picture was hung, and therefore what time she left you." She made a note. Oh good, we were on her "to do" list. "But I want to focus on why, for a moment. Why would she want to hurt you?"

I noticed that Helena never said someone had tried to kill me.

It was always "hurt," or "attack." A rare overt indication of the love I knew that she had for me.

I thought for a moment. "Aidan asked Lucy to send me the JPEGS of the Stevensons with book jackets in them. Would Myra know that?"

He shrugged. Myra knows everything that happens in the gallery, the gesture said.

"So she knew that I was looking at eleven pictures, two of which were very possibly forgeries. I e-mailed my results to you, Helena, but not to Aidan. Would she have seen an e-mail you sent him?"

"I didn't e-mail, we spoke." Her voice was absent as she thought it through. "So as far as she knew yesterday, you very likely knew of something suspect, and since all eleven paintings had book jackets in them, she might assume it had to do with your area of expertise. But before?"

Before what? I felt the way I always do with Helena, like a cocker spaniel scrambling along behind a grayhound that was outpacing me on idle.

"Sam. Someone knocked you off your cycle on Saturday."

I put my hand up to my face, where the scabs were healing. So they had. I wasn't sure I'd ever imagined a week where a hit-and-run became the kind of thing that slipped my mind.

"What would you have done to worry her before Lucy sent you those pictures?"

I thought back. "I e-mailed back and forth with her regarding the funeral, but only the time of the service, and sending flowers." I ticked over what had happened in the days between Frank's death and the funeral. "I had a strange conversation with her at the funeral, but that was after . . ." I touched my face again. "The only other time we spoke was when I paid a condolence call on Toby. We had a brief conversation." I tried to remember what we'd said. "I have no idea what we discussed—the gallery? Stevenson? Frank? It was meaningless chit-chat, the kind you have when you have nothing to say."

Helena made a note and nodded. She was ready to move down the agenda. "Let's leave Myra for the moment. Where does Celia Stein come in? *Does* Celia Stein come in?"

"I'm not sure. If it hadn't been that she approached me the day after Frank died, I'd say now she didn't. The only way I can make sense of it is that she found out what was going on and went to Frank. Frank would rather have died than—" I bit my tongue. Frank *had* died rather than let the gallery be exposed as sellers of forgeries. I started again. "Or, wait. Maybe she offered him a deal: if he paid her off, then she would keep quiet."

"Blackmail?"

"Jake said she started to have money three years ago, when she bought a big house."

"And why did she get in touch with you?"

Aidan spoke now, the first time since I'd named Myra. I'd become so focused on Helena I jumped. "Because of me. And your policeman." Truly I was going to slosh him for that "my" policeman routine when this was over.

"I don't understand."

"I had lunch with you the day after Frank died. The detective in charge of the investigation is your boyfriend."

"How would she know either of those things?"

He was bitter. "Because I told her."

"What, you rang her and said, 'Hey, crazy coincidence, but let me tell you about this woman you've never met?' Why would you mention me, much less that I was having lunch with you, or shagging a policeman?"

Give me patience, oh Lord, said his expression. "The Tate thing was Frank's baby. When he died, I had to take over, and I was supposed to have lunch with Celia to get up to speed. I said I didn't want to cancel you because of your policeman." Just wait until this was over.

I don't know if Helena saw me clench my teeth, but she jumped in. "You told her the day you found Frank dead?" He nodded. "And that day, she rang Sam's office." Another note.

And then, to add to the sense that she had us all under her effortless control, her assistant knocked. A call from the CID: my presence was requested, as soon as possible. Aidan went back to the Tate, and Helena and I took the cab I had left waiting outside. It was going to cost a fortune, but Helena would return to her office after the interview, and I needed to be able to get about. As we wove through the traffic, I tried to remember if I'd ever read a crime novel where the main preoccupation of the person on the run is the cost of the cab fare. I made a mental note to mention it as a new plot twist.

I knew, of course, that Jake worked at Scotland Yard, but I'd never been there. In fact, when we got into the cab and said "Scotland Yard," I realized I had no idea where it was. Victoria, as it turned out. At least my archive adventure hadn't taken Jake far out of his way yesterday. Even without sirens blaring, it took only three minutes from there to his office. Top Tip for Coppers'

Girls: If you're going to get yourself attacked, do it near the bf's office. Scotland Yard itself turned out to be an ugly 1960s office block down a tiny side street. I looked around as we got out of the cab. There was no reason, short of going to Scotland Yard, for anyone to ever walk down this street. Probably the point.

Helena took charge, bundling me inside, and then through the airport-style security in the foyer—metal detector, bag search, X-ray. We were given tags and escorted upstairs, where we were handed over to a second escort, who walked us down to where Jake and the same two detectives from the previous night were waiting in a meeting room. They hadn't been introduced last night, and they weren't now either.

I looked around, curious. Inside, the building looked like it had been decorated by the same people who did airport lounges—strident patterned carpet, sofas upholstered in clashing plaids, and walls finished in yellow wood with shiny varnish. The meeting room we were in had a sub-Scandinavian table and knock-offs of those Scan-style chairs with metal legs. The effect was spoiled by framed awards and citations peppered across the walls: Danish modern meets Quonset hut.

I looked at Helena. *I'd really be much happier if you carried the ball*, I telegraphed. She pulled out her legal pad, folded her hands on the table, and began. The men listened to her in silence, but after only a couple of minutes one of the two picked up the files and began flicking back and forth, hunting down documentary evidence for her story. The other two sat listening, neither accepting nor rejecting her—my—thesis.

When she finished, the three moved away from the table and

consulted in low voices. Then they returned, and the bigger of the two spoke directly to me. "We'd like to go over the two possible assaults on you."

I didn't sigh, but I thought about it. Helena's head never moved, but she shook her head in response to my not-sigh all the same.

We went over it again. And again. And again. They seemed puzzled by my part in the case, but since they never came right out and said so, I didn't feel it was possible to agree that I was puzzled, too. I'd started as Aidan's friend, and then, somehow, stuff just kept happening to me. I decided that "stuff just kept happening" would not be a useful contribution to their case notes, and kept it to myself.

Finally they stopped. I made a plea for the return of my handbag, and one mumbled about paperwork, but I saw Jake's almost invisible nod. I'd get it back. They spoke to Helena briefly about the practical details of the forgery side. For a case to be opened, someone would have to lay a formal charge. That would, however, follow automatically if one of the forgeries had been sold to any of the national collections. Finally, Jake took us downstairs, and we stood outside in the drive. Helena kissed me briskly and tap-tapped off to find a cab and get back to her office. And we stood in silence for a moment.

"We'll bring Myra in for questioning. Don't worry, sweetheart. It'll soon be over."

Dear God, I hoped so.

"Where are you going now?"

There was no point in being at the office if I was just going to barricade myself in and tell Miranda to repel all boarders. "Home, I suppose." I saw his protest and headed it off. "I might sit with Mr. Rudiger until you get back."

That won a grunt and a nod of approval. He looked at his watch. "Unless there's a delay finding her, or her finding a solicitor, I should be home by eight."

I gave him what turned out to be a fairly watery smile. Next time I got involved with violence and sudden death, I was going to stock up on tissues first.

I'd lied. I didn't plan to sit with Mr. Rudiger, although I had to ring his bell when I got to the house: I still didn't have my keys. He let me in with no more surprise than Helena had earlier. Memo to self: do *not* play poker with those two.

I told him I wasn't well and had forgotten my keys, and he nodded, even as his face said, *Fool yourself all you want, but don't think you're fooling me.* I knew I wasn't, but I was talked out.

I trailed around the flat, checking that every door and window was closed and locked. I looked in the cupboards, and behind the sofa. I felt like I was in a bad slasher film, but not a bad enough film not to do it. Then I went to bed.

I woke up feeling much better, if very stiff. The bruises from the books were getting worse, not better. I took them to the bath and soaked for a while. Then I pottered. I tidied a bit, watered the herbs pots in the garden before I jumped back inside and double-locked the door again. I put yesterday's clothes into the take-to-the-recycling bag: they were torn as well as black with grime that would never come out. All this made me feel like I was in control, and I decided that a visit to Mr. Rudiger would, after all, be a good idea. I started to hunt for my phone to text Jake to say where I was in case I was still there when he got home, before I realized that I'd have to do it Mr. Rudiger-style. I stuck a scribbled post-it note—"I'm upstairs. Sam"—on the door and went.

Mr. Rudiger and I had a routine. I always opened with a soft serve, asking if he'd like to come down for a drink/coffee/chat; he returned with, *Since you're up here, why don't you come in.* I lobbed back by hesitating politely—*If you're sure I'm not interrupting.* And so on. I like it. I like my professional life, where we drift, boundary-less between work and personal; I like the quasi-living together with Jake, a halfway house between the structured meetings dating requires and the unboundaried stream of living together. But I also like Mr. Rudiger's world, where borders are crossed only with a passport.

Match played out to both our satisfaction, I went in, as we had both known I would from the moment I'd knocked. We sat on his terrace in the late-afternoon shade, drinking iced coffee, which I'd made. He'd pulled a dubious, Central-European face at the notion of adding ice to coffee, but he'd politely joined me, although I think he was mentally holding his nose the whole time. I caught him up on the previous day's events. An hour before, I would have said "horrors," not "events," but Mr. Rudiger was always so calm that he helped me achieve some distance. After I'd finished, he sat quietly, not speaking.

"It goes back to vanity, doesn't it?" he said, finally.

"It does?"

He was very sure of what he was saying. "Vain people can't bear to be crossed. They are the center of their world, and if the circumstances don't allow the world to meet their needs, then the circumstances need to be changed. Their actions appear proportionate to them, because any situation where their needs aren't being met is an affront."

I'd heard similar ideas before, but I'd never had a real-life example to apply it to. "Werner Schmidt was affronted that the world did not agree that he was a great artist. That might well be the case. Myra?" I considered. She had certainly given me the feeling that she thought the gallery would collapse without her. "She's worked there for a million years. Maybe being its registrar, not a partner, was an affront to her vanity?" Mr. Rudiger turned his palms up, Could be. "Celia is vain. Her needs—money—were not being met, so she tried to blackmail Frank and it went wrong."

It sounded sensible, but I wasn't sure what it proved. Or didn't prove. Or if it proved anything at all.

It was after seven. Mr. Rudiger had heard Anthony come in, but no Jake. But with people on both floors above me, my empty flat seemed less threatening. I thanked him for his company and went back downstairs. I pulled the note off the door and dropped it in the recycling box. Jake would probably be home soon. Food stocks were low, but I wanted to do something normal, like make dinner.

I began to do that, but I wouldn't call it normal, as I turned over and over in my mind all that had happened. Normal, I told myself. I looked in the fridge. Several elderly, tired carrots, a semi-dead fennel, and that was it. End-of-week soup was the only thing I could think of, even though it wasn't the end of the week, only Tuesday. That reminded me, so in a further attempt to pretend my life was normal I emptied the bins. Wednesday was rubbish day.

I like making soup. You start with a few whiskery carrots, you put in some elbow grease, and before you know it, you have something comforting. Unlike Jake's job. There you start with a body and a question, you put in some elbow grease, and you end up with even more questions than when you began. If this were a crime novel, I thought as I chopped, we'd be on the last chapter. The forgery had been exposed, and now all that was left was to pull back the curtain and reveal the criminal mastermind, usually by having him show up on the detective's doorstep, waving a gun and curiously anxious to explain his actions.

It's not that I'd become jumpy or anything, but my eyes did just flick over to the back door. Closed. And locked. And then to the door to the hall. But I managed to stay in the kitchen and not walk down to check the front door, too. Honor saved.

And if the criminal mastermind wasn't ready to confess, the detective would stand with his back to the fireplace, explaining everything to the gathered suspects, playing eenie-meenie-miney-moe until he got to the guilty one.

I didn't think it would work for me. First off, I haven't got a fireplace. And then there were the practicalities. How did those invitations get issued? "Hi, Celia. It's Sam Clair. I know a splendid source of income has just vanished in a puff of smoke, but I wondered if you'd like to drop by for a drink. No? Pity. Another time, perhaps." That needed work.

I ran through a list of invitees. "Hello, Viv. You've really got nothing to do with this, and have barely featured in the scenario. Tradition therefore dictates that you must be the lead suspect. Like to come for supper?" Or, "Hi, Jim. I'm having a little soirée . . ." He'd be the easiest. All I'd have to do was say that Lucy was coming. "Oh yes, I thought I'd invite as many people as possible who have no reason to be involved—"

I stopped and stared out the window sightlessly. I had assumed—I assumed we had all assumed—that Frank had killed himself when he discovered the gallery was selling forgeries. But what if he hadn't? Who stood to benefit, not from the forgeries, but from his death?

Lucy and her sister. They inherited Frank's share of the gallery.

To the best of my knowledge, nice girls tend not to kill their uncles. Nice girls also tend not to attack editors they barely know. If they do, there has to be a reason for it. The reason to kill Frank was obvious. If the forgeries had become public knowledge, Merriam-Compton would have collapsed. No gallery could withstand a scandal of that magnitude. And Lucy wanted to make her career there. Why would she attack me, though? I thought back over our meetings. At Toby's, when I first met her, we had discussed the show she wanted to mount, and I'd—I clutched the paring knife more tightly—I'd mentioned the book jacket collages and even said I had the same edition of one of the books, and mentioned the William Burroughs. I'd followed that up by e-mailing Jim, who was besotted with her, and might easily have told her. I'd even mentioned *Kafka's Puppy*, which turned out to be a suspected forgery. She'd then seen Myra work herself into a snit with me at the funeral, and—I took a deep breath—she'd even asked me if I was brave enough to start cycling again.

I reached for the phone. A single ring and then, "Field."

Thank you, Lord.

"It's not Myra."

Silence.

"It's not."

"She's confessed."

That made no sense. "She killed Frank? And Schmidt?"

Another silence. Then his voice gentled, as though he were talking to a small child. "Why would you think Myra killed Frank? Why would you think Frank was killed at all? She confessed to producing the documents for Schmidt's forgeries. Although she is claiming she was coerced by Frank. She says he was the one who had briefed Schmidt, set the whole thing in motion." His voice said what he thought of that. "The thing is, it can't have been her in the archive. We have her health records. She's had a weak heart for years. She couldn't have attacked you in the archive. She's not physically capable."

I'd forgotten I'd moved on a few steps. "She doesn't matter. That is, she does, but—" I broke off and gathered my wits. "What kind of car did Frank drive? Or maybe Toby." More silence. "Humor me. Please."

He turned his head away and spoke briefly to someone with him. There was a pause. Then he repeated, his voice no longer in "humor" mode. "A Volvo XC90." And I mouthed along with him the next part, "Dark blue."

"I don't remember what they were, but do the last two digits of the registration match what the witness gave us?"

His voice was tight. "You know they do. Now tell me why. And who."

"Lucy. It's the only answer that makes sense. She's the only person with a motive to kill two people."

"Motive is for crime writers," he said, trying not to sound impatient. Then he backtracked. "*Two* people?"

"This all got turned around. Start at the other end. Start with a fraud that's been going on for years, that's being run by Frank, just as Myra said. He locates a forger, who is his ex-boyfriend, and Myra is co-opted—for money, I presume?"

"We think so," he said. "We're looking now."

"It's been going on for years, and everything is fine, because Frank had access to the material from the archive—cuttings, photos, even the glue. Then something happens. Schmidt starts to drink, or maybe the archive material begins to run out. Schmidt uses a book jacket that didn't come from the archive, not knowing there would be small differences." I was clarifying this for myself, too, as I went along, and now I stopped to think.

Jake's teeth were no longer gritted. "Go on."

"Lucy has been working at the gallery on and off in her holidays for years. She may very well have noticed something, picked up bits and pieces here and there. If the forgeries are discovered, the gallery will go under. But if Frank dies, even if the forgeries surface—even if Schmidt stands in the middle of Piccadilly Circus shrieking 'I'm a forger'—the person he forged for has killed himself in remorse. The gallery can continue, and that's what she wants. It was her future."

Jake's voice was kind. "Sounds good." The "little girl" was almost audible.

"No. Listen. It's not just motive. She probably thought I knew more than I did." I repeated the conversations I'd had with her. "She knew I was coming from the farmer's market to Toby's on Saturday, because we'd liaised over the kind of food I was bringing for visitors." I thought about that for a moment. "She's the *only* person who knew where I was going to be that Saturday." That had more effect. I could almost hear him sit up. "And she was at the Tate. I saw her. I waved to her." For some reason that infuriated more than the fact that she'd tried to kill me. I'd gone out of my way to be friendly to this woman because I felt sorry for her. Damned if I was going to be friendly to anyone ever again.

Then I remembered. "There's more. On the day I was hit by the car, she wasn't at Toby's all day. Jim said he'd gone up to meet her for coffee nearby. She could easily have borrowed Frank's car for that. It's hard to imagine anyone except family could have. And none of the rest of the family knows who I am."

"And Celia Stein?"

"What do you want from me, miracles?"

17

I went back to my soup making. I may not have a fireplace, but at least I didn't have to do my own dirty work, either. I felt much better. Or, I did until I heard the knock at my door. I'd been stirring the pot, and I was jumpy enough that the knock made me splash soup all over the floor. I stood there with the spoon in my hand, panicked, before I realized it was a knock, not the bell. Someone was at my flat door, not at the door to the house. Which meant it was either Mr. Rudiger, or Kay or Anthony. I'd heard Kay's voice a few minutes before, so maybe she wanted to go through to my garden—I was always happy for them to use it, and this evening it would be especially good to have company.

I called "Coming!" as I wiped my hands, and looked at the mess on the floor. It could wait.

It was going to have to. Because when I opened the door, it was neither Mr. Rudiger nor the Lewises. It was Jim Reynolds, looking tense. Which was reasonable, because slightly behind him was Lucy. Her expression was sober, judging, as though I'd come up wanting in some challenge. And apparently she was ready to back up that judgment, because in her hand she had a gun.

I stopped in the doorway, one foot still outstretched to take the next step. I grabbed at the frame for support, but she jerked the gun, a move-away gesture, as she pushed Jim forward impatiently. He was an obstacle to be moved, it appeared, not her partner.

Bollocks. I read too many trashy novels with happy-ever-after endings. A woman was standing in my doorway with a gun, and my first thought was, "Poor Jim, he really liked her."

It was also my second thought, because I was frozen. I had no sensible responses at all. I stood still, just staring, waiting. I couldn't think of anything else to do.

It's amazing what power a gun gives you. The handful of times I'd met Lucy, I'd thought of her as a nice girl, with equal stress on both words—that she was pleasant, and also very young for her age. The gun made her older. And much less pleasant, of course.

She repeated the move-away gesture more sharply, and pushed Jim a little more aggressively. I took a step back as she bit her lip, pulling her teeth along it, considering the problem—me being the problem.

"How did you get in?" I was disturbed to realize I really wanted to know, so that if a gun-toting nice girl showed up again, I'd be prepared.

"I had a chance to look around outside before your upstairs neighbor appeared. You really shouldn't leave notes on top of the recycling that say "I'm upstairs." It's all too easy for other people to stick them back on the front door."

So it would appear.

"We walked up with her, and then back down after she went into her flat." She shrugged. "No one suspects people who look like me."

No shit. "But . . ." I had no idea where that sentence was going, so I started again. "Jim?"

Jim hadn't said a word so far. He was sweating, and looked like he was in shock. When I said his name he shook his head, as though he wasn't sure who I was talking about.

Lucy was. "That's your fault, too."

"Me?" I realized my voice was rising to a whine. Any second now I was going to say "It's not fair," like an eight-year-old. I might stamp my foot, too.

"You brought him into this." She pushed her voice up to a falsetto, presumably in imitation of me: "Oooh, did you know that I'm a tragic geek who can identify something that no one else in the world has ever thought worth looking at? And then, I can call attention to it by asking a designer about them? And publicly display the problem at a conference where even more arts people will see it?" She dropped her voice back to its normal register. "Because of you, Jim knew the pictures were forgeries. Because of you, Aidan knew—he told me to send them over to you. *Everyone* knew. Because of you. And the gallery would have been bankrupted. What would have happened to me?"

Mr. Rudiger was right. It was all about her. "So Frank had to die?"

"Of course." She didn't even understand why I was asking.

I'd been standing talking to a woman with a gun, whom I was sure had killed two people, and I was frightened, but not terrified. Now, her sheer blankness brought back the same feeling I'd had in the archive. Fear has a physical location. It lives in your stomach, and rises up through your throat, looking for an exit. I had pushed it down in the archive. I needed to do the same now.

I swayed in the doorway. "Can I sit down?" I looked at the sitting room.

She considered it, rolling her lip through her teeth some more. "Not here. Is there a room where you can't see in from the street?"

"The kitchen. At the back. There's a garden, but there's no access to it from outside." I didn't know why I was being helpful, but in the short-term I couldn't think of anything else to do.

She gestured with the gun. She looked so comfortable doing it, I wondered if she'd been practicing, the way teenagers practice looking cool in the bedroom mirror. "Walk ahead of me, both of you."

I took Jim's arm. I told myself I was trying to keep him calm, but it was really for comfort.

The kitchen is small. Counters, sink, fridge, and cooker along two walls. When people come for supper, the kitchen table gets pulled into the middle of the room and we squeeze around it. The rest of the time it's pushed into the corner across from the counters, and there is just space for two to sit at it. She did the gun-gesture thing again: Jim was to go in one chair, me in the other.

"Sit. But keep your hands where I can see them."

I nodded and moved slowly to a chair, putting my hands carefully on the table. Jim wasn't as careful, but that's because he was barely thinking. She knew that, and was watching me, not him.

"I don't understand why you're here, though. If you kill me, where does it get you?"

She rubbed her forehead. It didn't seem any clearer to her. I wasn't sure whether pushing at this was a good idea or whether it would just make her angry. Which would in turn make her decide to get on with what she'd come for.

I kept my voice even. "Where did you get the gun?" I tried to sound as though I had merely an academic interest in what was happening. As far as I was aware, guns weren't handed out in freshers' week. Or they hadn't been when I went to university. Realizing I was capable of mental sarcasm helped me stay calm.

"Guns. Two." She waved hers again, like a child proud of her new balloon. *Look what I've got, Mummy.* "When Frank bought the Stevenson estate, Delia just packed up the entire contents of his studio. Everything. All the finished work, the half-finished, his files. She didn't sort anything, just had movers ship it out as it stood. When I went to intern for the gallery, they gave me the scut-work, the jobs no one wanted to do." This still rankled. "Frank had passed on the boxes with Stevenson's source files to Werner, but there were dozens more boxes no one had ever looked at, because it was like looking at the back of your cupboards. The contents of Stevenson's desk drawers, old phone bills, shopping lists, whatever." She waved her gun again, this time at the idea of heaps of unsorted items. "I was the drudge who was supposed to clean it out. The paperwork would be sold to a university archive, to earn yet more money for Delia"—another historic grievance—"and then the rest was ditched. All except the guns."

I had a flashback to that dinner with Reichel. He was the kind of man who expected women to sit and listen to him talk about himself, saying "You *did?*" admiringly at intervals. That was alpha-male vanity. This was just different vanity. "Guns?" I said, therefore, in an admiring tone.

Yes, that was what she'd wanted. She smiled. "There were two guns in one of the boxes."

I thought of what Jake had said. "But the one that killed Frank was Soviet."

She was the cat that had swallowed the cream, she was so pleased with herself. "And as untraceable as I'd thought it was going to be. Stevenson served in Vietnam. When I found it I did some research." Just what the world needed, a murderer with a library card. "Lots of U.S. servicemen picked up Soviet weapons in Vietnam, and then brought them home with them. For a long time they were quite common in the States. But never here, because there was no connection to Vietnam."

This was fascinating, but since she was planning to kill me with the results of her research, I failed to muster quite the enthusiasm she was looking for. If I stopped talking, though, she might decide she had to do something. I looked sideways at Jim. No help there. And I'd run out of questions.

I licked my lips. "Jake will be back soon." He probably wouldn't be, after my call to him, but it was all that I had.

She smirked at me. "And if he is, he'll find your note on the door again. 'I'm upstairs.'" Her voice was a mocking sing-song.

"But I won't be there, and he'll come back down." Why was I arguing with her?

"We'll have heard him go up." She waggled the gun once more. "And by the time he's back down, it will be too late." She was so sure of herself, leaning against the counter like a girlfriend who had dropped by for coffee. I stopped being frightened. Her casual stance was making me angry.

The soup, which had been simmering quietly, began to hiss. I was sure Sam Spade wouldn't have reacted the same way, but he and I had been brought up differently. I lifted my chin toward it. "Can I turn it down?"

"*Don't* move." She was fierce. But she had been brought up like me, and she pushed off from the counter, looking even more like it was a coffee morning, to turn it down herself.

Her boot skidded in the spilled puddle I'd left five minutes earlier—five minutes that felt like five years. That half pause was enough. Without conscious thought, I was out of my chair and at the stove, pulling at the saucepan, heaving the contents toward her in a huge arc. She threw up her hands to protect her face from the boiling liquid. She hadn't let go of the gun, but it was no longer pointing at anyone as she screamed.

My God, the scream. I may never get that sound out of my head.

And then everything happened at once. The room was filled with enormous men, all shouting. I don't think Lucy, burned as she was, even registered them. I stood there, saucepan in hand, prepared to launch myself at the first person to come near me. And then I realized one of them was Jake.

It probably only took twenty minutes before an ambulance came to take Lucy away under police escort. Jim went, with another escort, to be treated for shock. A paramedic looked at where I'd burned my hands on the pan, and then I was sent, with yet more escorts, up to Mr. Rudiger. Helena arrived at some point. Two detectives asked me for a statement, which I gave. And then gave again when they came back for details around midnight. And then we sat and waited.

It was nearly morning before I saw Jake again. He came up with a colleague, introduced as Chris. I prepared for another statement, but he shook his head and said wearily, "He knows about . . ." and waved his hand, to indicate the comprehensive nature of what Chris knew. Us, I assumed.

I wet my lips. "How is Lucy?"

"She'll be all right. Scarred, but all right."

I nodded. I didn't know how I felt about that. Jake sat down heavily beside me on the sofa, and took my hand, playing with the bandages.

"How did you know she was here?"

"We did a check on the car reg your friend Sam gave you. It belonged to a Marion Halcombe, address in Tooting. It took us longer than it should have, but we got there. She was married six months ago to a man named Jeremy Compton. She's Lucy's stepmother. So I came back to talk to you, get more detail on your conversations with Lucy. The post-it note on the front door—"

"Lucy expected you to see that and go upstairs. Why didn't you?"

He tapped my nose. "Because you don't leave notes for me on the front door, you leave them on the inside door." Thank God the man was a detective. His voice turned grim. "I organized backup, and—"

I tried not to sound too much like Pauline, untied from the railway tracks by Dudley-Do-Right. "And you came and got me." I was going to cry again, and I'd already spent the past week weeping over everyone I'd come into contact with. So I changed the subject.

"And Stevenson?"

Jake looked blank, so I clarified. "Why did Lucy make Frank's death look like Stevenson's suicide?"

"We don't know that she did. She's not in any condition to be questioned at the moment, and it may have been a coincidence. As far as we're concerned, it doesn't matter. She threatened to kill you, she threatened Jim Reynolds, she confessed to killing Compton in front of both of you." He shrugged. Not his problem.

I wet my lips. "What about Schmidt?"

Jake's expression became guarded. "They're going through the witnesses again, to see if anyone saw her. If she was there, she left no prints."

She'd hardly be the first criminal to wear gloves, but in the long run it didn't matter. Aidan would salvage his gallery. He'd had no connection, and Frank was dead. The only person who would care was Delia, who had loved her husband. And maybe Celia.

"What about Celia?" I'd thought she was guilty, even if I didn't know what she was guilty of. Maybe just of being beautiful and disdainful. In a properly organized universe, that would be illegal.

He rubbed his forehead. "We've been clearing that up. But what she's been doing isn't criminal."

"What has she been doing?"

"She wanted money, and wasn't getting what she considered her share from the estate. When Spencer Reichel was told that Merriam-Compton wouldn't sell to him, he was cut off from the prime source of Stevensons. She contacted him, and sold him some of the pictures she'd inherited, which she had every right to do. Then he gave her a job at the Daylesworth Trust, and in exchange she brokered sales from the gallery to anonymous 'collectors'—Reichel."

I sighed. "So much damage, for a few paintings."

Mr. Rudiger spoke. Since he hadn't said anything for hours, we all jumped. His deep voice made him sound like God, if God had grown up in Prague. "For a few paintings, and vanity."

He was right. Vanity, or entitlement, or just sheer greed. What a waste.

I turned to Jake. "When will your colleagues be out of my flat?"

His shrug said I shouldn't hold my breath. I'd slept in Mr. Rudiger's spare room before, and his nod, without my having to ask, said I would be again. I stood up. "I'm going to bed." I announced my plans firmly, so no one could be under any misapprehension. "I'm going to sleep for a week, and by the time I wake up you"—I pinned Jake with a particularly hard look "*you* will have spoken to your office about us. Because next time, I am really, really not doing this sneaking around crap."

Next time? Everyone in the room stared at me with varying degrees of disbelief. Well, almost everyone. Helena just smiled.